For Dan—
Tahoe City
May '24

RULE OF THUMB

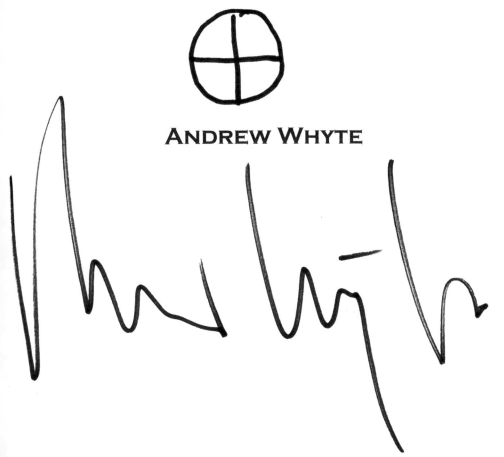

ANDREW WHYTE

MW00804312

For Dan-

Tahoe City

May 24

Red Queen, sittin' on a black highway

Waiting for her reign

And I scream, and I said that we could do it my way

But it just comes out as Elaine

And I had a dream yesterday

Gotta find out what it means

'Cause I'm comfortable here

But your gravity pulls me away, you see

And I wish, I didn't have to sing to make you understand

In life, you can compromise but with my Queen I won't

And these words won't bring me across the ocean to her land

And I thought that I would have to sing, but maybe babe I don't...

*   *   *

Copyright © 2018 Andrew Whyte

All rights reserved.

ISBN:0692107290
ISBN-13:9780692107294

DEDICATION

This book is dedicated to all of those
who continue to pick up hitchhikers

CONTENTS

Acknowledgments

*   *   *

Well I think I'm in love with impossibility

But that remains to be seen

I wanna fly, I wanna cruise around at light
speed

I wanna rescue my Queen

And you, sittin' in the median

An eagle waiting to fly

With your eyes closed, and your arms thrown
to the wind — I'll try

And I feel that you're feeling, that I feel
for you

And my breath, sends the wind that you feel
on your wings

And one moon, is a year gone by and I don't
know what to do

Another lonely day, and I can't help but
sing...

ACKNOWLEDGMENTS

I gratefully acknowledge the contributions
of the boys and men in my life, including:

Neil Young, Roger Weil, Hemingway, Albert Camus,
Scott Aborn, Tom Robbins, Carl Sagan, Matt Power,
Dan Garner, Sverre Eric, T.T.T., Michael Pan,
Hank Williams Sr., Kevin Hand, Kurt Vonnegut,
Sandy Sanderson, Woodie Guthrie, Stu Douglas,
M. Dubs, Budgie, George H. W., Jared Grant,
David Bumbeck, Bob Robson, Trevor Tall Fox,
and the real Audacy Myles.

*   *   *

Now I'm on the road, the clouds becoming blue

The wind is blowing cold, but then I turn and I see
you, my...

* Red Queen *

ANDREW WHYTE

PART I

CHAPTER 2001
Spontaneous Continuity

Sometimes the act of being in love compels one to have to take a train. This is the idea that I was preparing to run with as I jumped up onto the scaffold metal deck of the lead engine.[1]

Through the doorway, the conductor paused mid-sentence, and turned to me with a guarded and scolding look.

"Ah hello, g'day to you sir. Sorry to bother you chief, but my friend and I have just rolled over from Memphis," pointing backwards along the tracks, "and we're not much looking forward to freezing it out another night in a gondola, if you know what I mean — you see, we have to get to Arizona, I'm ah..." here goes, "I've gotta go get married," big smile here, looking embarrassed, "and um, just wondering if we might sit in with you — second engine back. We ah, you know, won't touch anything, or anything."

Pause here now as he's appraising my appearance and I'm standing bashful. Quick glance now out and down to the bank of the track where Chavez is staring north and chewing on a stick of grass, before panning back with a jolt to the present captain of our fate.

---

[1] Most freight trains nowadays are pulled along by two or three, or as many as six (heated) engines, and almost always, only the first engine is occupied by rail-personnel.

"Well, if you boys ARE or are NOT in that second engine... I don't want anything to know about it. I'm not allowed to. It could cost me my..."

"Thank you very much sir, it's like we're not here."

The getting married bit was a lie of course. The decision had been whether to hitch our way out in search of the highway, or to get onto this new and now immobile beauty that had just rolled up since we had gone to the store for tobacco and breakfast.

So after a jump down to the ground, and with no *small* wink to Chavez, we loaded our packs and the guitar up into the cabin, second engine back, and we were shortly steaming along in comfort with padded seats, heat, and a cooler full of ice.

We never knew what the name of that town was.

*   *   *

A couple of weeks before, it had gone something like this:

My dad woke me up with a shake and some words and passed me the phone in through under the covers. I had given him that bloody portable phone for Christmas the year before, and now instead of taking a message, he tended just to wake me up. I squinted at the clock: 10:30. Most of my friends would know not to call me that early, and that I'd been working nights, etc. Many of them worked nights too. Not Max.

"Woohoo! Hey sunshine, still in bed?"

"Yes Max, you are talking to me in my sleep."

"It's a beautiful day to be in New York brother... a beautiful day to be outside!"

"Maybe I can call you back..."

"No, hey listen: I've just quit my job and dumped my girlfriend. Are you still planning on going to Australia?"

"Yeah, but not till... well I'm gonna leave next month."

"And you're gonna hitch down through Central America first?"

"To Panama."

"Alright, well listen: you've heard of the Zapatistas right? Well this is history man! Subcomandante Marcos is going to lead the Zapatistas back out of hiding after seven years, and they're going to group up in San Cristobal on the 25th of February and begin a march to Mexico City."

"And?" I knew what was coming. Max was a writer, a socially conscientious guy, and very into the activist scene. I had been to visit him a few weeks earlier in NYC where he was squatting with twelve other people in some condemned building in the Bronx. We had ended up going canoeing on the river, collecting floating balls and throwing them at pedestrians.

"Well hey man! If you can assure me that we'd get down there on time for this thing, well... I could go with you, and we can hitch down there together! I've really gotta be in this march, man."

"Um, well Chavez... I told you about Chavez right? He's gonna hitch down here from Maine on the 20th and we're gonna make a split for Arizona. I've gotta stop in and see Morgan before we go. Now, that's about as farr ahead as we've spoken, but I reckon Chavez is thinking about coming south with me too..."

"Well that's fine, listen: I gotta take the bike down to Florida next week. Maybe I could buzz over and meet up with you guys in Arizona before you go down... Hey! Um, would you guys want to go in on a second bike and ride the..."

"No Max. We're hitching."

"Al*right*. O.K. Well, I'll let you get back to sleep man, but plan on it 'kay? Just like old times, you know? I'll be in touch with you, just gotta see to some things... hasta pronto hermano..."

Click.

I wasn't very surprised to find out later on that Max's most recent girlfriend had left *him* following some ex-girlfriend-including threesome gone awry, and by having 'quit his job', he had apparently meant 'gotten fired from his motorcycling-marijuana-delivery job'. But for right now, I hadn't even woken up yet, and lying there in bed, without having agreed to anything, I casually and sleepily wondered what I had just agreed to.

Hitchhiking with three would be a slow burden if not just short of impossible. Fuck, I thought, I should have told him so outright.

Max Forte was a year older than me. I had

known him in college. It was he who had provided me with my first front to go hitchhiking some years ago in '96. His girlfriend's father had owned a shack in Spain and my official plan had been to go over and work for the father-in-law type guy for the summer. But that was only the official plan.

1996 had been the light, the breeding grounds for my obsessions to follow. Max and I had met up in Spain as planned, and eventually thumbed our way to Istanbul and then halfway back before our differences impelled us to part.

Max was a realist (if I was an idealist) and could never understand or properly subscribe to the code of travel that I had immediately begun to create and adopt. Max would take a taxi if the price was right. He would stay in a hostel if the female company seemed promising. And he would draw unsuspecting euro-rail trash into long conversations, with the sole intent of leaving them off feeling inferior.[2] He was trying to live in our new world without really leaving the other one behind.

My own policy quickly became nothing but thumb, nothing but tent, never a campground, no exception. These rules would continue to evolve over the course of the next few years: '97 in South America, '98 back in Europe, and '99 in the Middle East. More on the code later.

Max's call had thrown my sleep, and I sat up and tried to shake out my head as I dressed. My immediate concerns were two:

---

[2] He would let them rattle on about the places they'd been, and the things that they'd seen, and then shut them down with, "Yeah but you guys are just taking the train," or "Yeah well, while you guys are busy *doing* places, we're actually being there."

1) How in the hell can we hitch with three people, three packs and a guitar, and...

2) Will the CDs be finished and delivered on time for departure?

Three months had elapsed since my unheroic return from San Francisco, and the band. What else does one do after college but move to California and start a rock band? But I had gotten what I wanted out of it: the CD. In the past, my travels had been subsidized by my guitar playing: busking[3] and smoky-bar hat-passing exclusively. But I had seen buskers with their own discs, and it seemed to me to be definitely the way to go. They were making better money. And they were transmitting with permanence. So with one and a half years invested in rock-banding with *Freewater* in the city, I had come away with my precious CD recording and plans to get back on the road.

The band, incidentally, had busted right after recording, so the production of the CD was left to me.

During these three months at home, besides making money, I had been hitching over to New York State to visit a computer-literate crony of mine to come up with the cover design. On the front, I put the title (**HITCHHIKER'S SONGBOOK**) and my name, and then in smaller lettering underneath my name: "**PLAYING WITH FREEWATER.**" On the back I pasted a big picture of my topless-self playing guitar. This would later prove to have been a

---

[3] Street Performing

good idea.[4]

*   *   *

Meanwhile, during one of the long nights back home, I found myself smoking pot at Lye Brook with an old friend of mine named Nick. Nick was the best musician I knew, and had been the essential member in the first band that I ever had. A high school band. Now Nick was telling me about his currents: his wedding band, his jazz band, and his plans to ditch both and move to Boston in the name of music and future prospects. As he spoke to me of these and similar chapters, I found myself chiding his appromatox horizons. Nick had never been on a plane, had never left the country, didn't even have a passport, and here he was digging himself in deeper. I'd like to say that it came to me in a flash, but really it was more like a building and self-reinforcing surge:

Three's no good, but four is two pairs (!).

Nick said "absolutely not" and that it "wasn't possible." Imagine my surprise then, when the next day I'm approached by his older-brother being somewhat possessive and asking me what kind of tomfoolery had I put into Nick's head?

The following day, Nick went to Town Hall to apply for his rush-delivery passport. He was going to take the train and meet us in Flagstaff.

---

[4] Was this whole project touching the darkness? Did the other band members know about my CD agenda in relation to my busking? No. Was the CD and its contents the only thing on my mind over that year and a half? No. Would I have left the band thing if we had been doing well and could splash along into fame? No. Did we get famous? No.

Travel is fatal to… narrow-mindedness, and many of our people need it sorely on (this account). Broad… views of… things cannot be acquired by vegetating in one little corner of the earth all one's lifetime. Mark Twain, Innocents Abroad.

The day after I got fired from my job, the UPS van showed up outside my parent's house with 37 boxes of CDs; 30 CDs per box. That was on a Friday. On Saturday, Chavez called from just in town.

"Hey, I'm here. Where do you live?"

"Good. Look around and read me something."

"Zooey's Deli."

"I'll be right there."

*   *   *

I suppose I should mention that the whole direction of the trip for me was helped along by the friendly but annoying bastards on table 5. When I moved back home and was dancing tables at the restaurant, I had some inquisitive customers who kept asking me about my life and what I was doing.

"Making money, filling tank." I droned.

"For what?" they continued.

"To leave." I summarized.

"To do what?" they persisted.

"To travel." I pleaded.

"To travel to where?" they hounded.

"To fucking Australia," I hissed.

One should never underestimate the power of the spoken word, for now I had an answer to everyone's question: Australia. That shut them up. Then when they asked, "And how do you plan to get there?" I held firm: "To hitchhike (you bastards!)."

"Ha ha ha ha," they roared, "You can't hitchhike to Australia!

Well that did it. <u>I was going to hitchhike to Australia</u>.

You are who you pretend to be, so be careful who you pretend to be. Kurt Vonnegut Jr.

*   *   *

Travelling with Chavez makes company seem good. He helped me to lug some CDs (his offer); he switched sleeping bags with me one night in Pennsylvania after I had had a zero sleep night (my sleeping bag was a piece of shit). This was late January. I accepted. Oftentimes, when travelling with someone else, I can't help but classify them in my mind as a liability. Not so with Chavez. In Memphis, when we tried for that first freight train that was going just a little bit too fast, we hit the ground in perfect unison. Me and Chavez. The ultimate wingman. This is a guy who I had met two summers before in the Yukon, and we had stayed in touch through mail-exchanging a couple of Tom Robbins books. He's a thick build, long hair, strong little fucker who once said to me that life was just a series of hellos and goodbyes. We were destined to be friends.

Chavez and I shortly thumbed down to Connecticut to stay a couple of nights with a

psychopathic old friend of mine from college.
There in Darien, we also began to refine our CD
music sales routine through the girls' dorms of
the local University. We divided and conquered by
hallway and floor, and Chavez sold more CDs than
I did.

My crazy friend Walter, meanwhile, is still
going to university. He'd have been done years
ago if he hadn't been so fond of starting fires.
Completely burned and destroyed hallways on two
separate floors in our old college dorm once, his
own floor, and that of his (and my) ex-lover.
Some sort of crazy romance gesture. — true story.

Anyway, this part was a series of goodbyes,
and from Connecticut we ripped down a highway
sign that said simply 'WEST' and challenged
ourselves to get to San Francisco-band-guitar-
player Pat's flat in Indiana by Super Bowl.

It was as we were closing in on Cincinnati
that we got picked up by the preacher. Chavez had
thumbed the ride, and he must have smelled it
coming 'cause he quickly stepped up and into the
back seat of the cab. I threw him a cracking
smile halfway through the ride's very first
words:

"Do you boys know that Jesus Christ died for
your sins?" he asked, in a drawn out, overly loud
voice.

It was a wet, late afternoon; I felt in fine
form to field this ride: "Which sins are you
referring to? Are you talking about sins which
we've yet to commit?"

"Jesus Christ, our Lord, knows of ALL sins:
those which have been committed, and those which

yur' still gonna commit." This statement was accompanied by an accusatory glare, and the plump preacher then elevated his voice to an even louder drone, reserved apparently for excerpts from the bible: "For it was then on the eve of our Saviour's crucifixion, that He spoke to Peter, and said, 'This night before a rooster crows, thrice will you disown and betray me!'"[5]

I paused for a moment until the weight of the elapsed silence seemed to balance the thunderous tone with which he had spoken.

"O.K. But wait... Isn't there a bit of a conflict there?"

The preacher looked steadily forward now, working his jaw as he stared out through the windshield.

I continued, "Under the assumption of everyone's having a free will to make decisions, and with Peter's having been human like the rest of us, how then could Jesus have foreseen and prophesized about Peter's triple betrayal before Peter himself had even confronted the reality of that future, and made such decisions?" He began to interrupt, but I raised my voice slightly, as if I'd just caught on to something important, "Unless of course, Jesus *was* God, and *could* see the future, because the future *had* already been written." I paused for a moment until the preacher began almost unperceivably to nod his head. And now a side cast glance to Chavez: "But if the future had already been written, then Peter didn't have any choice to begin with (and neither do any of us!), and why then, in that

---

[5] Matthew 26, Luke 22.

case, was Jesus picking on his own friends?"[6]

The preacher seemed not to hear what I had said, and continued: "Jesus Christ, our Lord, sacrificed his life for the sins of all mankind, and only through finding him, and embracing his word through the holy bible can you boys achieve redemption and escape the fires of hell eternal." This is what he really said!

Me, irritated: "Redemption from what?"

The preacher paused and frowned, scowled and turned, "Do you go to church?" he demanded.

"You could say that I'm in church right now," I replied, my smile becoming more sincere.

"You're not an atheist are you?"

"No. I don't think so."

"Then what is your religion?"

I raised my voice a little, "My religion is a kind which I live myself, and don't feel the need to go around explaining and pushing onto others."

Chavez cracked in the back. (There's always another ride.)

The preacher sighed and pretended to take interest in a passing road sign. "Well, this is as far as I go boys," he lied.

"O.K. Thanks for the ride."

Chavez was still laughing as the geezer

---

[6] I was going to end this sentence with, "…and how then, in that case, could it possibly matter what you say to us now?" But, I thought that the mean Jesus imagery would more proficiently push his buttons.

pulled away, out and along the same highway.

Priests in black gowns are going their rounds, And binding with briars, my joys and desires. William Blake, The Garden of Love

We did not make Bloomington in time for the Super Bowl, but ended up crashing on the floor of a guy named Shane's house with only 40 miles to go. We had met Shane at the bar where we had retired to after getting checked by the local cops. The cops had been called in to give us a shakedown after I had run up to a lady's car who was waiting for the light to change at the onramp. I had only wanted to ask her the score. She ran the light and then phoned the police. The cops thought that was funny. They knew the score.

In the morning we woke up and realized that our host was a pretty sketchy fellow, so we left before he woke, and walked back to the onramp above the interstate.

Our ride into Bloomington was with an old bearded Reki-healer who sang us a funny song about how his dog had fleas. When he dropped us off, he left crystals in our hands as he shook them goodbye. Great ride.

We walked through the outer suburbs, reading the streets, stopping for a beer, and then walking some more.

When we got to Pat's, no one was there.

We found one of the front windows to be unlocked, and after dropping our bags off and leaving a note, we headed into town to scourge the girls' dorms and sell a few more CDs.

That night, after reuniting with Pat, we all

went back into town to play an open-mic at 'The Cellar', which concluded with our returning to one of the boys' houses to have a big smoky jam. We played old stuff: David Allen, Waylon, Buffalo Spring.

The next day when we awoke, the apartment was again empty. We had a look at the map, and then discarded our aluminium WEST sign up onto Pat's mantle and left by the window through which we had come.

*   *   *

The first freight train that we managed to stick to crossed the Mississippi from Memphis and continued all night long. After our elation had subsided, we became very cold and somewhat frustrated by our attempts at achieving some sort of sitting-position that would not quickly wear a hole straight through the seat of our pants. We were in a roofless car known as a 'gondola'. The solution, as we found it, was to lay your pack down and spread-eagle it, belly down as if you were humping it. Sleep still wasn't easy, and we were feeling pretty ghastly when the train eased into some yard very early in the morning. It took us less than an hour to re-provision at a tiny southern shop, and then to crash the tent on a knoll of grass, careless to our being in full-view of an assortment of shacks and mobile homes.

As we were striking the tent in the late afternoon, another train pulled into the yard, and Chavez and I had a brief discussion about whether to jump on, or to seek out the highway. I was for jumping, just 'cause I didn't feel like walking out to the highway, which I guessed to be none to close, but Chavez did not want to freeze his ass on another open car. Agreed.

**You, you are on the road, must have a code,
that you can go by, and so, become yourself,
because the past, is just a goodbye...** CSNY

CHAPTER CHAVEZ

January 20th at about 9 o'clock in the morning.

A girlfriend of mine dropped me off on the side of I-95 in Portland, Maine, in the middle of a big blizzard. The snow was flying, falling heavy. We had just stopped at a gas station, and I had got myself a big cup of coffee before driving the final quarter mile to the onramp, where the split between north and south is.

She pulled over and stopped the car, and I got out and grabbed my pack, and walked around to the driver's side. She got out and I gave her a kiss and a hug, and then I walked to the southbound entrance, and she drove northbound, and that was the last I saw of her.

I remember just standing there, feeling really uncertain, and not knowing how to look back. So instead I just walked down the onramp, and started waving my thumb at the oncoming cars.

It wasn't long before I got a ride down to the Maine border in a rickety old pickup truck with an older gentleman and his son. He dropped me off somewhere near Kennebunk. And then I got another ride, and another ride, and another ride, and before night fell, I was in Manchester Center in Vermont, where Mr. Audacy lives.

I called him from a little bagel shop or something not far from his house, and had him pick me up and take me back to his parents' house where I met his folks, and then he and I went out and had some drinks and got ready to leave.

When morning came, his mother gathered us into her Subaru station wagon and dropped us out on highway 7, where we hitched up to Middlebury College to spend a couple of days with Audacy's brother Charlie.

Together with Charlie and two of his girlfriends, we indulged in some psychedelic experiences, and spent a wintry afternoon roaming across the snowy, wind-swept valleys of Vermont. Everyone took off on their own for a while, and I built a bit of a stonewall on the rise between two of the fields.

When I went off to find Audacy, he had a stick in his hand and was scratching out a sentence in the snow. He had written it in a wide circle, and I can still remember: *"It's a hidden trail that marks our glory, these tracks in the snow don't tell no lies."*

The following day we hit the road for real, and hitched about ten miles west and over to the next route. We got dropped off there and waited for about 8 hours in the cold... freezing cold. You gotta remember that this is the middle of January in the northeast, and it's just not too warm that time of year.

Finally, we got picked up and made it on down to where another friend of Audacy's lives in Granville, and we had a warm place to sleep for the night.

In the morning, we hitched from there in eastern New York, kind of upstate, and down to Connecticut, where we got to Walter's house.

We spent a couple of nights at Walter's father's place, and Audacy played on the college radio there. We got into all sorts of mischief, including stealing Walter's father's Range Rover and going back to campus to see some girls and, I don't know, we were just binge drinking and screwing around.

When we left Walter's, we hitched out of Connecticut and across N.Y. State on our way to Bloomington. We were going to try to make it there by Super Bowl Sunday.

The hitch across from Connecticut to Indiana was bitterly cold. Just a real cold spell during that time. Audacy wore a winter jacket that he stole from a pile that was left outside of a church, and he had a shitty summer sleeping bag, probably good to about 50 degrees, while I had packed a zero degree, down, mummy bag.

It was one night in Pennsylvania: We'd been hitching all day and we made it to a truckstop and had our dinner and a coffee there. Then we walked back out to the onramp. It was well after dark now, maybe 10 or 11 o'clock at night, and we hitched and hitched and hitched and nobody stopped, and it was just getting colder and colder. Our fingers and toes were frozen, and no matter how many circles we paced in, we just couldn't warm up, so finally we made the decision to pitch the tent in an open field, whereupon, just in pitching the tent, when we had to take our mittens off, our fingers absolutely froze. I could hardly work the zippers to get in and out of the tent, and I was only barely able to get into my sleeping bag.

At some point in the night I awoke to find Audacy next to me shivering terribly, and I knew that even with all of his clothes on, you know, his wool hat and his coat and his pants and his long-johns and his mittens and all that, he still didn't have enough warmth, so I remember sort of rolling over, still in my sleeping bag, and just sort of leaning on top of him a little bit to try to warm him up, and Audacy woke up immediately with a start, and screamed out, "What are you doing?" and I was like, "Jesus man, you know, you're just... your freezing to death! I'm trying to warm you up," and then he fell right back asleep.

So we packed up in the morning, still freezing our asses, and walked over to the onramp and got a ride within the hour. It was a big truck, and Audacy got into the bunk in the back, and fell asleep for 3 or 4 hours. I forget the truck driver's name, but he was a crazy old guy, almost autistic in his mannerisms. We rode with him across to Indiana, and almost made it to Bloomington that day, but not quite. We fell short after being picked up by a few different police officers for hitchhiking out on the interstate, and they kept on removing us and depositing us along the highway at the next county line. At that point, we had begun joking about the possibility of crossing the entire state in the backs of these cop cars.

When we made it to Bloomington, we stayed a few nights there with Pat, who was the guitar player in Audacy's old *Freewater* band. Audacy played some music there in town, and we went back to a party that lasted till early in the morning.

Then we started heading straight south.

We hitched down into Tennessee and it got a little bit warmer as we went, but not too much. The daytimes were warmer but the nighttimes were still bitterly cold in the tent.

It was probably two weeks into the trip when we made it to Memphis, and from where we got dropped off, you could see a railyard not far away, and we both just sort of looked at each other and decided that we should give it a whirl. So we walked over to a little mom and pop store that sold hardly anything at all, and bought some beef jerky, some peanuts, a small bottle of whisky, two Colt 45s, and I bought myself a pack of Camel unfiltered cigarettes. Then we walked over to the railyard and sat behind a pile of railroad ties, drinking our forties and just sort of biding our time as we waited for a train to come by.

This is all at about 11 o'clock in the morning.

We waited about an hour before we heard something coming along the tracks, and we peeked out from around the corner of the railway ties, and sure enough there was a train rolling our way. So we got our packs on and crouched behind the pile of railroad ties, getting ready to run out and jump on this mother.

As it approached, I could see that it was going pretty fast, and just as I was about to open my mouth to argue this point with Audacy, he just bolted and made a B-line for the train and I really didn't have an opportunity to discuss anything, so I just stood up and made chase.

We were running at full speed, and I was going just fast enough to be able to keep up with the train with my pack on, and I remember running across this patch of pavement. Audacy was maybe ten feet ahead of me, and at the same time that he jumped up, I did too, grabbing onto the side-rail of the ladder, and the both of us had one hand of the train, and one foot on the ladder. About a second later, the train bucked, and this together with its forward momentum caused us to wing around and smash up against the side.

Anyway, we were both thrown from the train.

I remember a sickening feeling of falling in slow motion and then hitting the ground and skidding along the gravel. I scraped along until finally coming to a slow stop just a few feet from the tracks, with the train just rolling by.

I started to drag myself up, and I looked over and saw Audacy slowly getting to his feet as well, with his guitar flung a few feet away from him, and we both just kind of got up and looked at each other, and had this moment of collective "FUCK!"

I looked down at myself and my palms were bleeding, and my elbows were bleeding, and my knees were bleeding, and I had torn through my jacket and pants. But we just kind of dusted ourselves off and walked back behind the railroad ties, and sat back down to collect ourselves.

We were both in a state of shock, I guess, but we decided for some reason not to give up. We were both hurt and tired, but we waited again for another hour, and sure enough, another train came rolling by. This one was going a lot slower, and we managed to grab hold, climb up the ladder, throw our packs in, and then jump in ourselves.

At first it didn't seem to be that cold inside of our car. The sun was still out, and it was bearable. But once the train left Memphis and cleared the bridge, it started picking up speed to 40 or 50mph, which isn't terribly fast, but on a train with all of it's shaking and moving about, 50mph is a lot, especially with an open top and the wind coming straight into the car.

We rode that train through the daylight hours and into the dark, and as the sun set it became colder and colder, and we were just sippin' on our whisky and smoking those camel unfiltered cigarettes to stay awake. The floor of the train was vibrating so much that mostly we just stood up and leaned against the walls and rode it out.

At one point in the night we had both become so exhausted that we had no choice but to lie our packs down, and just sort of crouch over them, and we were just vibrating and jerking all over, and it was the coldest night that I've ever had in my life, as close as I've ever come to death through cold.

The train pulled into another big railyard at some time around 3 or 4:oo in the morning. We had no idea where it was, but we were so happy to be out of the wind when it stopped.

We sat in that car for three hours because the railyard that we had pulled into was a big loading and unloading zone, maybe fifteen tracks wide, and they were shuffling all of the cars around. There was no way of determining which way the train was going to go, or if our car was

going to be put onto a different locomotive, or
what. But we couldn't very well get out because
there was lots of activity and guys driving
around on four-wheelers and spotlights and
railworkers everywhere, so we waited until
morning when things started to die down a bit,
and then we climbed out of the car, and down the
ladder we went, and made our way out of the
railyard as quickly and as clandestinely as
possible.

I still I have no idea what state we were in,
but we walked up onto a big hill and the morning
sun had just peeked through, and the frost on the
grass was melting into dew, and we sat shivering
on top of the hill, feeling so sick from having
been shaken all night long, and being so cold,
and not really having any food. We really had no
choice but to pitch our tent there in the sun, so
we crawled in and got in our sleeping bags and
slept until afternoon, just to try to warm
ourselves up and get control of our bodies again.

When we had come to the point where we could
walk around and talk, we packed the tent away,
and hiked a quarter mile out to this little store
in a very small town with a black community, and
we were the only white people in sight. We
learned that it was maybe ten miles back out to a
main road, so we were faced with a decision of
either trying to hitch that dirt road out to a
larger highway, or to try and get back on the
train.

We decided to make another try for the train,
so we walked back to the hill and put our stuff
down there, and we could see that one of the
trains was getting ready to take off again. It
was pointing in what seemed to be the right

direction, and this time we tried a different strategy. Audacy walked down to the lead car where there was an engineer getting ready to go, and he gave him some bullshit story about trying to get to Arizona because he was going to get married there, and then he ran back over to me and said, "Come on let's go right now," and we grabbed our stuff and jumped onto the second engine.

We had seats, we had a coffee maker, we had warmth, and we sat down and listened to music on his little mini-disc player, telling stories and talking, and just thinking that we were so cool, riding in that second freight train engine.

Sometime around ten o'clock at night the train came into a town. It didn't stop, but it slowed down, and we decided that it might be a good time to jump off to get something to eat. So we took our packs outside and climbed down the ladder. I threw my pack off the engine and then just jumped and hit the ground rolling, and Audacy did the same, while trying to hold his guitar up.

Now, as we stood up, we looked around and realized that there was an enormous metal fence with razor wire all along the top, and we thought "Well, what the hell is this?" So we start walking along the perimeter of the fence until we spot a kiosk up ahead, and as we approach, the man inside notices us, and we scared him because he didn't expect anybody to be coming from that direction. He reaches down near his waist and pulls up a double-barreled shotgun and then cocks it and levels it at us, and we were like, "Whoa, whoa we just want to know where we are. What state is this? What town is this?" And he yelled,

"Texarkana!" And that was the first person that we met in Texas.

Turns out, we were just outside of a federal penitentiary, but it wasn't really a big problem. We just slipped by and kept on walking, and we were in Texarkana, Texas, on the corner of Arkansas and Louisiana.

We walked into town and it seemed to be pretty deserted. We bought ourselves a couple of big beers and sat down in a vacant parking lot to drink them, smoking cigarettes and just kind of relaxing after the train. Then we found a restaurant not too far away, a little Italian spaghetti restaurant where we had a real cute waitress. We were all dirty and dusty and we sat down and had ourselves a real big dinner and got our energy levels back up before leaving and walking around Texarkana for an hour or two.

There was really not much going on. We found one coffee shop and sat there for a while before deciding to go and find a place to camp, out in one of the town's little parks underneath a tree for the night.

In the morning we collected our stuff and walked 5 or 6 miles before stopping at a Burger King to get a cup of coffee. From there we somehow solicited a ride with an old lady and her son, in the back of a pickup truck that got us on down the line, and out of Texarkana.

*   *   *

We began our hitch west, clear across Texas through Sherman, Gainesville, Wichita Falls, and all the way up to Amarillo.

Somewhere around Amarillo, we got picked up by a really big Indian guy, and we were telling stories about hitchhiking, and this guy had a terrible scar on his neck, and after a few hours, the story came out:

Some years ago he had been driving that same stretch of highway, and there had been another guy hitching. Well, he pulls over and picks the guy up and they're riding for a while, and out of the blue, the hitchhiker pulls a knife on him, and as the knife came out, our Indian ride pulled the car over very quickly, slammed his fist into this guy's head, and as he did so, the guy cut his throat. Then as he's bleeding, he gets out of the car, goes around to the passenger side, drags the guy out, and then kicks his ass. Then he made him take his boots off, and left him on the side of the road with no boots and no wallet, before getting back into the car and driving to the next town to call the cops. He went to check himself into the hospital, and he gets all stitched up and he's OK. And sure enough the cops find the robber guy walking down the road, no boots, no wallet, and you can't really get that far without any boots. But we just couldn't believe that our guy would still be picking up hitchhikers (!).

We drove with him for two days, spending one night in a motel that he got somewhere in western Texas or New Mexico. I slept too close to a space heater that night and melted part of my sleeping bag.

When he dropped us off, we continued west through Albuquerque, and then spent the night in Gallup after we had bailed from one of our rides cause he was such a young pompous ass. He was so full of himself that we just couldn't ride with him anymore.

So we got off in Gallup, New Mexico and Audacy played two bars that night. One was kind of an empty honky tonk joint, and then we got word that there was another place that was a little more happenin', and that turned out to be an Indian bar, and everybody in there was Native American. Kind of a rough scene. So we walk in with our two big packs and Audacy's guitar to sit and drink, and some local Indian girls are hitting on us, and Audacy gets up on stage and plays a couple of songs with the band, and then we go out to the parking lot and smoke some ganga with some sketchy Indian guys who are all clam-baking in one of their beat-up cars.

About that time we were both pretty drunk and pretty high, and we knew that we had to get out of there, but the Indian women were still chasing us around, so we walked a mile looking for a place to sleep, but didn't really find anywhere. Ended up camping out in a Walmart parking lot in the dog shit area.

In the morning we went off to do some laundry. As dirty as the freight trains are, we wanted to be a little bit cleaner for our arrival to Flagstaff.

So we left Gallup, and after having walked for many miles along the blue highway, we decided to try the interstate. Our second or third ride is with this crazy crackhead Mexican guy, speaking Spanish. Audacy's in the front seat and I'm in the back, and the guy is just totally loony. The car is filthy and you don't dare to touch anything, and Audacy's kind of giving me the vibe like, "get ready to jump out of the car," and unbeknownst to me, because I didn't speak Spanish hardly at all, the guy was asking Audacy if he'd ever sucked cock for coke, and all sorts of really shady sketchy shit, but he dropped us off right on the outskirts of Flagstaff from where we were able to walk into town and hitch a couple of short rides, and before we knew it, we had found Dave McConnelly's house and we were drinkin' beer with him and his brother and their girlfriends and hanging out in Flagstaff, Arizona, waiting for Nick to show up the following night.

CHAPTER THREE
Texas to Flagstaff

The HITCHHIKING RULES of the CODE:

I - don't upstage other hitchhikers.[7]

II - don't fall asleep on a ride.[8]

III - don't steal from, beg from, or ask anything of a ride, *ever*.[9]

*   *   *

From Texarkana, we started a slow and grueling hitchhike west northwest to clear Texas and rejoin the interstate. We travelled along highway 82 and spent a night on the floor of a

---

[7] It is a wild discourtesy to hitch anywhere near one kilometre in front of another hitchhiker, even if (you're) dropped off there, and not in view of the other person.

[8] …unless proffered, or unless there's two of you leaving someone awake to talk.

[9] This includes going further for you, and out of their way.

motel room with a Native American trucker, watching "The Matrix" and being careful not to be spotted by reception.

The interstate sped our travel, and we made Flagstaff in good time for the full moon. Avalanche Dave wasn't home when we got there, but his bird and some of his flatmates had caught word of our impending arrival, and gave us a warm welcome. Hobbit-like Avalanche Dave later appeared, together with his younger brother and other happy faces, all exchanging lofty banter regarding the next day's "pimp and ho'" party, which had been scheduled for Dave's birthday.

The two boxes of CDs had arrived.

The following afternoon we went to the railway station to pick up Nick. And there he was: fresh, clean, and visibly without a clue as to what he was getting himself into. He was all smiles, but you could tell he was nervous on account of his hands being kept in his pockets, and his whistling too much.

First thing Chavez said to Nick was: "Are you ready?"

Nick, laughing: "Who said I wasn't?"

We both smiled in elation at the arrival of Nick, and all together adjourned to Avalanche Dave's to consummate the occasion with anxious but steady drinking, amidst a myriad of females who were attiring themselves as whores.

A tall, blond-haired guy named Happy was not going to be able to make the gala that evening, and offered me his thrift store getup: white-collar French-cuffed shirt, brown corduroy vest, dapper pants, sunglasses and wig. I jettisoned the pants and wig, and wore the outfit for the next several weeks.

The following morning included a diner breakfast[10] and featured a visit to the Flagstaff Radio-Shack, and the purchase of two handheld Citizen Band radios.[11] This provided us with some entertainment for a little while as we ran around the parking lot: "Breaker, breaker motherfucker!

When we got back, I placed a call to that girl down in Bisbee to alert her to our proximity, "...So we're just waiting for Max now, and he's supposed to be getting here today."

The telephone rang a little later, just as we were starting to play a song.

"...Goddamnit Max, why am I talking to you in Texas?"

"Hey, this is really a cool place, man! There's like a warehouse here that has been taken over by activists. And everyone is so involved. It's great! And there's this girl..."

"No Max."

He wanted to change everything, and motorcycle off with some new bird and then meet up with us down in Mexico (the prospect of consistent nook I'm sure playing no small part in his reasoning).

I was mad. Max had proposed to be the third originally, a situation which I had avoided by

---

[10] Two eggs, three strips of bacon, short-stack of pancakes, maple syrup and hash browns.
[11] 9 batteries required; batteries sold in packs of 8.

recruiting a forth, who would now become the third if Max bailed. I told him as much over the phone and softly threatened him to get on his fucking bike and meet us in Bisbee in two days time.

He called back ten minutes later to tell me that it was a "GO". And I expected of course, that his new girlfriend had decided not to.

As Avalanche Dave drove the three of us back to the highway later on that afternoon, someone spotted the postman finishing his rounds, and Chavez was let out to inquire about a package that he had been hoping to receive before departure.

The postman had Chavez's package.

It seemed that we were right on time.

So off we dropped Chavez at the first exit and then Nick and myself at the next, and soon lamented to find that the range on the CBs didn't carry very farr.

Plan was to meet in Bisbee by the following night.

Wandering Aimlessly with his eyes on the steeple
Lost traveler hoping her thoughts haven't left him
Of plans he bears many although lost in the canyon
With the sun setting slowly on his dreams once
forgotten
Or left behind waiting for her absent inclusion
Cause he's going to be with her or he's going to
go crazy
As the hope is left waiting and the plans remain
changing
From an edge of the abyss he dreams of her beauty
And the story unspoken with its actors unwilling
And the mind starts to swim when the blackness
divides

Hearts beating backwards, tree vein cunt lizard
And with music to follow as I open a beer.

CHAPTER CHAVEZ

There were three of us now: Nick, Audacy and I, and since Nick had scant hitchhiking experience, it was decided that Audacy would go ahead with Nick, and that I would hitch by myself. Our next destination was Bisbee, Arizona.

So I hitched alone out of Flagstaff, shooting for Benson, but that night got stuck in Phoenix at an onramp right in the middle of the city, and it was real shitty. At one point in the night, a car pulled over with a flat tire, and it was this young girl who was on her way to work at the airport. I didn't really have anything else to do so I helped her to change her tire, and when I did that, she gave me her name and number and told me that she'd hook me up with some free plane tickets.

So I spent the night there, and just camped out in one of those little hips or valleys, and in the morning, started hitching again from that same onramp, right in the city. After a couple of hours, I started walking down the freeway, and must have walked through half of Phoenix when I finally got picked up by these two guys who looked like they were out of a Quentin Tarantino movie, looked like they were straight out of L.A., hair all slicked back with the dark sunglasses and Hawaiian shirts and all that, and they were pretty sketchy. But they dropped me off somewhere around Tucson, where I got picked up by a carload of young Indian skater kids, a bunch of

punks smoking weed, and they dropped me off out
in the middle of the desert at the turn-off to
their reservation.

I remember sitting in the middle of the
desert, pretty much D.T.H., knowing that I had to
make it to Bisbee, and knowing how far it was and
how little time I had to get there. I was pretty
much fucked, and didn't think that I was going to
make it there that day, and it was just hot as
hell. There was no shade, it was just desert.

But about a half hour later this guy comes
along, pulls over in his little car, and turns
out to be this German guy who was some sort of
journeyman cabinet-maker, I don't know what the
hell he was, he was weird. Nice guy though. Late
twenties. Had on a crazy costume, looked like he
was Amish or something, and had a big black wide-
brimmed hat, and like a black corduroy jumpsuit
with a black bowtie and a white shirt underneath.
Looked like quite a character. Anyway, he was
just driving around Arizona and had a few weeks
to kill, so he took me all the way down to
Bisbee, and we got there about a half hour after
Audacy and Nick had shown up, and about ten
minutes before Max Fortes rode into town.

Fortes had just come over, after much delay
and procrastination, from New York City, and had
ridden his motorbike down from there. So it was
perfect timing. All four of us arrived at pretty
much the same time.

We all met up in front of some little opera
house in Bisbee, which was a real cool town. An
old mining town I guess. So after stopping at the
bakery to eat some free day-old bakery stuff, we
went up the hill to Morgan's place and kind of

unpacked, and then spent the next three nights in Bisbee.

The first night we hung out in the café all night drinking, and playing a bunch of music. The next night we went up into the hills and Audacy started a big fucking raging bonfire in the middle of the dry season, and it was windy as hell with border patrol helicopters flying all over the place, and after a four to one vote in favor of *not* having a fire. Anyway, nothing burned down - got lucky again - and the night passed.

CHAPTER FIVE
A Big Arrival

Hitchhiking Lingo: D.T.H. = Too high to hitchhike

= Too High To Hitchhike

= T.H.T.H.

= Double T.H.

= D.T.H.

e.g.: My second and third rides were both skinning up when they pulled over, and I got D.T.H. and had to wander off into a field to sleep it off for a while.

*   *   *

So there we ambled, Nick and I, by the side of the road, and he was stretching his arms and clapping his hands as I tried to give him a brief rundown of how we might display and maintain our flow. I told him how we should try to keep at least one of the car doors open at all times when one of us or our things were still inside. And then I forced myself to shut up, and after indicating that he was expected to do the hitching, I had a smoke and aligned the packs with the guitar put in front.

I watched Nick as he nodded and then whispered to himself, stepping up onto the road with a bit of a laugh. I stood silent and lived vicariously through Nick as he took in the vein of the road, extending up to the horizon in each direction. To the left tracing home, to the right calling onward. Destination: Infinity.

Nick was letting out a laugh with each car that passed us by, but the laughter would lessen with each pass until after a few minutes, he was no longer turning to watch the cars drive away, but was instead focusing early on the oncoming cars.

It didn't take long.

*　　　*　　　*

Three rides and five hours later and we're in a ride with a tattooed guy that we had solicited from amidst a horde of lot-lizards[12] at a gigantic truck stop, in a car that smells of ginger and puke.

We had been mostly travelling along blue roads up until now, but anyway, we get left off at a bad exit on the interstate. And with a pulloff lane but no real onramp, we were kind of what the cop wanted to call "fucked".

---

[12] Trucker whores.

"You boys gotta get off of this here federal property, and go back and find the highway."

"Well, how farr is the highway from here?"

"It's a good ways off... Now I'm not gonna give you boys a ticket, only just a citation. And then I'll be expecting you to clear on off of this here interstate. Now if you just sign here..."

"Well *I'm* not signing *my* fucking citation," said I.

This comment spawned reactions.

From the cop it was a raising of the voice, finger shaking, clipboard waving and standing akimbo. From Nick it was more like surprise, an increased level of anxiety, and a faint sense of distress. The cop went on and on about how he'd gladly have us spend the night in jail, and then continued by giving us the exact location of the prison which, as he pointed out, was not very farr away.

Nick's glance to me was maybe like a bit of an appeal, or at least that's what I imagined. Furthermore, the afternoon's hitch had been kind of more roadside than not, and a prudent estimator would already be pinning us behind an arrival to Bisbee by tomorrow afternoon (excuses, excuses right?). Bear in mind: <u>sex played no small part</u>.

Anyway, I signed the fucking citation.

Then it's the next day, and me and Nick are scrambling for the back of a blue P-up truck ride occupied in the front by none other than the

three guys from ZZ Top. I mean it really looked
like them! They said nothing when they stopped,
but the one on the passenger side did the
quintessential 'hop-in' gesture as we approached.
It was exactly from a video I saw once.

So there we were in the back of the ZZ Top P-
up truck, and I was beginning to crunch up the
cardboard sign with which we had hitched this
ride. It read: 'BENSON'.

Let me go off on signs for a minute. As a
general rule, I'm against signs. Signs usually
tend to provide an excuse to the mentality of the
driver for *not* picking you up: "Oh, I'm not going
there," or "I'm not going that far," which really
makes you want to scream, "Yeah, but you're going
that fucking way!" Especially when there's miles
and miles until the next fork or exit.

But. When one finds oneself to be a few
unwanted miles out in front of a major fork or
junction, sometimes the declaring of one's
destination (thisaway or thataway) can assist the
driver in forecasting whether or not the
application of brakes, or *autostop*, is even
worthwhile.

I still prefer no signs however.

I once met an English guy who had a sign that
said 'FURTHER'.[13] That was my favourite sign that
I ever saw.

Anyway, back in the P-up truck ride, I was
folding up the sign that said 'BENSON', and with
my magic marker, I idly realized that with this
same sign, by adding a 'B' to the end, I could

---

[13] On the other side it said 'HOME'.

46

create an abbreviation for our next destination:
'BSB'. It was a bit of a stretch, I knew, but as
I held up the folded wad to show Nick with a
laugh, a red P-up truck began to overtake us in
the passing lane, and on seeing the sign (I may
have kind of displayed it), he gave us a big
thumbs-up and decelerated to pull in behind us.

As our exit approached, we banged on the roof
of the ZZ Top guys, who silently slowed onto the
shoulder and gave us the thumbs up. Our new guy
awaited us down on the off-ramp, and his name was
Steve.

Steve had been the drummer in a famous punk-
rock band, whose name Nick and I both pretended
to recognize.[14] Now he was all hipped out and
rolling a joint as he drove, and he had a
beautiful baby boy who was strapped into the
backseat of his extended cab.

Steve wasn't really going to Bisbee, as it
turned out, but he decided to drive us there
anyway, after finding out that we had come all
the way from Vermont.

So forty minutes of driving and another joint
gets smoked, and we're pulling into Bisbee with
Steve asking us where we want left off.

"Anywhere," said we, rounding the corner and
onto Main Street. And before the truck had even
come to a stop, there out in front of the bar on
the street corner before us, stood:

1) Morgan, arms waving, totally afire,

2) Her sister, Flori, all smiles,

---

[14] People often pretended to recognize the name of my band too.

47

3) Max, Cheshire grin, rising from having been leaning against his bike,

4) Chavez, pack at his feet, chatting to:

5) Some other guy, dressed up as a strange looking Mennonite.

This part was a series of 'hellos', with only one goodbye as rock-star Steve passed up our offer to buy him a drink to make his way back towards Benson. The Mennonite guy turned out to have been Chavez's last ride. He was with some European travelling guild, whose members dressed, worked and travelled by a code. It was actually pretty cool, and we would meet more of these guys later on.

As for right now, I knew the balance was in the mix with the four of us coming together for the first time. Introductions... on to organization, which concluded with a plan for me and Morgan to drive all of the packs up to the house to drop them off, sexetera, so as to then be able to return to the bar with everyone — all hands free.

Tinge of anxiety for me right then as we're pulling away, and I pause from talking with Morgan to look out the window at Nick who is standing tightly with his arms crossed, watching us pull away like a lonely schoolboy. Max is standing out in front of him, chatting it up with the others, and probably opening up with one of his famous travel stories where you really just had to be there.

*   *   *

When we got back into town, the boys were

more or less as we had left them, only that they
had moved inside. We drank for a while,
acclimating to our new group, and then afterwards
we piled into Morgan's sister's sedan to drive
back up to the house, and I found myself behind
the wheel. Morgan was directing our movie from
the passenger seat with Nick seated upon her lap.
Chavez, Max, German friend, and Morgan's sister
were all in the back.

So you can imagine my sense of concern when
after our first turn around the corner, the cop
lights come on in the rear-view mirror. I pulled
over right way and waited, trying to lower the
general sound level inside the car. Someone
slipped me a piece of gum from the back as buddy
approached the driver's side window:

"Um, good evening. My, it looks a bit
crunched up in there. Ah, where are you guys
coming from?"

"Just coming from the bar," I said, trying to
focus a neutral stare. I supposed that he had
been spotting us all along.

"And which bar is that?" he asked.

"Um, I don't know the name," I stammered,
trying not to crack a smile at the hopelessness
of our situation, and then to everyone: "What was
the name of the bar that we were just at?"

But before anyone could come up with a name,
Morgan suddenly ducked her head over towards my
window, "Hi Bob," she sang.

His voice changed as he said, "Oh, hi there
Morgan, how's it going?"

"Oh, pretty good, you know."

"Looks a bit squished in there," he scolded uncertainly.

"Oh, we're just going up to the house," she assured him.

And then he continued to me. He said: "Ah, we pulled you over to inquire as to whether anyone has a camera in the vehicle?"

This to me was the least of all expected things that he might have asked.

"No," I began, and then lifting my head slightly towards the ceiling, I asked, "Does anyone have a camera with them?"

"No," chimed everyone, in a dilapidated chorus.

"Oh, cause we're just pulling over cars 'cause somebody had a camera stolen."

"Well it wasn't us, Bob," Morgan's sister put in from the back.

"Oh, I didn't see you there too." Apparently this cop was a regular patron at the bakery.

"Are you coming in tomorrow?"

"Oh, we'll probably be around," he said, hedging back from the window, "Well then, you guys drive safe."

The girls overlapped: "Goodbye Bob," with "See ya Bob," and I realized that we were in the clear.

Black boots black boots black boots black boots black

My boots are so black that they couldn't be *blacker*
Black boots black boots black boots black boots black
He wanted his freedom, yeah but not to be without her

CHAPTER NICK

I don't remember how it was approached to me, to go on a trip. But I remember that Audacy was back in Vermont, and I was sort of at the end of a rope, and I needed new things. I had been spending too much time in my own head, and doing that kinda stuff, and it was time for outside adventures; it was time to move on and see the rest of the world. And I had never been out of the country before, except for Canada, but that doesn't really count. And so I went with Audacy to get my passport.

When I first met Chavez, I knew I would like Chavez right away. We met up at Audacy's house by the school, and he had hitched down by himself all the way from Maine, and I knew right away that we'd be friends. In a way he reminded me of my older brother. But it wasn't that, it was just a good first impression, so I was excited to get going and meet these guys.

Now, I had been around New York City for a while, but for me, the trip really started happening at Grand Central Station, which is a sweet place, and I had been there once before; oh, and let me tell you that the last song that I sang before I left was called 'Whistle Down the Wind,' and it's a song about having to get out and go see the world.

Anyway, Grand Central Station. I had my pack.

And I had brought my bible with me, I don't know why. Anyway, I read a bunch of the Old Testament there, and the stories seemed to fit a traveler's perspective, especially Exodus for example.

I realized that this trip was more about Audacy, and where he was going, and what he was trying to do, so I felt like a supporting character, and I said that all along, but from my own angle, I was looking for new experiences.

Anyway, Grand Central Station. Three days on a train across America, which was fun. And I had never been on a train before. There's wacky people on trains. I didn't meet a single person who wasn't interesting.

I got to Flagstaff a day or two after they had arrived, and as soon as I got off the train it felt like I was stepping off of a boat, I felt... not-grounded. And there they were, right at the train, come to meet me. They're all smiles and happiness, and its right before Dave's birthday, and the Pimp and Ho party.

So we spent a couple of days up in Flagstaff, and I had never hitchhiked before, so Dave drove us down to the interstate that led towards Phoenix, and I started hitchhiking with Audacy. He was standing there by the side of the road singing some chant about his black boots, and I remember that he told me: "You're too clean, you need to get dirty."

Our first ride was with a Native American dude and his kid, and we rode in the back of a pickup truck, and it was a good feeling, which was a good omen.

Second ride was with a man and a woman from

New York, and they smoked us up and gave Audacy a beer. And I'm not sure how many other rides we got, but we were supposed to meet Chavez in Ely, and there were three exits, so we went to the last one, and no sign of Chavez, so we camped out outside behind some Truck-World place.

Those two had the walkie-talkies, which, as Chavez took off first, it was about thirty yards until they lost reception. But Audacy was using the walkie-talkie on channel 19 to try to get some truckers to pick us up. But that was a no go.

Let me also tell you that the first night of sleeping out in the tent, it was cool. It felt completely different. The ground felt like rocks, and my back was getting used to the new situation for me, and I was excited.

So that was one day, from Flagstaff to Ely, and I remember we went into a bar and tried to get to play, but they had some country DJ on in there, and it was a no go, but me and Audacy went into the back room and played stick, and there were three huge Mexican-Indian dudes in there giving us a rough vibe, and it was like, both sides of the track.

There was one other ride that got us to Ely. It was this old man in a pickup truck, and he had his wife and his kids in the cab with him, and the last thing that he said to us was: "Don't get caught around here when the sun goes down."

Ominous.

From Ely to Bisbee we had a bunch of rides. In Tucson we were on the freeway and a cop came and gave us a nice little piece of paper. I still have it.

I remember two rides. One when we were in the back of a pickup with three Harley guys, and somehow Audacy made our sign turn from Benson into Bisbee, and it worked, and the other one was with a kid who had played in a band that had opened up for Greenday. And he was a nice guy.

I liked how the landscape changed, especially from Flagstaff, 'cause now we were in the south, and it was still cool.

So we get to Bisbee and we jam in a coffee shop. With Audacy's chicky chicks. As soon as we got there, it seemed like we had arrived at the exact same time as Chavez, together with that dude who looked just like Mark Harding, or Jack Black. It was that German guy who was working around the world. Wearing long-ass black chaps and shit. That's when I met Max Fortes, who also arrived within an hour of us being there, and we were at a bar that had swinging doors, and I thought that was cool. Like that Merle Haggard song. The real West. Bisbee was a cool kind of artsy town, and it seemed like a communal area of interesting minds.

Now: Max Fortes. I remember this very clearly. It's that: he didn't pay much attention to me, he shook my hand and we mentioned each other's names, but then all the guys took off on me during my first conversation with him, and I was basically snubbed and he ignored me.

Then of course the fire that Audacy built, that we all recommended not to happen, what with all of the helicopters that were looking for illegal immigrants, and right there on the border. But it worked out well, and the fire kept

us warm, and we all slept in the same tent that
night, huddled together.

CHAPTER SEVEN
When words went wilting

Well, the CB radios that we had purchased in
Flagstaff were the sort that had a detachable
antenna, and once we had unpacked and done a
fresh inventory in Bisbee, it was discovered that
we had already lost the antenna for the unit that
Nick and I had been carrying. I did some phoning
around and found that there was a Radio Shack
back near Benson, and Morgan offered to make the
drive. We took a few of what she, and other
people from New Hampshire call *road sodas*, and
the two of us had a pleasant drive backwards
along yesterday's route, as I recounted the hitch
across and she told me all about Bisbee and
working at the bakery.

When we found the store, a friendly young
Mexican employee opened the box on a new radio
and gave us the accompanying antenna with a wink
and a nod, refusing to accept payment for the
replacement.

Mission accomplished.

So then we loaded back into the car and
started back.

Let me sing you the song of half-hearted love.

It wasn't until we were over halfway back to
Bisbee that Morgan insisted on breaching the
subject that we had so successfully been avoiding

up until that point: The future.

"...And how far do you think you'll go?"

We had just been laughing, and the laughter was still in the air. "How farr? I don't know. As farr as the road takes me, I guess."

"And to Australia?"

"Sure, well... that's the plan."

Short pause now, as the laughter recedes.

"Well it's no fucking English Channel you know!" Her tone had changed, becoming angry.

I said nothing, and sat thinking about how I could turn the conversation. But I didn't get the chance.

"And what about after?"

"After?"

"What about after, goddamnit! Are you gonna come back?"

Her voice had begun to pitch hysterically.

My hands began caressing the air, "It's been so nice just the way it is. Just leaving things unsaid. We both know the way things are. Can't we just leave everything unsaid?"

There was a brief moment as she stifled a sob and her driving became more erratic, "No, goddammit. I can't do it. I can't do this. I want to know if you're gonna come back," and now she began to cry, "I want to know what's going to happen... like, am I supposed to *wait* for you?"

"No." I closed my eyes to say these next words, "Don't wait for me."

*   *   *

God is a Joker.

I am courageous.

If in the end I should fail, I wish to have played well, and will have borne my track and my search across lengthy planes, such as I may know

The extent to which happiness can be maintained fluctuates proportionally with the perfection of the supplement with whom bound, which in turn fluctuates proportionally with the extent to which she is sought out.

God is a joker

I am a seeker.

*   *   *

And I know she's waiting there,
She loves me to this day…
Cortez the Killer, Neil Young

We finished off the beers on the way back and tried to cheer ourselves back up, but things were different then, and I felt like I had just packed my last item and was ready now for departure.

CHAPTER MAX

Well it's always hard to know where to begin a story, and this one could begin back in Spain in 1996, but I'm going to start at New Year's Eve, 2000-01.

I had been invited to a party at this amazing 19th century Robert Baron mansion, owned by a bunch of artists up on the Hudson. I had been in Vermont over Christmas, and the party was meant to be a formal, bohemian affair, so I was hitchhiking in my tuxedo, and it was snowing when I caught my last ride.

They were a group of Oaxacan carpenters and I told them that I planned to soon be crossing through Mexico, and they told me that I should go to Oaxaca City, and that it was the best city in all of Mexico.

The party was amazing. I stayed up all night on New Year's, and then went back to the city and spent a couple weeks in New York getting ready.

And then the inauguration of George Bush was set to take place in Washington D.C. on the 20th of January. There was to be a big gathering of people from all over the country coming to protest the inauguration, and I went down there two nights before the thing started, and was staying on the floor with some people in northwest Washington.

A producer from this radio show came up to me and a friend of mine, and he knew that we had been kind of involved in radical activism in New York City, and he said that they had an extra pair of tickets to the inauguration. Now, the only people who were getting tickets were these heavy-duty Republican donors, who had come from all over the place. But somehow, this producer had gotten hold of a pair of tickets from some kind of infiltrator, and they wanted to give them away to someone who would be sure to cause a ruckus during the inauguration.

So me and this woman were given the tickets, and we started debating about the different things that we could do. We knew that we'd be searched before we went in, so that there'd be no point in trying to carry signs, or anything like that, so we ultimately decided that we would write messages on our bodies, and then take our clothes off and march through the middle of the inauguration. So we wrote all of these political catchphrases and stuff, in permanent marker, on our chests. I think I had 'Hail to the Thief', and 'No Mandate', and a couple of other things.

So the original plan was to wait until Bush had his hand on the Bible, and then to take all our clothes off. The inauguration was held outside, and it was a freezing cold rain, you know, January 20th, it was miserable mid-winter, and all these Republican donors were sitting outside on the steps of the capital, and all of these Republican donors in their fur coats were sinking down into the mud in their folding chairs.

I was sitting next to a couple from Tennessee who had raised fifty thousand dollars for Bush. Then Cheney went and took his oath of office. Everyone was there, Bush was there, Clinton was there, Bush senior was there, everybody, all the Supreme Court, all the Senators.

We were about 100-150 feet away from Bush. We could see him, but he probably couldn't see us. He was behind plates of glass, and it was so cold that there was just no way that I was going to take all of my clothes off, so we backed out a little bit, and decided that we would just take our tops off and walk through. So we did that, and we got about thirty feet before we were swarmed over by secret service and capital police, and escorted off the premises, where they took our pictures and wrote down all of the stuff that we had written on us, and asked us if we had any ill intentions or violent impulses towards the president, to which I replied, "I don't think that he's actually the *president*, but I don't want to hurt him." So they let us go, and we just left and went to the inaugural parade where people were throwing eggs at the presidential limousine, and that was pretty exciting.

So, my stepfather came down from Vermont, bringing my motorcycle on the back of his pickup, and he dropped it off for me. It was pretty cold, but my plan was to head out across the country and meet up with Aude in Arizona somewhere.

So I headed south, freezing, freezing cold, one of the coldest days I ever rode in, stopping at every rest stop along the way to warm my hands back to life with the hand dryers in the bathrooms.

I met up with this friend of mine, this girl, and she rode on the back with me.

We went down and visited my Dad in South Carolina, and went through Savannah, Georgia, and Gainesville, and it was getting warmer by then, followed along the Gulf Coast, Florida to New

Orleans, and then spent about a week there exploring the city.

When we left New Orleans, we rode out across Louisiana. We crossed into Texas, and slept in the high school football bleachers in Orange, and then finally got to Austin where we stayed in an artist's warehouse. We spent a bunch of days dumpster-diving and hanging out with circus performers, and then headed out across Texas, and I think I stayed in one place - Van Horn, Texas - in a little fifteen dollar motel.

I was riding a 450cc, horizontal twin, 1984 Honda Nighthawk, which is not a bike that's really designed to drive across the country with. It's very small, could barely do 65mph, and I had these handmade saddlebags on it, which were stitched together with dental floss. Everyone I met thought I was crazy for trying to cross the country in the winter on a little Japanese bike that was 15 years old, but it worked out.

So I crossed Texas, crossed through El Paso, crossed that little stretch of New Mexico, and made my way to Bisbee where I met Nick and Chavez for the first time, who were to be our third and forth travelling companions.

Now, my plan, such as it was, was to catch up with the Zapatista march in San Cristobal de las Casas, in Chiapas. It was going to be an indigenous march in which all of the Zapatista indigenous rebel leaders led people from their stronghold in Chiapas, and up to Mexico City. So that was going to take place on the 25th of February, and I wanted to kind of get down through Mexico as fast as possible to be there.

Someone's last ride into Bisbee had been with

this German carpenter/journeyman guy, and I guess
the carpenters' guilds' would have been like the
woodworkers' guilds, which would have come from
like the Renaissance times in Germany. Part of
your right of passage is to spend a year
travelling around the world, offering up your
services as a woodworker, dressed in the
traditional garb, and he had this broad-brimmed
black hat, and a white shirt, and black pants and
a black vest made out of these kind of antler-
buttons and very heavy corduroy-suede, like a
finely tailored outfit, and that was sort of your
signifier as you travelled around. And I liked
the idea of it because journeyman, you know, it's
a step up from apprentice, but before being a
master, and you have this notion of like a
journeyman, and that's actually what this guy was
doing. I forget his name, but he had bought a car
and was sort of driving himself around America,
getting odd jobs at woodworking and meeting
people. Quite a conversation starter.

So I was totally enchanted by Bisbee, which
was a beautiful town, a copper boom town. Most of
the buildings had been constructed in this art-
deco style and very nicely done, built along this
canyon right on the Mexican border.

We stayed a couple of days there with Morgan
and her friends. I forget their names. The one
guy had a sailboat in Alaska, and the woman,
Sophia, worked in a bakery. We went camping one
night up in the mountains, and then got ready to
go.

CHAPTER NINE
Bisbee

There was something else that was going on while we were in Bisbee. Max was trying to organize a place where he could store his bike, and he told us that his first choice would be to sell it, but that either way he had to come up with a solution quickly. So he spoke to the boyfriend of the girl who ran the bakery, and the boyfriend told him that he may have a bit of extra space in his garage. The guy was also interested in perhaps buying the bike, as he thought that it might suit his girlfriend as a first bike to own. Max said that he'd be glad to wrap the whole thing up, and that he'd be willing to part with the bike for a thousand dollars. The boyfriend took that into consideration, and then asked if he could take the bike out for a spin. Max gave him the keys.

After the guy had taken off on the bike, Max went to find a telephone to place a call to his stepfather back home. Long story short: The boyfriend came back and said that he'd buy the bike. Max replied that there had been a development, and that his stepfather had forbidden him from selling the bike for anything less than fourteen hundred.

We all thought that this was kind of a shit move to pull, especially when the guy had offered to store the bike for free. But Max told me to 'shut up and stay out of it', and that he 'knew what he was doing', and finally there was no sale, but the guy adhered to his offer to store the bike for free until Max's return.

That second night in Bisbee we camped out up on the mountain, and I fixed dinner.[15]

I don't remember what we did that next day, but I remember that there was a lot of drinking going on come nightfall, and at some point Morgan and I made our way upstairs to make a slow, sad and rather detached form of love before passing out on top of each other.

*　　*　　*

The next morning came quickly. The four of us were scuttling about, trying to make sure that we hadn't left anything behind. Coffee was being made, and Chavez was in charge of packing the car.

M: "Has anyone seen my glasses? Hey you guys, has anyone seen my glasses?"

C: "Yeah, they're on your head, Max.

M: "Oh... right."

A: "I swear, this boy'd go riding off to look for his pony with his glasses on his head and his pencil behind his ear.

M: "Yeah shut up, OK? I'm just trying to be sure."

---

[15] **Recipe for Barbed Wire Shishcabob:** This is a really easy road-feast to make. You buy a ½lb/person of cubed beef from the butcher, and then also some peppers, a few onions, some people like mushrooms, and definitely lots of wine. Then you find and break off a five-foot section of barbed wire (barbed wire will break if you bend it back and forth enough times). The barbed wire unravels into three separate finer strands, and with these you start weaving a grill by bending them back and forth every 16 inches or so, and then you hold them all spaced together right by running the last piece of wire through in the opposite direction. So the only thing left to make now is the actual skewers, which you can usually set your company to making with whatever kind of knife. It works best if you strip off the bark.

*   *   *

There was an energy and excitement in the car on the way to Douglas that I was guiltily trying to suppress for Morgan's sake.[16] We unloaded from the car at a parking lot that was within sight of the border, and after bidding farewell to both she and our German Mennonite friend, we took some deep breaths and exchanged some looks and some smiles before turning ahead and not looking back.

*   *   *

Spits and grains and the essence of who you are and who you want to be: Come sit beside me. There is but one woman in the world who appears in different faces, said the girl. But the girl became fire. But the fire kept me warm.

These are crazy times in a crazy world gone mad, and the music now rhymes with the ragged edge of metal and concrete, or else a life and a time in our minds, which may never have been, and ought never to be, except for right now.

It's so much easier to follow the tread of a sole, but only keen eyes will find where the barefooted go, and with no fallback plan, you can't ever miss, so tie down, light up, and follow your bliss (with me)

---

[16] I'm not sure if I can properly describe the feeling of building energy all during this time. On the eve of adventure with four varied but strong young lives converging into a single vector. The feeling that you get, as a male, walking down the street with the four of you striding abreast, loyal and strong, expectant and focused, arrogant and reckless, and in a word, seemingly undeterable, unstoppable, like being on coke, and probably the reason that so many were killed in the old west. No longer a drifter, but a faction, no longer an aimless wanderer, but a platoon, a force to be reckoned with. It's a strong feeling.

PART II

CHAPTER TEN
Into Mexico

The TRAVEL RULES of the CODE:

I - don't pay money for any ride.[17]

II - don't pay money for any accommodation.

III - try to pay for everything.

*   *   *

Once we had cleared customs into Mexico, we made the long walk through town and positioned ourselves out on the highway. Nick and I set up our shit by a road sign, and sent the other two further down, and they kept on pausing and turning around, and we kept on yelling, "Further! Move further down, you bastards!" until they were finally out of sight. We waited a fair while for our first ride, and then ended up talking them into picking up the other two as we drove past.

It was Nick's first exposure to Latin American driving, and it was all he could do to not scream out every time our ride dodged left to overtake a vehicle with oncoming traffic whistling towards us. The sense of 'safe-space' was immediately reduced upon crossing the border, but over time one begins to take comfort in the fact that the oncoming truck can always just veer

---

[17] This includes the guys that'll pull over to try to shake you down for juice money… like what Sal Paradise and Dean Moriarty were doing.

off the side of the road to avoid collision.[18]

So those guys drove us all the way down to
Hermosillo, where we had some dinner and then
started to tramp southwards out of town. As we
cleared the streetlights and into the darkness,
Max pointed out a railyard to our left, and
petitioned that, as there were probably not going
to be any good places to pitch a tent anyway, we
might as well pitch there beside the tracks —
just to see what happened.

I was too tired to argue, and it was decided
that the best way to position the tents was close
together with the doors facing each other, so
that any intruders would be forced to enter
themselves into a flanked position.

And then we were asleep. Sweetly sound
asleep.

It seemed that not an hour had gone by when
Max's voice pitched up out of the darkness,
calling for us all to wake up and strike the
tents. I was not about to move, and I thought
that I could hold the guys on this one. "What?
There is no fucking way Max. No. Shut up and go
back to sleep. There'll be another train in the
morning." But Chavez had a hard time sleeping
with tenacious Max striking their tent down
around him. I then appealed to Nick: "Nick, don't
do it. If we stay put, he'll calm back down." But
then as I opened my eyes and looked, Nick already
had his socks on and I could see that his eyes
were all wide awake. "FUCK."

We didn't pack, but more like just chucked

---

[18] *Giving one's life over to the ride.

and crammed everything into our bags. The train
was pulling by now and Max was off, running
willy-nilly, ready to jump onto any old car. He
and Chavez were about to stake claim to a gondola
that was stacked full of scrap metal, and I had
to raise my voice to get their attention, "No
goddamnit! If we're going to get on, we have to
stay together." Chavez jumped back down off the
gondola and we scurried back alongside the track
with the train slowly pulling by. A dozen or so
cars later, we saw two grainers coming towards
us, side by each, and we quickly orchestrated our
ascent.

The way that we got on, with two of us going
up each of the closer ladders of the adjoining
cars, we were able to squat onto the platforms
and then pass our things in through the holes.[19]

It was a bit of a chore getting our stuff in
through these 20-inch diameter holes, and we had
to unpack some stuff to get them through, but
eventually everything except for the guitar made
its way in. The guitar wouldn't fit, so I left it
tied off just outside of our cubby, lying flat
down against the metal grate.

Straight away, as we attempted to become
situated, the train began to slow down, and after
just another minute it came squeaking and braking
to a stop in a yard on the outskirts of town.

The four of us waited, our senses working

---

[19] Grainer cars are generally used to carry sand (or grain), and
because of some structural reason, each end is sloped on the actual
container, and a solid metal brace holds the thing together and
stretches up from the platform to the top of the container. Now for
some reason they decided that the empty space enclosed by the metal
walls of the brace should have a circular access-hole in it, about
20 inches wide. When you get into this hole, you are fully obscured
from view, and well protected from the wind.

overtime.

From their side, Max and Nick were first to
spot the approach of the railyard bulls, by the
stride of their flashlights. They were chatting
as they came strolling down the line of cars
towards us. We all stayed put and hid as they
started past, but after pausing to check the
connection between the cars, the one guy's
flashlight caught sight of my guitar case.

"Oye espera. Que lo que es esto?" he asked,
beckoning to his co-worker and beginning to lift
the case.

I poked my head out of the hole, "Buenas
noches."

The guy positively almost fell over
backwards. "Que estas haciendo alli?" he cried,
as the two flashlights trained in on me.

"Estamos en camino. Nos vamos hacia el sur."

"Pero quienes son 'nosotros'?"

"Somos cuatro, viajando," and with this I
told the guys to stick their heads out of the
holes and smile. The Mexican rail workers were
further taken aback. I continued, "y seguro que
no vamos estar haciendo ningun dano, jefe. Es
nada mas que necesitamos la vuelta."

The two guys exchanged a bit of a look before
the lead guy turns and says: "En este tren, no
van a llegar."

I plead on: "Oye jefe, no es demasiado tarde.
Solo tendrian que seguir en sus caminos, haciendo
sus trabajos, y nosotros nos quedamos aqui,
tranquilitos, hasta que se vaya el tren."

"No, ya te dije," he sang on emphatically, in his Mexican accent, "Que en este tren no llegaran. Si ustedes van p'hacia el sur, deben estar en el otro, deben estar en ese tren alli!" and with this, he indicated another train which was three tracks over, and remarkably, was also hauling two grainer cars, side by each.

So after a quick word to the guys, we repacked, dismounted, thanked the rail workers, and loaded onto the adjacent train, getting back into our same positions as before. A few minutes later the train started rolling, and the underling guy lifted his arm up over his head and delivered us an awkward wave as we pulled away.

We began to speed into the darkness, and Max pulled out his sleeping bag and spread it out inside the chamber of their car to go back to sleep: just another day at the office. Chavez and I sat on the grate on our side, chatting over the noise and keenly observing Nick.

Nick was like a kid in a candy shop. Big eyes and stunned. When we yelled across to him, he smiled with delight and raised his voice up over the steely clang of the train, "I just can't believe it!" he yelled. "Wooooooo..."

> **Rock me mama like a wagon wheel,**
> **Rock me mama any way you feel,**
> **Hey, mama rock me.**
>
> **Rock me mama like the wind and the rain,**
> **Rock me mama like a southbound train,**
> **Hey, mama rock me.** Bob Dylan

CHAPTER CHAVEZ

So there we were, crossing into Mexico, and everything got a bit weirder. Audacy was the only one who could really speak Spanish, Max had his pinkie on the handle but didn't really grasp it, and Nick and I were pretty much worthless at the onset.

So we crossed the border and walked a good three or four miles through that sketchy border town. Luckily it was a small town, and we crossed to the southern outskirts of Agua Prieta and then split up into pairs.

Back in Arizona we had bought a couple of short-range CB radios. Audacy had one and I had one, and each pair was going to keep ahold of one as we went. They were good for about seven miles, so we would pick a spot on the map and try to make it there by nightfall, and if the town was small enough you'd be able to raise each other on the CBs. That was the idea anyway. We'd try to remember to turn the radios on for the first five minutes of every hour. Sometimes it worked, mostly it didn't.

So we walked to the edge of Agua Prieta and hitched. I was with Max first, and Audacy and Nick were together. We walked down the highway to separate ourselves, and then after about an hour of waiting there and watching the half dead dogs run around, and just kind of soaking up Mexico for the first time, a car pulls over and its these two pretty big Mexican guys who looked like business men, in a rather small car, something akin to a ford focus, not very large at all, and we come to find that Audacy and Nick are already squished into the back and had talked them into pulling over to pick us up.

So our first ride in Mexico, it was the four of us, two big Mexican businessmen, a guitar, and four packs. I've never been so cramped in my life. We had three people in the back, one person lying across them, and then packs and guitar stacked on top of that person.

That went on for four hours or more.

They dropped us off in Hermosillo by nightfall and we had a walk around. It was sort of a bigger town, not a city, but a big town, and we got some nice rice and beans and eggs at a sort of indoor/outdoor café and I made a call to a girl back home, and then we just walked around. We had some Pacificos, which is a Mexican beer, and we just sort of chilled out. When the time came to pitch a camp, we walked out to the south side of town and pitched our tents close to some railroad tracks, just figuring "Why not?"

So we all get into bed and we're sleeping, Max in my tent with me, and Nick and Audacy are in Audacy's tent, and sometime around midnight or one o'clock in the morning, Max wakes me up, shaking me, "Get up, get up, we have to go right now, get up, pack everything!" and I'm like: "What the fuck?" And he said that he heard a train coming, and I listened, and sure enough a train was coming. He jumps out of the tent and wakes up Nick and Audacy, and all three of us are pissed at him, we're like: "Fuck you Max, we're sleeping." Luckily though, this is one of the few times that Max was really helpful: he *did* get us all up, we *did* get all packed, and we *did* jump on that freight train.

The one that we got on, however, wasn't going anywhere. It stopped right in front of us. So we're sitting in this freight car, and there're these two Mexican guys walking up and down the cars, checking the connections, so we all hide and we're hiding in the little hole of a grainer, and we get everything inside of this little hole, and there's just enough space for everything except for Audacy's guitar. Now as the guys walk along with their flashlights, looking at things, one of them notices the guitar and stops. He takes a closer look, and then climbs up and starts to reach for the guitar, and Audacy sticks his head out and engages him in Spanish, and I'm not sure exactly what he said, but it was essentially: "We're just travelling, trying to get down to southern Mexico, we're not dangerous, we mean no harm." And the guys were like: "We? Who else is here?" and then one by one we all crawl out of this little space...

CHAPTER 12
Desert Picture

The train left the highway and began a gradual climb up into the mountains. I sat with Chavez, and tried to record the abrasive sound of the freight train with my mini-disc.

Later on, I followed Chavez up the ladder and onto the roof of our car, quarter moon, and we sat there, magic carpet, arms out and cross-legged like on the cover of that Neil Young album. I almost shat myself the first time we went through a tunnel. The all-round feeling was one of total exhilaration, and even the darkness of the night couldn't obscure the sensation of the view.

When the coldness of the early morning drove us back down the ladder, I too crawled into the hole, and after jettisoning some dried human excrement from the corner, unfurled my sleeping bag and tried to catch some sleep.

When I awoke, dawn had broken and we were higher up in the mountains, weaving through some tiny village and it was all flowery with bougainvillaeas amidst the deep, lush green. We were all awake now, and together ascended onto the roof, from where we waved to the few early-waking, dirt-sweeping villagers who disbelievingly spotted our presence.

The sun rose up and had warmed the life back into our bones by 9 or 10:oo when the train slowed and pulled up into another yard. This time, after our positive experience from the night before, we disembarked within full view of the rail yard chief and greeted him with respect. I inquired as to whether the train would be continuing onward, and he replied that it wouldn't, but that a southbound train was due to arrive later on in the morning. He suggested where we might get some breakfast, and advised us to return to the tracks by noon.

So into town we strode, and after twice asking directions, we found the place, and the little old man consented to cook us breakfast. There were two other travelers there already (Tom and Anna) who had come down train-jumping all the way from Canada, and were now headed back up north. We sat and breakfasted with them, and Tom showed us his collection of peyote buttons and then took me and Chavez off on a walk to smoke a huge spliff.

When we got back to the breakfast-house, the boys were a bit frenetic about our noontime return, so we bid our host and our fellow travelers goodbye. And when we got back to the tracks, the Mexican army had arrived.

They had come in on a freight carrier of some sort, and were presently milling around on a central track between the trains in the yard. There were at least a hundred of them. As we approached the first bunch, I casually asked if they knew which one of the trains was going to be continuing to the south. They gestured to the train on our right, and pointed us down the aisle of cars in which the rest of their group were assorting. We walked in ragged formation down between the two trains as every one of these 18-year-old kids with machine guns glared at us with mischievous curiosity. When we arrived to the end of the cul-du-sac, blocked off by the caboose of a train on the centre track, we encountered the majority of the unit, also milling around and smoking cigarettes. I repeated my question as to whether they knew if this was the train that was to be heading out southbound, and the wiliest of the pack stepped forward and unhinged and slid open the door of a boxcar. He spoke with a laugh, casting countless comedic glances back towards his companions as he assured us that we had arrived to the right place, and that we had only to jump up into the boxcar, "<We've been saving it for you, ha ha. Choo choo>!"[20] Inside the boxcar that he had opened, the floor was covered with lye. I stepped back against a visible,

---

[20] Boxcars can only be opened from the outside.

enclosing human snare, and said with a smile to the guys in English that absolutely no one was to board the boxcar.

Max was in Lala land, "Why? What's the matter? This boxcar could be OK. Gracias amigos, gracias." And he made a move to get up into the car.

I tried to intensify my voice to Max without allowing the stress to be perceived by our surroundings, "Max, will you fucking look at me." He did, confused, and then stepped back.

I turned to Chavez and we quickly redirected our posse down the aisle between the trains, leaving the army with some vague comment about our wanting to be in a different compartment. We traced our path back down to the end, through the group of soldiers, and then walked around and back south along the quiet side of the train.

It wasn't a minute passed by before the four most belligerent of the army-folk reappeared around the end-car, toting their guns, smirking and side glancing, honing in on our vulnerability. (My father had always warned me about crooks with badges, and here they were.) I sat in the middle of the entrance to our boxcar, with Nick and Max to my sides. Chavez took point. The army-boys snarled up to our position and stood two to each side of Chavez, facing our empty boxcar. They began taunting us, and I kept answering their inquires with a joking aspect, trying to keep the whole exchange as light as possible, waiting for the fucking train to go. They stood questioning us, fantasizing about how the situation might unravel.

Meanwhile, our friend the train yard-chief

had noticed our situation from afar, and upon entering into our proximity, the strangest of things occurred: the hostile army contingent turned into a small bunch of uniformed boys. He came over and stood with us and the difference was palatable. And he stayed on with us for the next few minutes, right up until the train shuddered and began to move away.

Our waves to that man as we rolled away were most sincere. And in my mind, I was convinced that he had prevented an upset.

As our accelerating train slipped us away from the inquest, we began to fully appreciate the romance of our scene: being on board a boxcar-freight train, straight out of the movies, with a view to the West and rolling down through the afternoon.

Everyone shed some clothing and got comfortable. Nick and I improvised a little guitar and penny whistle compilation, and the whiskey and cigarettes were placed into the middle of our circle. The train would speed, slow, stop and then accelerate again as we came and went through small towns. At one point, it pulled up and came to a stop only 50 metres away from a small stand that was selling ice-cold beer, but thirsty as we were, none of us could summon the nerve to attempt the dash.

A little while later, Nick spotted a small child who came running up alongside the train, seeming to have every intention of making the jump. When he heard us yelling out shouts of encouragement, he startled and almost recoiled, but then decided instead to reach forward and throw in his lot with us. The four of us grabbed hold of his arms and lifted him up onto the platform, and then sat back, delighted with our new purchase. The guys now had a chance to practice their Spanish in peace. Nick quietly offered the lad a cigarette, and then a few minutes later when the boy had begun to grow more comfortable, he took a pull off of our flask of whiskey and we all had a laugh at the sour face that he made.

The boy carried no baggage. He was simple perhaps, but polite and kind, and although he couldn't make heads or tails out of our map, he was quite confident that the destination of our train was Mazatlan.

*   *   *

The novelty of our newcomer began to wear off with the setting of the sun, and we simmered back down into the serenity of our circle. Nick was strumming lowly on my guitar, and Max and Chavez were fading out.

Night fell.

The Mexican boy was the first to notice our approach to the city. He stuck his head out of the open door and stared patiently ahead. I asked him if we were arriving, and he pointed to the glow and said, "Mazatlan."

The boys came to, and we packed up our things.

A few minutes later we bailed from the rolling train as it made its approach into the railyard. When we started down the tracks, following our decelerating train in towards the city, our young friend ducked into the grass for a moment and Max was the first to put an unexpected two and two together:

"Hey, you know our young friend, the boy?"

"Yeah," we nodded, glancing over to observe our travelling companion as he squatted in the grass.

"Well..." Max concluded, "He's a girl."

Our young friend then jogged back to catch up with us, and as we got closer into the city, our paths parted, and she turned and yelled goodbye to us with a wave and a smile.

CHAPTER NICK

We crossed into Mexico from Douglas, and they made us buy a $20 entry visa, which I thought was funny for some reason. I remember asking Audacy if he was going to miss that girl in Bisbee, and he said something like, "Not as much as I would miss finding the girl who's down my road."

My first impression of Mexico was that it looked just like it does in the postcards. It was pretty neat.

We basically walked through town, and got out of town. Our first ride was the four of us in the back of this little sedan, and I was pretty much sitting on Audacy's lap as we drove along with two Mexican businessmen, and they loved it. They took us all the way to Hermosillo, and that was cool. The night was warm. We had beer, and I had a coca-cola, and I was thinking, "I'm really in

Mexico 'cause I'm drinking coca-cola out of a glass bottle."

That night we walked to the edge of town and slept in the tall grass about 50 feet off the road, and the next day, we just got up and we were off.

The next night we were in more of a city, but we had to walk all the way across town, and the sight of four gringos walking with our packs was interesting for a lot of the onlookers, and all the little girls, fresh out of school, were giving us the eye, which was *encouraging*.

We camped beside the train yard. That was Max's idea 'cause he really loves the trains, but I think we were all really into it. We camped at 11 or 12:oo, and the train came at 2 or 3:oo, or maybe earlier, and we got up and packed, and it was amazing how fast we packed.

Chavez was the first one to the train, he jumps up: a whole car full of broken glass, he jumps down. We run along to another one and get up, and we're all safe and sound, and then the train stops in the station, and we're just sitting there. And then the bull comes over with another guy and wants to know what the hell we're doing, and he tells us the train is stopped at the station and that it wasn't going anywhere. He said, "If you want the train going south, well that's the train over there." So we flew over there and jumped onto it. Me and Max were on one platform, and Audacy and Chavez were on the other. Max fell asleep, because he was in his element I guess, and I think Audacy eventually fell asleep too because me and Chavez spent a lot of the time just yelling back and forth between each other, and I remember singing a song for a while, *"I'm goin' down, oo, oo, I'm goin' down."*

Anyway, so we watched the sun come up, that was cool. We got to a really small town, and we got off the train and that's where we met Antonio. He was neat, and he told us that the train was leaving at noon. So we planned on meeting back there.

We go into the town and there was an ox-cart, and I mean, this was like the *real* Mexico, the off-the-beaten-track Mexico, the Mexico that the tourists don't see. And the town had one big hill, and I just kept thinking that a whole lot of these people would have never travelled beyond this one town, and that they were just forever looking up at that one hill. And as we were taking off on the train later on, I remember just watching that hill disappear.

I just imagine those people, the woman who fed us breakfast in the morning, and we met that Canadian dude who was going north, who was trying to get his discoteque up and going, and he was hairy, sweaty, smelly, full of cocaine, and definitely needing a couple days of sleep.

So we're off to Mazatlan, which was fun, and it's a boxcar, which I've always wanted to ride in a boxcar... All these things were cool to me. For some reason, I always just knew I would. In Mexico? Well then sure why not?

So that was a long trip. The pulling and the pushing of cars. There was shit in the corner, and I remember playing songs in there, and that was fun. We pick up Wajishi, in his dirty-ass coat, and that kid was alright, and we drove all the way to Mazatlan with him.

Mazatlan. Ground. First time we see the beach. We get there late. We try to go into a bar or two. There was one spot that was kind of lit up like Vegas, with lots of blue neon. Anyways, so we're down on the beach in our two tents, and the guy knocked on our thing, thinking we were homosexual activity...

CHAPTER 14
Arma Blanca

Mazatlan was a piss hole.

The street downtown was lined on both sides with hotels catering to the American college scene, discoteque music blaring out from the neon lobbies.

We continued south down along the shore, looking for some place or another where we could buy ourselves a cold beer and just relax. Finally, across the road from the beach, we spotted a little pub that appeared to still be open.

After our second drink, it was determined that we were in a gay bar. No matter. I went up and talked to the bartender and inquired as to the municipal laws about camping on the beach.

"Si, se puede," he assured me, "Todo el mundo lo haga."

So after one more drink, we headed back across the road and down along the shore, traversing the seawall from the sidewalk promenade and down onto the sand.

We had the tents up in no time, and I was so exhausted that when I finally came into this comfortable sandy lay-down position, I let loose with a sighing exclamation: "Aahhhhhh."

Less than a minute passed by before there was a scratchy knocking on our tent, and I got myself back up with no small amount of frustration, and stuck my head out the door. I found myself looking up at yet another military-police sort who was telling me to come on out of the tent with my hands up (which is impossible). I ducked back in and chucked my pants back on before getting out and standing up to address this guy, and as I did, I noticed his partner up on the seawall, training down on us with a big semi-automatic.

He asked me what the hell we thought we were doing.

I told him that we had been travelling, and that we were now trying to get some sleep.

"<You're not sleeping>," he sneered, "<I could hear you>!"

I pointed out that we had checked with local sources to ensure that camping on this beach was legal.

"<Oh yeah? And who told you that>?" he asked.

"<The folks over at the bar>," I said.

"<That bar over there>?" he asked, pointing across the street.

"<Um, yes>."

But now the guy was shaking his head in

disgust, and casting a look of angry disbelief up towards his companion. He turned back to me and said, "<Do you know that we are a catholic country here>?"

"<What>?.."

"<...And we don't permit immoral acts>[21]."

"<Immoral acts>?"

And then dropping his voice, he added, "<...And we don't like you fucking *maricones* coming down and doing what you do on our beach...>"

"<Whoa, wait. We're not *maricones*. We're just trying to get some sleep>."

Now he flashed a provocative smile, "<But you forget: we could hear what you were doing in there>."

"<No, wait>," and now quickly in English to the boys: "Hey guys, these cops think that we're fags and having gay sex on the beach, so come on out of the tents and act... tough." I was about to say 'macho', but as it's a Spanish word, I figured the cops would understand it.

The boys came out, grunting and spitting, and as the cop checked them out, I continued, "<You see, we aren't *maricones*. These are my *compadres*. We come to Mazatlan looking for women. And now we arrive and search in town, but it seems like there are no women. Where are all of the women>?"

Max echoed with a horny smile, "Si, donde estan las mujeres?"

---

[21] "...Y no permitimos actos imorales."

This seemed to put the cop at ease, and he changed his tact, "<Are you boys carrying any weapons>?"

"<Weapons? No.>"

"<Not even a knife>?"

"<Well, of course I have my knife-of-travelling.[22]>"

"<Let's see it>."

I reached into the tent and produced my 'Tramontina'. The cop measured it against his palm[23], and then shaking his head, threw the sheathed knife up to his friend on the seawall. "<This knife is forbidden in Mexico. This is a white arm.[24]>"

"This is no white arm. This is my knife for cooking. This is the knife that we make sandwiches with, that I've brought all the way down from Canada>." He was still shaking his head, and his overhead partner was nodding in ascent, perhaps imagining how the knife might look on his belt.

"<It is a white arm>." he maintained.

I became emboldened: "<Well do you know what? This knife was given to me as a gift, by my grandfather, only the year before he died>."

This brought about a change in their expressions, and they exchanged a look, knowing full well that what I had said was a lie, and yet

---

[22] "…mi cuchillo de viajar."

[23] In most Latin American countries, it is illegal to carry a blade that is longer than the breadth of your palm.

[24] "Esto es una arma blanca."

hesitant to risk proceeding for fear that it might be the truth.[25] All eyes now turned to the silent cop above, who seemed to be the higher-ranking of the two, and he waited another long moment before nodding with a shrug and throwing the knife back down to the cop on the beach.

"<We don't see this knife, eh? Put it away. You guys are gone in the morning>?"

"<Yes>."

And with that, they walked off to continue their rounds. We bedded back down, and slept for the rest of the night in peace.

CHAPTER MAX

There's this real looking-glass sense when you cross the Mexican border. The streets are all dusty, and the pavement gets really fucked up. There are hungry looking dogs walking around, and little dirty kids.

I guess that Nick hadn't really travelled that much before, Chavez had some, and Aude and I had quite a bit. But it was still pretty strange, in a disjunctive sort of way. Like a real sense of being in a new country, and the weather was pretty nice. It was windy, and the light was very bright.

I don't remember the exact order of rides, but I think our first ride was with an off-duty cop in a station wagon, and he took us west, kind

---

[25] Catholics deep down.

of parallel to the border, and this guy has
loaded his car up to the gills for us. He kept
trying to pass trucks on these uphills, which is
rather terrifying. Mexicans love to pass on blind
corners and hills, and he took us a ways and then
we got another ride with a couple of guys that
took us to Hermosillo.

I remember buying peanuts for a bunch of
little kids at a roadside stand, these little
dirty Mexican street kids. The Spanish word for
peanut is *cacahuete*, but in Mexico they call them
mani.

The first night we slept in a field on the
edge of a town, and the second night we were in
Obregon. At the edge of town there was a railyard
and I was pretty keen on riding a train, so I
convinced everyone to camp out right next to this
railyard — kind of in an out-in-the-open kind of
place, and sometime in the middle of the night a
train came up and sided, and I yelled at everyone
to get up and break camp, and we were gonna go
get on this train, and they were all kind of
pissed 'cause everyone was asleep, but we broke
camp and everyone climbed onto this train.

This was the middle of the night, like 2:oo
in the morning, and I remember a rail worker
walked by and saw us, and just pretended not to
see us, and I realized that they were more scared
of us than we were of them, you know? And another
worker came by and Aude talked to him, and I
think he was like, "You guys are on the wrong
train, you gotta get on *that* train, *that's* the
one that's going south." So we climbed onto the
porch of another grainer, went in, and the train
started rolling out, we rolled, and it was cold,
you know? It was cold. Sonoran desert, Sinaloa,

and the middle of the night, it was probably in the 40s. So we were really fucking cold.

And then the sun came up, beautiful sunrise, and we were going through the desert. God, I remember holding onto the ladder of the train, and it braked in the dark, and it cut my hand open 'cause the train stopped so quickly. And we ended up in this town called San Blas where there is a major junction in the rails. Trains go back northeast up the copper canyon, which is supposedly one of the most beautiful rail lines in the world, or south towards Mazatlan, which is on the Pacific Ocean, kind of a port town, and a big spring-break place.

So we got off in this yard, and there was a yard worker there and we talked to him. He was really friendly, this old guy, and he told us that the train to the south was going to leave at noon, so we could just come back then, no problem. So we went and found a little rail shack breakfast place by the side of the tracks, not a hundred yards away.

We were having breakfast there, like tortillas and scrambled eggs and coffee, smoking cigarettes, and a couple of Americans come out of this little room that they'd been sleeping in, and this girl's got gold jewelry on and stuff. They were a couple of clean-cut kids from San Diego, and they were trying to get over to Baja to pick up their sailboat and sail it back up. They wanted to ride a train up into the copper canyon 'cause they had heard that it was so great, but they were the least likely looking train-hoppers you've ever seen in your life, and all the railyard workers thought they were crazy, with this beautiful blonde girl with jewelry on going train-hopping in Mexico, where the favored weapon of rail gangs is a railroad spike with a piece of baling wire that you swing around like a medieval weapon.

Dangerous anyway.

You have to bring lots of water 'cause it's fuckin' hot.

So we hung out there for the morning, and then walked back into the railyard, and there were a bunch of army guys who were working on the trains, you know, opening and unloading them and stuff, and we found out which string of cars was heading south and we went and got into an open box car, which smelled pretty bad. People had been shitting in the corners and using dirty Mexican comics to wipe with. But we sat there in the open mouth of the boxcar for a while and figured it was a good as any.

You want to get a boxcar that doesn't have a load in it because the load can easily shift, and it's really dangerous. And you always want to jam the door open with a railroad spike to make sure that it doesn't slide closed.

So we were sitting there when a bunch of army guys came by, and I wasn't too worried about them. I guess the other guys were a bit more worried, and they were a bit menacing maybe, but just when we thought things were going to get worse, our old friend from the morning came by and scared them off.

Aude gave everybody copies of his CD that he was carrying with him. He was travelling pretty heavy, and I was travelling as light as I could, so I had a little... I think he called it my 'little schoolgirl pack'. But you know, the one thing that I've learned in all these years is to travel as light as you can.

So we get on the train, the train pulls out, and we ride. It's a boxcar, which is a nice ride, down through the desert of Sinaloa, and it was really hot. So we rode down towards the coast, and it was really just like... crazy desert, you know? You go past herders and through ranch country, and it's very dusty and very, very hot, and loud too. We got a little bit of sleep, but it's kind of hard to sleep on trains.

In Culiocan, this kid gets on the train with us, who at first we all thought was a boy, and was smoking cigarettes with us, and eating our food. I think that all the kid had was a dirty blanket and a bag of corn chips. He was travelling without even any water, so we gave him some of our water and stuff, and he rode with us all the way down to Mazatlan. Later on when the train stopped, we realized that the kid was a girl: a 12-year-old girl, dressed as a boy, train-hopping by herself, going to see his sister in Mazatlan.

We got there in the dark and split off from the kid, and we ended up going and sleeping on the beach. It was this real gnarly ugly spring break scene, holiday bars and shit, and we went and pitched the tents right on the beach in the middle of town below this seawall.

We were half asleep when these cops came by and kicked at the tent. We got out, and they were yelling at us, and Aude turns to us and says, "They think we're *maricones*, they think we're fags." So the police searched us, and Aude had a sheep knife on him, and they threatened to run him in for "arma blanca", but he said "<I need my little *cuchillo* to cut my cheese>," and he finally guilted these douche bag cops into leaving us alone.

It was pretty exhausting.

The whole thing was exhausting.

Mr. Audacy has a rather difficult philosophy of travel, which is that you never pay for a ride, which is... I'm not an absolutist in that sense. I'm fine with paying for the occasional ride. I've travelled enough to not feel like I need to be an absolutist about it. But I respect the philosophy, even if I don't necessarily agree with it all the time, in all circumstances. But that often meant that you had to walk the fuck from the middle of Mazatlan to the first good hitchhiking spot, which could be damn far, and damn hot.

CHAPTER 16
Drawing Straws

The way we decided to work the travelling in pairs thing was this: each morning we would get up and have a look at the map, and then choose a coastal town (the smaller the better) 200-250 kilometres to the south, where we would try to meet up for that night, and always at the south end of the beach. In case for some reason one of the pairs was delayed, or got a good ride taking them past the primary town, we would also choose a secondary town which would be a further 200 kilometres down, which was our do-not-pass-go destination; a place where we would heave to, and wait for the others no matter what.

So in the morning, Chavez and I drew the short straws, and we sat ourselves down at a café on the edge of town to drink coffees and blue steel cans of Mexican peach juice as we watched the other two hitch from the roadside. Suddenly they ran ahead and were off on their first ride, and we paid up and hauled our things over to the very spot that had been freshly vacated by our companions.

Our first ride that morning was in a gravel truck, and we both sat up in the cab next to the driver, Chavez in the middle. After an hour, the truck began to climb into the mountains, and in a freak display, the sky opened up and it started absolutely pissing rain. The trucker put the windshield wipers on and a few minutes later, the passenger-side wiper got caught up on a piece of rubber that was sticking up from the back of the hood. I unrolled the window and told the guy that I could fix it.

"No, dejalo."

I figured that he was just being polite, and I went to lean out the window.

"<No, leave it>," he repeated, over the symphony of the rain. "<This truck doesn't belong to me, it belongs to the company>." As indeed it did. And sure enough, after a few more impossible attempts to perform its designated function, that wiper broke.

We arrived to our 'primary' late in the evening (the name of the town was Division) and made the short walk to the beach. We found an

empty little thatch and wicker family-run
restaurant with tables and chairs in the sand,
and a woman came out from inside and declared
herself to be open for business. She brought us
some large beers and then returned to the kitchen
to fix up some dinner. I watched over the stuff
as Chavez walked south with our CB, scouting out
to the end of the beach. Our meals were ready
when he got back, but he hadn't seen or heard any
sign of the boys.

We ate dinner and had another beer, and then
Chavez led me down the beach to a gigantic sea
turtle that he had spotted just before, straining
and flippering as it laid its eggs in a humungous
crater in the sand, and as we looked more closely
with the flashlight, the ancient turtle actually
had tears coming out of its eyes. We began to
feel guilty for our intrusion and Chavez turned
to continue on down the beach with the CB, while
I returned to where our stuff was at the lonely
restaurant to ask our hostess if it would be
difficult to come by some marijuana.

"No," she said, and then to someone else, out
of view: "Oye Ricardo!"

"Que?" came the response, drifting in from
the back of the house.

"Donde esta esa bolsa de mota que teniamos?"

"No se. Sobre la nivera!?"

So she finds the bag of weed, and drops it
down onto the bar between us. The bag easily
weighs over an ounce.

"<This you can have for five American
dollars>," she says, "<I can put it on your

93

bill>."

I tell her that we only want a quarter of it,
but that she can add two dollars to our bill. She
accepts, and watches neutrally as I extract a
handful from the bag, and then we both give a
curt nod before I return to my beer at the table.

There was the sound of a dogfight off in the
distance, and the moon was waning over the
lapping ocean, and as the woman returned to her
kitchen, I sat down at our table to roll up a
nice joint.[26]

Chavez got back and had not found the boys.
We smoked the joint as we sat finishing our
beers, and then paid and thanked the woman before
heading north along the lagoon to find a shady
spot to pitch.[27]

*   *   *

M: "What, he's still in the tent? Oh, c'mon,
it's like nine o'clock! <zzip> Hey!"

A: "Augr, this is becoming a theme."

M: "Hee. Buenos dias compadre."

A: "Good morning Max."

M: "Hey, levantate baby, you're gonna make us
late for the prom."

So Chavez had gotten up early and gone off to
have another look at the south end of the beach.
When he had gotten back over there in the
daylight, he'd spotted his own tent pitched not a

---

[26] Heaven is here on earth.
[27] We would usually try to pitch the tent on the west side of a
tree, so that we could sleep in for longer in the morning.

stone's throw inland from the shore.

So the four of us returned to that same wicker-place, and after stories and over coffees, we drew straws.

It was me and Nick.

Ours were the long straws, and the other two sat down in the shade and waited for us to hitch off. A few rides later we got picked up by a computer salesman who was headed inland and down to Guadalajara. He was willing to drop us off as farr as Tepic, which was 80 kilometres past our 'primary'. Nick and I talked it over and decided to take the ride all the way.

When we arrived to Tepic, everyone was dressed up fancy and the pueblo was preparing for fiesta. We made our way into the inner square to have a look around. I had run out of rollie tobacco and we lowered the bar and bought some shit-ass filtered cigarettes called 'Boots', but then chucked them out and got our first pack of cheap-ass, cherry-tipped 'Faros', which were destined to become our tailor-made smoke of choice during our travels in Mexico.

We sat down in the square and took to street performing, and found that almost as many people bought us sodas as threw coins in our case. But we made enough to buy some street food and a bit of stuff for later, and it was well after midnight when we cut out of town and made our way back down along the highway.

Bread, cheese, peanuts, chocolate, apples, oranges, onions, tuna, avocado, salami/pepperoni, wine, beer.

It was dark and everything was jungle and

hills. We were looking for anything. We came up to a P-up truck that was pulled off to the side of the road, and as we passed by, I knocked on the window to ask the startled guy if he wasn't leaving town. He told us that he was, and to climb up into the back. But then, just before pulling out onto the highway, the guy takes two long tokes off of a spoon with a strange pipe made out of aluminium foil. Nick and I exchanged a nervous look and then clamped our arms around the roll-bar for the ride of our lives. When he finally pulled over to let us off some ten miles from town and we were jumping down, I asked him:

"Oye, que estabas fumando alli? La mota, o la coca?"

"La coca," he replied, with a sheepish grin.

And then he was gone, and we were off into the hills.

"Was it coke?" asked Nick, "It was, wasn't it?"

As it happened, the hills didn't work out so well. They were much too full of barking dogs. We ended up walking about a kilometre further on down the highway, and then camping about seven feet off to the side of the road on an unpaved pull-off.

The ditch is more interesting.
Neil Young

If you're tired enough, the trucks don't even wake you.[28]

---

[28] Two things that should not be skimped on when you're hitchhiking are your boots and your backpack (And your sleeping bag in

CHAPTER CHAVEZ

It was one of the most magical nights of my
life, not because it was a train, not because it
was Mexico, not because we were hitchhiking, but
because of all of those reasons and a thousand
more.

Nick and I never slept at all that night,
Audacy and Max had taken the little cubby holes,
so we stayed up all night, and at one point, I
climbed up onto the roof of the grainer. There
was a sort of ladder that goes across the top
that you could hold onto, and I just sat up there
and watched the moon and the stars, and I could
see the landscape changing from the scrub-brush,
deserty mountains of Sonora, and as we went south
it became more jungly and more tropical, and I
will never forget that night, just sitting up on
top of that train and looking at the stars.

When dawn broke we could see that we were in
a much more tropical place. The train stopped
somewhere, a few hundred miles south of where we
had got on. It was a very rural train yard where
they were switching cars. We walked just outside
of the railyard to what they'd call a store or a
restaurant, but really it was just a place where
somebody lived. It was some old gay Mexican's
house, and we went into his small courtyard and
he cooked us some breakfast, and we met a couple
of other travelers there and hung out with them

Pennsylvania). Colours are always best dark. Green black blue. My
pack is tent and my black is dark blue. Don't show flash, dirt or
presence. Dark fly on the tent is invaluable. As for a tent: as you
will. Mine's six hard years young (been given away twice in
different countries and returned), ratty as hell, and I love it.
But I've had a travelling friend grown wildly prolific with a small
piece of tarp, carried or stolen. From the outside, no one would
want anything that I have.

for a while. I remember we smoked some *mota*, and swapped stories, and chuckled at the gay old Mexican guy, 'cause he was very strange. We actually got some peyote from the Canadian train-jumper guy. He had a bag, and Audacy and I each ate a button.

So when the time came to leave, we paid the gay old Mexican and said goodbye to the Canadian pot-smoker, and walked back out into the railyard. This time, we're all really high. Well, I was anyway.

I remember walking back to the train and the Mexican military guys were there, and I just remember being very nervous. There were more than 150 of them, and as we walked past them, we kind of caught the attention of four of them. We walked back in between the two trains until we were out of sight, and then stopped for a second to collect ourselves and decide how we wanted to do this. We got around a corner into the next aisle of trains where we found a boxcar that was empty, and Nick and Audacy and Max all jumped up into this boxcar and were sitting there with their legs over the side, waiting for the train to start moving. I had seen those guys following us, and I thought for sure they were going to come around the corner, and sure enough they did.

I had stayed outside, just because it occurred to me that it would be a very bad situation to be in to have all four of us inside of a boxcar. Our backs would be against a wall. So I stayed out. And these four guys come walking straight up to us and they stand right next to me, two on each side, and they were looking very hostile and very not-cool. They start asking about drugs, about marijuana and cocaine and all that kind of stuff. They want to know what we have on us, and Audacy's doing all the talking, and meanwhile I am keeping in constant eye-contact with Audacy, just trying to get a feel for which way this was going to go. The biggest of the four of them stood to my immediate right, and then there were two to my left, and another one to the far side on my right. My plan was that if a gun was drawn, I would kick out the knee of the guy standing to my right, and then turn to my left and punch that guy, and then hopefully by that time, Audacy and the guys would be out of the boxcar and taking the other two.

As things started to become more edgy in their tones, I noticed that down the train to my right was the old man who had given us directions to the gay old Mexican's house, and as soon as he saw me look down that line to him and then saw the military guys standing on either side of me, he stopped what he was doing and came straight up the tracks.

Now, as soon as he arrived, the four army guys all immediately became friendly in their manner, started joking, and everything relaxed. The guy commanded some sort of respect from them, and it immediately changed the mode of the encounter.

Now, Audacy did a few things on this trip that I wasn't so psyched about. But the only one that I can remember (and I can't begrudge him for it, cause this is how it went) was that Audacy gave each of these four guys a copy of his CD that he had been selling for ten dollars, and I was really angry that he gave them those CDs because I felt for sure that these guys were going to jump us, rob us, do whatever they wanted with us, and then there he was giving them CDs! He gave one to the old man too, who was the only person that we should have given one to in the first place.

Just after he gave them the CDs, I threw my stuff up onto the boxcar and climbed in and the train started moving, and we were off, riding south through the desert from Navajoa.

A young kid jumped on the freight train sometime that afternoon, and rode in the same boxcar with us, a little Mexican boy, 8 or 9 years old. Well, night came and we pulled into a bigger town which turned out to be Mazatlan, and the kid got off the train and was kind of following us, and at one point he stopped to take a piss and pulled down his pants and squatted, which kind of shook our reality a little bit. We had thought all along that it was a boy and here it was maybe a girl, and we had been feeding it cigarettes and whiskey. Probably not the best idea at any rate.

So there we were in Mazatlan, walking from the train that we had just jumped off of, and down towards the beach. It was a big kind of gringo touristy area with a lot of discotecas and nightclubs, and a lot of people just boozing. So we walked around, went to a bar, had a couple of beers, and then pitched our tents down at the beach next to a big seawall.

We got all set up, the tents were pitched with our things inside, and we were all laid down when we heard someone yelling at the tents. Audacy peeked his head out, and sure enough there's two Mexican police officers with big guns, accusing us of all kinds of things, and

Audacy was just kind of laughing it off, and they asked us if we had any weapons, and Audacy showed them his knife, and they wanted to take the knife, and I don't remember what story he told them.

Anyway, they didn't take the knife. They accused us of being gay, and having gay sex on the beach or whatever it was, and Audacy just laughed it off and said something to the equivalent of, "We're all about the pussy man, leave us alone." So the officers left, and we slept in peace for the rest of the night.

I can't remember how many days it was before we got on the lorry. There was one day that we kind of took off and just stayed on the beach all day, playing soccer with some kids, and had a barbeque in a beautiful little Mexican town, hanging out with another gringo guy who had driven down there in his station wagon. I think his name was Bob...

CHAPTER 18
A Day Off

The next day, the hitchhiking was very slow, and by late morning we were starting to wonder if we were even going to make our 'secondary' that day. There wasn't a lot of traffic, and Nick and I were keeping our spirits up with championship-of-the-universe stone-throwing: breaking bottles that we had propped up on the fence on the farr side of the road. Finally a car comes speeding by and then doubles back around to check us out, and that was when we got picked up by Bob.

At first we didn't even realize that Bob was a gringo, but once it came out[29], our conversation switched to English, and by after lunch, we were all having such a good time that Bob decided to drive us right down to Monteleon.

When we arrived, it was still mid-afternoon, and Bob drove his station wagon down the washed-out, four-kilometre lane that led from town, and down to a beautiful and deserted fat-sand beach.

Of course the guys weren't there.

The three of us went swimming, and then as we lay drying off in the sand, Nick brought up the notion of taking a day off from the road and spending it here at this fine and secluded spot. Bob lent me the bicycle that had been strapped to the roof of his car and I headed back into town to buy some provisions.

After peddling back out along the riverbed road, I came into town and stopped first to pick up five big rolls. Outside of the bakery sat two wrinkled old men, laughing and drinking canned beers, and they advised me on where one might procure some rolling tobacco, and I detoured off onto a side-road to a little faded green house that sold nothing but.

After that it was on to the *mercado* to pick up an onion, a couple of avocados, some tomatoes, and a half-kilo of cheese. I also paid for ten beers to be picked up on the way back. Next was the fruit stand for five peaches, bananas and directions to the butcher. From the butcher one procures the salami, and here I'm almost all the

---

[29] Bob sneezed, and I could hear the English "Achoo", instead of the Spanish "Hitzche".

way back to the highway. So I look up and decide on a whim to take a look at the spot from where we'll probably be hitching out on the morrow, and lo, the final business in town, a small café off to the left, and who is seated out front with coffees and comic books, if it isn't Max and Chavez.

So I come peddling up like I'm Kermit the frog, and the sun is still shining as the boys spot me reaching the curb.

A: "Doctor Livingston I presume."

C: "Heyyyyy..."

M: "Nice bike."

A: "Yeah, it's buddy's who gave us a ride. Did you guys just get here?"

M: "We've only just finished our coffees. Man, we just had a killer ride..."

C: "Where's Nick?"

A: "We're down at the beach. He and buddy are waiting, I'm just collecting some sandwich material."

C: "Yeah, we were just thinking about ordering some food."

A: "There's enough here for all of us. If you guys just want to start down the street, it leads all the way down to the beach. I'll just go pick up the beers, and then catch up."

M: "How far is it?"

A: "Augh, just a few clicks. It's a really nice beach"

M: "That'll take too long to go both ways."

A: "Both ways?"

M: "*Well*, what about keeping on? You could peddle that bike of yours down to the beach and get Nick, and your buddy can give you guys a lift back out. It's still early, and I think that we could get a couple more rides, you know?"

A: "...?"

C: "Max's worried about getting to San Cristobal in time."

A: "Oh come on Max. Your thing is still five days off, and at the rate we're going, it'll only take us three."

M: "Can you guarantee me that we'll get down there on time for this thing?"

A: "What? Man! There's plenty of time to take one afternoon off. We've been going hard, and today is the first time Nick's even had the chance to take a swim. Wait till you get to the beach and you'll see."

C: "So then you can guarantee Max that we'll be in San Cristobal on time?"

A: "Chavez? Are you guys fucking kidding me? We're hitchhiking here. There *are* no fucking guarantees. All that I can say is that we're ahead of schedule."

C: "Audacy, this is important for Max, that he be there. If it were me, and if it was important to me, I'd like to think that you would take that into consideration."

A: "Yeah, well, I would. But this is silly. Don't worry, OK? We're going to make it there on time. OK?"

M: "..."

A: "OK?"

M: "...OK."

A: "Good. It's just one afternoon. Now let's go to the beach, and just relax, and have fun. I'll catch up to you guys with the beers."

So I caught up a little ways down the lane and put Max's pack on to carry the bottles of beer, and he carried the groceries. When we arrived back to the beach, introductions were made, and then I went for a long swim with Nick and Chavez.

When we had dried off, I went about trying to organize some firewood, and walking over to where our stuff was, I was going to see if I couldn't enlist some help. Max was standing over the grocery bags with a spoon in his hand, finishing off one of the avocados.

"Max! Those are for the fucking sandwiches!"

"Hey, I only ate one. There's another one in there still, and lots of bananas too if you want."

A: "..."

CHAPTER NICK

Chavez and Fortes were off on their own, and me and Audacy got a scary ride.

He was a Mexican guy. He looked like the bad Mexican dude from *The Three Amigos*, and he had the cowboy hat on and the big boots, and a suit, businessman, driving around. He opened his first beer as he was picking us up, and after a half an hour, he was on his 6th. He was an interesting guy, beer in one hand, beeping at every girl, laughing, smiling, and listening to the music. And this is when I discovered that in Mexico, there are only three songs: Fast, Slow, and Waltz.

So he dropped us off in Tepix, and that's where we had an altercation with this drunken dude who was on the highway and was trying to hitch in front of us, and Audacy and he had words.

So we arrive into Tepix, to the most beautiful square, and I saw a most beautiful girl, and we were eating food.

Walking out of town, we saw this dude who was in his truck, and as we were passing by, Audacy knocked on the window to ask if he was leaving town, and he said, "Get in back," and we got in the back, and then he lit up this crackpipe and took off. He dropped us off a couple miles down the road and told us that we could sleep at his house, but that he just needed to pass it with his wife. So he drives off down the long road, and Audacy leaves it up to me whether or not we should trust this guy, and I said, "Let's not

trust such a crackhead," and, "We don't need
him." So, we hide in the woods.

Dogs are barking at us.

He comes back out, looks for us, and then
goes back in.

Now the dogs are really barking at us because
we start walking up the hill towards this house
that had no lights on, but the dogs were outside,
so we turned back and camped, literally, 5 feet
off the road.

A passing car woke us up in the morning. And
that's where I saw the first snake I had seen on
the trip. It was 5 or 6 feet long, and it was
crossing the road.

So we were going to meet up with Max and
Chavez in Monteleon. That was my favorite town,
and that's where we decided to stop for a day or
so, and enjoy the beach and everything.

Our ride into Monteleon was with a University
of Colorado professor, who was telling us that he
had heard 240 indigenous languages during his
travels in Mexico. So he was with us when we got
there, and as Audacy was running off into the
sea, the professor said to me: "You know, in
Spanish, Audacy is the most polite charismatic
person, but in English he can be a real asshole."

That was the first time that I ever jumped in
the Pacific Ocean, and I liked it.

The town was really cool. There were just
five roads: two going that way, three going the
other way. Cobblestone, or some sort of rock.
And the people in town were really nice, and to

get to the beach you had to pass the garbage area where they would all meet up on Sundays to burn their garbage together, and we had to pass by a pepper field where they were picking peppers.

That night, we had a huge bonfire on the beach, and the University of Colorado professor (he mentioned that he had been to Vietnam, and was referring to kilometres as 'clicks'), he became kind of freaked out about the fire.

CHAPTER MAX

The pacific coast highway begins right around Mazatlan, and it's amazing - nicer than the US coastal highway even. It runs right along the beaches and cliffs, through Michuacan, through Acapulco, all the way down to Puerto Escondido and Puerto Angel.

In every little village in Mexico there's these things called *topes*, which are speed bumps, so in every truck that we were in the back of, you'd get tossed up into the air at the *topes*.

So we continued on down, and I was probably the one who was advocating going faster than anyone else 'cause I had this *thing* that I wanted to get to, but we made it to a beach, and this was after we had started splitting up into pairs.

Aude had insisted that we get these walkie-talkies (which had a range of about 50 yards, and didn't turn out to be very useful at all) to try and stay in touch, because it's rather hard to hitchhike with four people, and a lot of the time we'd be split up into two groups. It would

alternate. Since Aude and I spoke Spanish, we
stayed split up most of the time, and the system
that we worked out was that we'd pick a town that
both pairs would be aiming for, and we'd go to
the south end of the last beach in town and camp
out there, and wait for the other group to catch
up, which, when you're talking about the Pacific
coast of Mexico, was absolutely preposterous.

We met this crazy ethno-linguist, Vietnam vet
guy who was driving himself around Mexico and
trying to save dying indigenous languages. I
don't remember what his name was, but he would
punctuate every sentence with the phrase:
'mothafuckas' ...whether he was talking about
missionaries or about the Viet Cong. He told us
that he had gotten kicked out of the army for
roughing up a prisoner during an interrogation.
The guy had a big handlebar moustache, and he was
a bit irritating.

We hung out at that beach for maybe two days,
and it was beautiful. Somehow we got split up
that night and Nick and I tried to find everybody
in the dark, and then ended up sleeping in the
middle of a dirt road next to a pineapple patch.

A couple of times when we'd pair up, and my
pair was behind Aude's pair, we would catch up a
little bit by getting on these rickety old
American school buses that were plying along the
same route that we were going on.

...So we broke the rules, and I wonder if
anyone else has confessed to that as well.

But we made our way down along the coast,
stopping at different places, and one night we
stopped at a beach that was a turtle sanctuary,
and there was a guy guarding the turtle eggs with

a machine gun in the dark, and I was afraid that
he was going to shoot us, but we were looking for
Aude on the southern end of the beach, and we
probably walked for three miles down this beach.

That's the problem when you try to meet up
like this. There are stretches of beach that run
for 30 or 40 miles, you know? And you're walking
in the dark.

Also, below the tide line, there were these
bioluminescent organisms in the sand, so that
when you stepped into the sand in the dark, these
little starbursts would light up underneath your
feet, like little constellations and galaxies.
You could see the outline of your footprint
traced in bioluminescent organisms living in the
sand.

We slept at the end of the beach that night,
and then walked back in the morning and found
Aude and Chavez.

That was the day we got our really long ride.
A truck pulled over with these two little
indigenous guys. It was a truck driver and his
son. They were really short, like 5 foot 2, and
the boy was fifteen. They had just dropped off a
load of pineapples in Mazatlan, and were driving
back empty, so we crawled into the back of their
truck, which was a big wooden container, open on
top, where they would have fastened a tarp over
the load. And this thing had a hole in the floor,
and the only thing that the guy asked us was to
not shit in the hole, which was over the back
axle in the bed of the truck, so if you had to
piss, you'd have to lie down spread eagle, and do
it down onto this spinning axle which was about a
foot below the hole. It was fairly nerve racking.

CHAPTER 21
Not a five-minute drive,
but a ten-hour ride.

We loaded our stuff into and on top of Bob's car, and he drove us back into town. We had coffees together, and then bade him farewell and watched as his station wagon turned north back onto the highway. The rest of us ordered toast and had another coffee, and then we drew straws.

Me and Max pulled the long straws.

So we all walked out of town together, and when we came up onto the highway, Chavez and Nick went to take their turn in the shade.

Max and I had hitched a lot together before, and all of our inherent disagreements had long since been thoroughly argued and put out for public display. The whole frustrated relationship had actually worked itself out into a pretty tight little system, and as we took to the roadside, I passed him my rolling tobacco and said that I'd take the first shift of thumbing if he'd roll me up a nice 7-6.

This goes back to a method that we have, whereby every rolled cigarette can be described by a two-digit number. The first number denotes width: 1 being the skinniest prick, and 9 being the Bob Marley whoofer. The second number is for tightness: 1 being the loosest roll, and 9, merely a headache-provoking guitar-playing prop that will self-extinguish every time that you put it down. The standard, in both cases, is a Camel unfiltered cigarette. A Camel unfiltered cigarette is a 5-5.

So Max and I thumbed a P-up that was going to Puerto Vallarta, and the driver-man with his gold-rimmed smile and his big sombrero had no qualms about letting all four of us jump up into the back of his ride.

Sombrero-man dropped us off in the middle of the city where we guzzled another steel-can juice, and Nick ran off to buy some smokes. Then we began the walk out of town together and found ourselves on a confusing bit of highway clover. As my peripherals became symmetrical, I noticed that our flow had drawn short, and I turned around to witness Max chatting it up with some cab driver.

"Max, what are you doing?"

Max, with his great smile, twisting around, but still leaning onto the cabby's door, exclaims, "He says that he'll take us all the way to the edge of town for only forty pesos!"

"Fucking hell!"

"Well... that's only ten cents each! We'll save having to walk five miles!"

I looked to Chavez for support, but he just put his hands up and made an expression like he didn't want the decision to come down on him. So then, in one synchronized movement, we all turned to Nick, who perceived the focus and paused for a moment, and then this is what he said:

"I don't know, it seems like hitchhiking's worked out well enough for us so far, I figure, why not just give it another go?"

And right then, with a smile spilling onto my

face, I could have kissed that boy, and I felt
that it was the biggest moment of the trip so
farr. Chavez suppressed a grin, and Max turned
from the cab and said nothing more, and within
thirty seconds, we caught a lift in another P-up
truck that took us right out to the edge of the
city.

From our new place out on the periphery, we
resumed our pairs, and Max and I hadn't been
hitching for more than ten minutes when a
humungous truck pulls off onto the gravel
shoulder of the highway, and we weren't sure
whether it was pulling over for us or if it was
just braking down. I ran over and jumped up onto
the running board to speak with the trucker. The
man was in his sixties, and travelling with his
son. He said that they were going all the way
down to Acapulco, and that he didn't care if
there were two of us, four of us, or ten of us,
as long as we didn't mind riding in the back.

So the son stepped down and opened up the
side panel, and the four of us loaded into what
was due to become our home for the following two
days.

The sweetest part about a ride like this,
secluded from the hosting entourage, is that you
don't have to keep up the conversation the whole
time. We would see them when they stopped for
gas, lunch or dinner, and we would have our
dialogues then. But for the rest of the time, it
was just relaxing and trying to stay cool, moving
around the back and chasing the shadows when the
truck would make a turn, and eventually coming to
find that there was really no place that was
completely in or out of the sun.

That night, things cooled down, and we stayed where we laid as the father and son went to sleep underneath the truck.

In the morning, Nick ran off to get some more smokes, and Chavez and I skipped over to a fruit stand for a pineapple and a large melon. It was even hotter than it had been the day before, and the four of us sat in a circle on the floor in the back, quietly passing around the skinned pineapple, taking bites out of it as if it were a gigantic ice cream cone.

Then we sat back, with our sticky hands, and Chavez went to take a piss through the hole in the floor. When he got back up, he gestured to Nick for a smoke. I was already rolling one up, and Nick passed Chavez a cigarette and then lit one for himself as well. Max reached out his arm and clicked his fingers, and he said: "Nick, can I get one too?"

This scene and sequence of events had become so commonplace between us that it hardly warrants any mention here, except for Nick's unexpected response. This was apparently the feather that was to break the camel's back.

"No."

"Alright, come on! I'll buy some the next time we stop."

"Max, you said that yesterday, and you said that the day before. You've been saying that for the past two weeks, and you haven't ever bought a single pack. Get your own smokes."

Max looked around to appeal to us, but we stayed out of it.

"Oh come on! We're a commune here. We've all been sharing our things. I share my... my chocolate, and my apricots. And these guys got the fruit, and it just so happens that we're stuck in a truck right now, and I don't have any cigarettes!"

Nick sat quietly, and kept on smoking. Max was wide-eyed, shaking his head in disbelief:

"Oh, that's just not right, it's just not right!" and then turning, "Well Aude? Can I have one of your rollies?" He didn't like asking me, 'cause of our past stuff, and 'cause he knew I had a hard time finding them in Mexico.

"Yeah, you can have this one," I said, passing him the one that I had just lit. "You should buy a pack soon though."

"I will, I will! Next time we stop."

So into Acapulco we came, mid-afternoon, and our father and son friends dropped us off on the near side of town. We stretched out and regrouped, and then started the long walk into town.

It felt like we had arrived to Florida. The signs were still mostly in Spanish, but the people who were in the street and running the businesses were predominantly blue-haired, American ex-pats.

Coming into the town centre, we stopped for about half an hour to have a coffee and wait for Chavez to go pick up some touristy knickknack for his girl back home. When he reappeared, we heaved our stuff back on and continued the hump through town. After a few minutes of walking through the heat, a familiar truck came honking by and pulling over, with father and son waving out of the windows and telling us that they were, after all, continuing on to San Cristobal.

I never really understood the reason why.

Something about watermelons.

So again we loaded into the back of the ride, and again they spent the night underneath the truck, and by the following morning, when they stopped outside of San Cristobal, we were about ready to be *out* of that panel-truck. To our friends however, who had seen us through all the way, we were immensely grateful. They grinned and declined on our offer to take them out to breakfast, and then they were off. Off on their happy business.

CHAPTER CHAVEZ

After Mazatlan, we got dropped off in a little seaside village, and it was Audacy and I, and we were looking for Nick and Max, and as I was walking up and down the beach with my little short-range CB radio, I came upon a giant sea turtle laying eggs, and called Audacy over to watch for a while before we left it alone. He headed back, and I moved down along and got attacked by a dog on the beach.

Dogs in Mexico are, I guess, just part of the culture really. There's stray dogs everywhere, and dead dogs lying in the ditches. They basically just breed unhindered, so there's a lot of, just, vagrant dogs.

Now, the morning after the sea turtle, we met up with Nick and Max, who had been camped not too far off, and we were walking along the Pan-American highway, or Route 1, and we had split up into twos, but we weren't so far away that we couldn't see each other, and this lorry pulls by. It's a big box crate truck, maybe like an F-350 engine in there, a panel truck really, with walls but no top on it, and the guy pulled over and then picked up all four of us, and we spent the next two days in the back of that truck, pissing through a hole in the floor, and eating watermelons and pineapples, and making a huge mess. Audacy was riding naked in the back of the truck, and there were a couple of times when we went through roadblocks that he had to jump up and put his clothes on real quick. I spent most of my time just sitting up on the metal bar that ran the length of the truck, and watching the landscape roll by.

A couple of days later, we rolled into San Cristobal and bid our truck driver farewell and good journey, and Max, in one of his moments of supreme clarity and intelligence, gave away the only map that we had, which was a nice gesture, but we really needed that map.

CHAPTER 23
San Cristobal de las Casas

We began our march towards the downtown, passing down long streets with brightly pastel-painted buildings on either side. We walked east into town until spotting a café, and then crossed the road and went inside. The place was an old-fashioned Cuban-looking venue with a big, sunny courtyard in the middle.

We unloaded into a pile, and the boys set down to writing postcards, eating toast, and drinking coffees. I set off into town to find a roadmap that would span from our currents, and down into our Guatemalan future.

When I got back to the café, I slid the new map up under the back-pad of my pack and took a caffeinated load off, while the others took turns at achieving their particular errands. Nick set off on his own to seek out the post office. For Chavez it was a call back home to his ever-sweetening baby. And for Max, who had made us strip down before splitting up, he set off with our grimy garbs in hopes of accomplishing the laundry.[30]

When everyone had returned, we continued on towards the centre of the bustle and made our way into the *plaza central*. Here, the Zapatista event was more acutely perceivable as the square grew increasingly populated by thin, strong men in black balaclavas, together with their governmental army counterparts, various merchants, and many journalists and media personages from around the world.

We arranged our base-camp at the edge of the square, and sat about busking, jaunting off on errands, and generally killing time.[31] Max ran

---

[30] Later on, when he returned from having picked up our things, he noted with pride that they had charged him extra, due to our clothes having been extremely dirty.

[31] Chavez found an old photograph postcard that we all ended up buying. The picture was of four banditos, posed with their guns in front of a freight train that they had brought to a stop. The flipside of the card described how the banditos had come upon a

around assessing the state of affairs according
to any and all good-looking women and media
correspondents. He found out that the march was
going to begin in two days time, and that it
would be leaving from that very square.
Subcomandante Marcos was due to appear at some
time between now and then, and was expected to
address his followers before leading them up
towards Mexico City. Max was very keen to march
in their support, and began cornering us
individually to persuade us to come with.

I questioned two of the girls that Max had
been chatting with, and they mentioned that any
foreigners who wanted to accompany the procession
were required to pay a fee of $100 U.S. dollars
for the privilege of lending their support. That
sounded like crap to me, and it didn't seem to
wash with the others either. The outlines of a
division were beginning to form on our horizon.[32]

Meanwhile, as the evening wore on, and with
Max off running around to suss things out for
himself, Nick and I played music at two different
places for free beer and a hat-pass, and then
applied our earnings to a pasta meal, followed by
a pub crawl. We ran into another friendly member
of that German travelling guild who was dressed
up in the same manner and hanging around outside
of the discotheque, trying to score some weed. He
advised us that the quickest way out of town was
towards the east.

We found Max, and he reiterated his intention
to stick around for the march, and told us that
he had found himself accommodation for the night

---

photographer in the passenger car, and had taken time out of the
robbery to make him take the picture.
[32] The outlines of a horizon were beginning to form on our division.

on the floor of some hostel with one of his new journalist friends. I gave him the name of the town where the two girls were living who we planned to visit in Costa Rica, as well as the name of the school that they were running down there. He told me that he hoped to catch back up with us, but that for now he was committed to the march.

And then we said goodbye to Max.

By this time we were pretty hammered, and we staggered out through the seemingly endless barrios until at last spotting an empty rise up behind two crumbling cinder block buildings. Up onto the rise we climbed, and pitched the tents, and were almost bedded down when a single dog began to bark, setting off a wildfire of K9-alarm that spanned for miles in every direction. We sat and tried to muffle our laughter, and as lights began to turn on all across the valley, we laid down and punched out.

In the early morning, we struck camp and strode quickly down to the road to avoid any confrontation over our hurried choice of a campsite. We dragged ourselves on down to the nearest café, put our stuff down, and had a reflexive look around. Three: the number that we had been so carefully trying to avoid. No matter. There was nothing that could be done about it now. We'd just have to hitch with three.

CHAPTER CHAVEZ

We arrived to San Cristobal in the morning, and went to a beautiful little café with an outdoor courtyard, where we had some really good coffee, and I sat and wrote for a couple of hours before leaving my pack with the others and having a walk around the city. I went to the bank and got some money and did little things like that. It was just a nice, pretty, relaxed day that we spent there.

Max spent a good deal of his time getting in touch with the other journalistic forces that were in town, and before long we made our way in to the *plaza* where all of the action was. The Zapatistas were coming out, and the Zapatista women were selling these little dolls of Zapatistas on horseback and with guns and all that. The Zapatista men were there, some of them on horseback, some of them on bicycles, and some on foot. They all had big guns and rifles, dressed all in black, head to toe. Black facemasks, black headbands, black pants, everything, and man did they look bad ass.

With the arrival of the Zapatistas, so too did the Mexican army arrive, and they were there more or less in full force, big machine guns, running crowd control, and it got a little bit tense I suppose, but we didn't see any violence.

We sat there in the plaza all day playing with the little kids and watching things start to take shape, smoking our Mexican rice paper Faros and taking turns at jaunting around the old part of the city.

There was an incident where Nick was taking photographs of some of the army guys, and they approached him and wanted his camera and film, and Nick got all clamped up and I could tell that he was pretty worried at that point, but Audacy

came out and talked them down, and it turned out
to be not a real problem.

We split up with Max that night. He went off
with his journalist buddies to do journalist
stuff, and we went across the plaza to a bar
where they played music for a couple of hours.
There was really nobody there, but we got some
free drinks. After that, we jetted around the
corner to an Italian restaurant and had ourselves
the first nice meal that we'd had in a while,
before walking back out into the plaza and going
into another bar where Nick and Audacy played
between sets for some Mexican funk band who ended
up giving us a CD.

After that we heard that the place to go was
this nightclub just across the way, so the four
of us crossed over (Max was back with us at this
point), and continued to get more and more drunk
until we were all dancing, and we had a lot of
fun in there, and I felt useful for once and
scored some pot off of some guy in the nightclub.
Upon our leaving, there was a disagreement about
where we were going to sleep, and Audacy of
course was adamant that we just camp out
somewhere, and Max of course was adamant that we
didn't. So it turned out that Max went and stayed
with some buddy that he had met, some other
journalist guy, and it was decided also at that
time that Max wanted to stay in San Cristobal,
and that the three of us, more or less, wanted to
get out of there. So after saying goodbye to Max
that night, Nick and Audacy and I sat on a dark
unlit corner in the street, and smoked ourselves
a little *porro*. There was an eerie moment when a
guy in a little Zapatista outfit came cruising
out of the darkness on a bicycle and rode by real
slow and just sort of stared us down.

After that, we walked, and we kept walking, and at this point it's late. It's probably 2:3o, 3:oo in the morning, and we were walking through the streets of San Cristobal and into the neighborhoods, looking for a place to wedge the tent in and get a couple hours of sleep. We finally did find a place where a house had been torn down, so we hiked up onto this little hill and pitched our tents as quietly as we could, and I swear, I was probably zipping up my tent-fly when one of us made some noise that set one dog to barking. Within seconds, there must have been thirty dogs barking at us as we crouched up on this little hill in our tents, high and drunk and tired, and we just sort of looked out over the city and saw all the lights coming on, and we were so tired that we just started laughing and then went to sleep.

In the morning I woke up and unzipped my fly, crawled out of my tent, and noticed that I had pitched my tent pretty much on top of a dead dog. Then we packed our stuff and walked out of there.

CHAPTER NICK

Me and Max hitched together for a while, and Audacy and Chavez were ahead of us, and Max had a competition with Audacy especially, about meeting up, because he didn't want to prove to be a worse hitchhiker, so he talked me into getting a bus and taking us to wherever it was. I don't know if he ever told anybody this, but we took a bus.

A Mexican bus was interesting. Went into a washroom, and paid to get toilet paper and stuff like that. It was all interesting.

And then we met up with those guys, and they were going on about how they had seen a tortoise on the beach.

Early on the next day we got a ride with a papa and his son, who were driving a long ways. We spent two nights with them, and they slept underneath their truck.

When they finally dropped us off at a gas station, the first thing I hear is this Phelonius Sphere Monk, blasting out of the gas station's loud speakers, and I couldn't believe it: jazz, here! And I knew that I'd like San Cristobal right then. And I did.

San Cristobal. Three security guards. Right outside the bank. Army men. I take a picture of them playing with the Zapatista dolls. TABOO. And they came over to me and they wanted the camera, but I don't really know what they wanted, but I remember being tall in Mexico, and Audacy even taller.

That night we went to a bar and played in between the sets of a really good Santana cover band, and then we got invited to a rave, which was cool.

San Cristobal was a neat colonial city with lots of vibrant colors.

And then of course we were walking out of town, not wanting to pay for a hostel. Me, Audacy and Chavez go looking for some place to sleep in the city, and up and up this hill we go, and out of nowhere comes this Zapatista dude on a bike, and he just glared us down, and that was *freaky*.

How cool was it that he didn't kill us? Ha, ha.

And then the dog alarms. We set off the trap. 1, 2, 3, and before you know, every dog in Chiapas was barking. That was great. We slept behind someone's house on an incline, and the blood rushed to my feet when I woke up in the morning, and what a feeling!

We got out of there, and we left Max behind. It was just the three of us.

Our first ride out, in the back of a pickup, there were all these cows in the middle of the road, and our ride basically just kept crashing them out of the way with his bumper.

We arrived at the border right around nightfall, and they didn't want to give us our twenty bucks back, but we got our twenty bucks back, and we got out of Mexico just fine.

CHAPTER MAX

We sat in the back of that truck for 900 miles down along the coast of Mexico, getting tossed up in the air over every *tope* that we passed, stopping occasionally at little roadside stands to get beer and cigarettes and water, and amazing fresh fruit, pineapples, biggest pineapple I've ever seen, and Aude had this style of cutting the pineapple where you just cut the skin off of the outside and hold onto the blossom stem on top, and eat it like a caveman chicken leg.

Yeah, and it was hot. It was really hot.

We made a game. If you took a beer can, because of the way that the wind blew over the top of the truck, you could throw it and it would bounce back to you. It was kind of like Steve McQueen in the Great Escape, when he's in his prison cell, throwing a baseball.

They stopped at night, stopped for a couple of hours to sleep. The kid would drive sometimes, and we were driving on the edges of cliffs, with this fifteen-year old boy driving this rickety old truck, you know? And they were so nice, those two. And we didn't realize until the end that they were going all the way to Chiapas, all the way to exactly where we wanted to go. It was like one of those small miracles of travel. We stopped one night at this truck stop and ate some fish, and the woman came out with a stuffed rattlesnake and stuck it in Nick's ear, and he totally flipped out.

So that was a long ride in that truck, 'cause it wasn't going very fast, but we got to San Cristobal two days later, just after sunrise, and that's where the Zapatista revolution was going to be. So we stayed there for the night.

Oh, and that was the other rule: that you're not allowed to pay for any place to stay, which, as far as I know, we didn't. We had very good weather. I don't think it rained a single time.

The boys didn't want to march north towards the capital, which was understandable (we had plotted our entire route to avoid Mexico City as much as possible), so we made the plan that I would catch up with them in Costa Rica, at Ingrid LeBlanc's house down on the Nicoiya Peninsula.

So, we parted ways, and they headed down south.

*   *   *

I went on the Zapatista thing for a few days, but it was really just a Zapapolooza traffic jam, with about a hundred buses that were just going nowhere fast. And usually by the time that *my* bus got through, the rally would already be over in whatever town it was. So after two days of that, I was in Oaxaca, and I was like: that's enough for me.

I spent a day in Oaxaca, and met this hilarious Australian anarchist/activist kid who was also sick of the march, so we made plans together.

I hitchhiked alone from Oaxaca back towards San Cristobal, and was waiting by *el Arbol del Tule* which is supposedly the biggest tree in the world, when this taxi driver pulls over and picks me up. He's got a skull with sunglasses mounted onto the hood of his taxi, and I usually wave off taxi drivers, 'cause I don't want to pay them, but the guy said 'No, no, c'mon,' and he and his ten-year old boy drive me up through the mountains, and in the middle of the mountains he goes: "Maximo, te aprendes de oofos?" And I said, "<What are oofos>?" and then I realized that he was talking about UFOs. And he told me this story about how he had seen a UFO in this exact spot in the mountains, and that it was very commonplace to be picked up by aliens.

He took me as far as Tuxla Gutierras, which is at the base of the mountain below San Cristobal, and I slept that night rather miserably in a building site, being bitten by

mosquitos, in kind of a seedy little shithole of
a town.

When you go up to San Cristobal, it's
amazing. All the little Indian women are there in
their peasant dress, walking up the mountain road
in single file with loads of wood on their heads.
It's an amazingly beautiful place. Really cool.
Old colonial town. I met back up with Wayne, the
Australian guy, and he and I hitchhiked, and
crossed the border into Guatemala with these
Quebecois travelers in a van.

CHAPTER 27
Into Guatemala

We started east out of the city, emerging
from the barrio into a red sand desert. And as
the landscape changed, so too did the people,
together with their means of transport. Almost
every vehicle was a P-up truck now, and we caught
a series of short rides with openhearted
families, farmers and workers, who had grown up
in a culture that held a positive view of
travelers, and the goodness of ride-share.

So in and out of these rides, with the cattle
in the road, and our windy hairdos, and the
handsome Mexican Indians whose children would
stare at us in amazement.

The sun was down when we reached the last
shop on the Mexican side, some seven kilometres
from the border. We turned out our pockets and
pooled together the remainder of our peso-change,
and then sent Nick into the shop to spend it on

what turned out to be whiskey, chocolate, bananas, cashews, candy, and chips.

While Nick was in the store, I stood roadside with Chavez, chatting with a cabbie who couldn't understand why we didn't want to load up with him.

"<It's not expensive from here to the border>." he said.

"<Yes, but we travel by a code>," I replied.

I had become very dismissive towards taxis, and I turned to watch Nick emerge from the light of the store. The cab driver didn't pull away, but instead followed my gaze over to Nick, who came walking up to our spot, looking quite pleased for having accomplished his Spanish language shopping mission. We stood there talking and packing away the groceries, and still the cabbie sat watching us. Then he called over:

"<Hey rubio, I will give you and your friends a ride to the border for no charge, as a gift>," and I suspiciously thought to turn him down, until he added with a proud smile, "<I too will travel one day>."

So we thanked the cabbie, loaded in, and shared our tall green can of Pringles with him as he drove us the few remaining miles over to the border.

After an unsurprising amount of procedural confusion (for three people hitchhiking in the dark over any border), we stepped out through the border turnstile from the serenity of Southern Mexico, and into the sketchy rundown carnival atmosphere of the Guatemalan border town.

Latin, Star Wars, Old West.

I exaggerated my own sense of confidence in an attempt to balance Nick's visible anxiety, and we walked down the street with all eyes upon us, dogs gnashing at our heels, and young boys laughing as they pelted us with stones.

We had to get the hell out of there.

I ran up to a P-up truck that was slowly making its way through the throng of people, and asked the two men inside if they would give us a lift.

"<No, we're not going very far, only just up here>."

"<We only need a couple of miles, just to get away from the border>," and then from behind me came a yell in English, "Fuck off!"[33], and I turned to see Chavez trying to help Nick ward off some young kids who had seemingly dared each other to try to touch him. Nick was circling defensively as they laughed and continued trying to sneak up on him from behind. I turned back to the men,"<...anywhere is better than here>," I said.

The driver smiled and pointed into the back of his truck, "<We're not going very far>."

"Monton de gracias."

I threw my pack and guitar up into the truckbed, and as the boys clambered in, I walked around front to sit up with the men in the cab.

Our border-rescuers dropped us off at the

---

[33] Nick's voice.

first small town, whose sole and central feature was a well-tended soccer field. As we descended from the road, Chavez wondered out loud if we might try to pitch the tents right out there in the middle, in accordance with the ancient Chinese hitchhiking proverb: *if you can't hide from everyone, then don't hide from anyone at all.*

When we got down the hill, we saw that most everyone had already gone to bed. On the southern edge of the field, however, there was a one-table-restaurant with its lights still on and a few people about. We walked out onto that side of the soccer field and put our stuff down on the quarter-line. The boys sat down, and I headed over to the trailer-café.

There were three generations of women in the kitchen, and I addressed the eldest, inquiring as to the possibility of our camping the night in the field. The old lady asked where we were from, and then turning to her middle-aged daughter she asked if there was a soccer game on for the following morning. The daughter took over and said that there was no match scheduled. She told me that there shouldn't be any problem, and that they would keep an eye out. I thanked them and gave my best Boba-Fett nod to the men at the table and then headed back over to where the boys were waiting.

We erected the tents, and then sat down on the grass to light our candle in preparation for our feast of cashews, bananas and whiskey.

Just then, from out of the dark, the young, 3rd generation girl from the kitchen shyly approached our spot, and as she stepped up close to us, we could all see that she was beautiful. She told us that her name was Gwendi, and that she had been sent over to invite us back to the café for dinner.

"<Thank you>, I said, smiling up to her, "<please express our thanks to your family, but we already have our dinner here>."

She glanced at Nick, who was breaking a banana off of the bunch, and then she smiled and said, "<Why don't you come over and let us cook you a proper dinner>?"

"<Thank you, but we have no way of paying you.[34] We have only just arrived across the border, and everything is closed>."

"<You won't need to pay us>," she said smiling, "<You will be our guests>."

And with that, and an unnecessary translation for the boys, we grabbed our bags, left the tents where they were, and followed Gwendi back over towards the lights.

The older ladies whooshed away the men who were in the chairs, and then started setting large bowls of tortilla ingredients down on the table. Hot black beans, cold red beans, white rice, scrambled eggs, lemony onions, hot peppers, chopped cilantro, and red and green salsas. A tall stack of tortillas was wrapped up and kept warm for us in a blue dishcloth. The ladies sat smiling and watched us eat, refilling any bowls that became depleted.

When we finished, they started asking us all

---

[34] "…No tenemos como pagarles.

sorts of questions, and I sat and translated both ways. Then Nick and I played "Viajero Perdido" for our hosts[35], and they smiled and clapped. I gave Gwendi one of my CDs, and she was bowled over,[36] and then we thanked and bowed to the women and returned to our spot out on the soccer field.

We bedded down and had a conversation through the walls of the tents about how fine Gwendi was, each of us horny and imagining different compromising and erotic situations, and we dreamily discussed out loud the possibility of taking her with us; and replacing Max with a girl.

In the morning, we were awoken by the CD, blasting out from an outdoor speaker behind the café:

"Well I don't know where I'm going, and I don't know how I'll get there, but I'm happy just to ride with you, and we can sit down and tell each other what we have and haven't done and what we want to do..."

We folded the tents, and Gwendi was laughing as she danced around with chickens fleeing from underfoot. She beckoned us back over to the café where her grandmother had fixed us some coffees, and we sat at the table in a state of bliss, admiring both the hospitability of humanity and the green mountainous extravagance of our surroundings.

---

[35] Nick plays just about every instrument. The one that he chose to travel with, because of its lightweight and packability, was the melodica, which is a small plastic keyboard that you blow into. That's what he is playing here, and at just about every street and bar-gig that we play.

[36] ...It's all about the picture on the back.

After coffees, we bade farewell to the friendly family and made our way back up to the highway. The CD was still playing, full blast, and we could hear it all the way up to the road:

"I am a ball of burning lightning, I am orgasmic carnal sin, I am pain beyond worth screaming, autumn teardrops in the wind, I am a sheep that's just been sheared, a virgin girl who just got knifed, I'm not aiming at feeling nothing, I'm raging with passion and being alive…"

PART III

CHAPTER 28
Guatemala to Costa Rica

We're not from anywhere when we're walking down the road. Didn't I tell you that the road goes on and on and on?

I think that I must've cut class on the day that they were teaching us a lesson in humility, and I don't mind telling you that I've had some pretty good rides in my time. Records have been broken and there have been stretches of straight-through-the-night Olympian hitchhiking that even Sissy Hankshaw would pause to admire. I have never, however, experienced such ideal hitchhiking like what we had in the country of Guatemala.

Ninety-five percent of the vehicles are P-up trucks in Guatemala, and from border to border, we were passed by only two P-up trucks that *didn't* pull over to give us a ride. Not that anyone is going very farr, but they're certainly willing to give you a lift. It's very good for your arm and leg muscles, getting in and out of all of those truck beds. And there wasn't any time in between. You'd jump down from one truck and the next one coming up would be pulling over just to ask if you needed a ride. It was amazing.

So we spent the bulk of the day just jumping in and out of these rides, slowly travelling through some of the most beautiful countryside that any of us had ever seen. By mid-afternoon, we had come into sight of an enormous freshwater lake that was stretched out between the mountains. We took a few hours off and had a swim, and then a walk around the marketplace (avoiding some Germans) and I bought a hand-sown hackisack for one dollar.

The people of Guatemala were all dressed up in the brightest of colours, and the women especially wore these embroidered shawls with intricate patterns that apparently indicate the towns and regions where they come from.

A cool from the lake and a beer for the afternoon left us feeling sufficiently refreshed to get back on the road, and we decided to hitch a bit further, but not to go too farr as to leave the lake.

The hitchhiking was just as easy now as it had been before, and by late afternoon, we came rolling into the town that occupied the lake's south shore. We made our way down to the water's edge and pitched the larger of the two tents underneath a knarley tree behind a stonewall.[37] We decided that we ought to keep a watch at the camp, and Chavez volunteered to be the first to stay behind. He asked me if I wouldn't fish the candle out of my pack for him before we left, and I dumped out the contents of my waterproof tote-bag[38] and waited until he had it lit before Nick and I walked up into town.

It was Friday night. The town was coming alive. Nick and I joined into an impromptu soccer game with the kids in the square. A marching band was warming up, and food vendors lined the

---

[37] We all started sleeping in my tent.
[38] Candle, playing cards, knife, cord, flashlight, bug-stuff, firestarters, corkscrew, spoon, hackisack, safety pin, duct tape, compass, matches, boot-wax, iodine pills.

street, still preparing their stalls.

When the band expands into the square and causes a halt in the game, Nick makes some comment about how sweet it would be to have a joint right now, and I agree. We head over to the street corner to ask the sketchiest-looking guy around where one might find *un pocitillo de mota*. He points us along to another guy on the opposite corner, and after repeating our surreptitious inquiry; the guy turns on his heel and mumbles for us to follow him.

So down the alleys we go, arriving eventually to a dark little cemetery where our man tells us to wait, and we have a bit of a time talking him in to getting us only the smallest amount. Then he disappears into the shadows and we sit down amongst the gravestones.

N: "Do you think he'll be back?"

A: "I don't know. You tell me."

N: "Yeah, I think he'll be back."

A: "Yeah."

N: "...I can't believe where we are. This is a crazy place. I've never been anywhere like this place before. What did you say to him? It wasn't *poco*, but it was like..."

A: *Pocito*. It means less than a little bit. Actually, I think I said *pocitillo*, which means even less then that."

A few minutes later, the guy reappears and gives us a disturbingly large satchel, and we pay him and thank him before weaving our way out of those streets, and back down to the shore.

Chavez was writing postcards when we arrived, and those two kept a look out while I got into the wind-stop of the tent to roll the dope up into as few joints as possible, and even though I twisted up double-papered 9-9's, I still couldn't manage to roll it into fewer than four. We sat out on the jetty and watched the moored fishing boats bob in the reflected starlit waves as we passed around the first of our four fatties.

Nick tends to become quiet and introverted in thought when he gets toked, and Chavez expressed his interest to view the festivities that were taking place up the way. I hid the three remaining *porros* in a knot of the tree, and then headed back up the road with Chavez.

When we got back up to the square, things were going *off*.

*   *   *

There is something that has been lost to our new-age western society, but that still exists to the people of Latin America, and that is: the basic and continual public celebration of being alive, and it heightens with the arrival of every single week-end.

When westerners stay in to watch Saturday Night Live, or head out to get pissed at some invite-only party, Latin Americans get all gussed up, and together with their families and in-laws, take to the streets to celebrate and reaffirm their senses of attachment, community and love.

It's saddening that the trend of modern day affairs lends itself to a philosophy under which the arrivals of babes are more often perceived as lamentable mishaps, and the elderly, as mere nursing home financial liabilities.

In the more ancient world, the elderly are revered for their experience and wisdom; and the newborn, looked upon as gifts from the sun-god. I hope that the aimless blade of science doesn't slash every pearly gate.

*   *   *

So Chavez and I had a go at the soccer, playing on opposite teams. Then we strolled around eating candyfloss and corn nuts while I tried to avoid the street corner guys from before. We combed the streets, admiring the singing populace and then staying away from a large fight that broke out, and Chavez kept an ever-looking eye out for a place that sold talking-with-baby international telephone cards.

In the end he found one, and did his business. I waited for him on a park bench across the street. When he finally hung up the phone and walked back over, he had a guilty look about him, and I asked:

"What's up?"

"She wants to come down."

"Down to where?"

"Maybe Costa Rica."

"What do you want?"

"I don't know," he said, rubbing his neck, "I do miss her though."

"Well."

When we got back to the shore, there was one

less joint stuck up in the tree, and Nick was acting pretty spaced out. He passed up on his turn to adventure, and we chatted delirium till heavy lids.

CHAPTER NICK

I love Guatemala. Guatemala is cool. The mountains and the valleys. I've never seen anything like it. And people just kept picking us up. It was way too easy. I remember having to pee and not having the chance because we'd jump out of a truck and say thank you, and another truck would already have stopped just to ask us if we needed a ride, so there we go, we're taking rides.

I don't remember how we heard about the lake, but that big lake surrounded by the mountains was gorgeous, and we got dropped off at the far end of it where we went looking for weed, and someone tried to sell us an ounce for $4, and we ended up getting only a ¼ and then smoking some fatties. That was interesting: all of those different back-ways, and trying to get to the dealer's house. But it was all cool.

We went back and smoked some big fatties, and then Audacy and Chavez went into town and came back to tell me that there had been a big ruckus, and I had an insane part of my trip, stoned, watching the lights glimmer off the water, and some guy over in the dark, puffing on a cigarette over there. And there was a church right next door, because we were kind of camped out on a lawn with a long wall, and on the other side of the wall in the church there was a girl singing, and there was a circus keyboard sound, and this girl kept singing and singing, and the music kept going and going, and there was a drummer and a tambourine player, and it just seemed like the pitch kept on getting higher and higher, but never went higher and just stayed, but just had such intensity and people clapping, it seemed to go on forever. It was totally freaking me out! I was inside the tent, outside the tent, the guy over there was smoking a cigarette... so I was just going crazy.

And then Audacy and Chavez came back and said, "This is the most insane city." But we were all happy to get the fuck out of there the next day.

CHAPTER 30
Alligator in the Water Feature

In the morning we baptised ourselves before leaving the lake,[39] and by early afternoon we had made it to the border.

The highway ran alongside of the shore, and the countryside that we passed through in El Salvador was in a smoking ruin. The region had just been hit by a mega-Richter earthquake only the day before,[40] and one of our first rides was with a red cross truck that was carrying a

---

[39] Nick was too Catholic to kid around about the baptizing thing.

[40] This kind of untethered my goat. Two years of San Francisco and I had never even felt a tremor. We found out later that the day after we left the country, the same region was hit by another quake of almost equal proportions.

humongous plastic bag full of fresh water.

We noticed some changes as we crossed the border. Besides the devastation left by the earthquake and the flattened aspect of the landscape, we watched the girls become taller and so very much better looking. And as farr as our rides went, they were now almost all aboard full-size trucks.

We got dropped off on the shore in a place that was too small to be called a town, and walking one block down to the beach, we find a clump of three palms, casting a moonlight shadow, and we whisperingly pitched our tent up on the darkest spot in the sand.

There was a fat guy in the morning who owned the two buildings that stood between us and the highway (his house and the restaurant). He had come out to tell us that we were crazy and that he himself had been robbed on that very stretch of beach only the week before, and had been relieved of everything right down to the gold cross around his neck, etc. We expressed our appreciation for his concern, but pointed out that the night had already passed and that now we were on our way. He shook his head and invited us in for coffees, and we sat with him in his courtyard for a while, sipping our coffees and admiring his prize-fighting cocks.

*   *   *

The hitchhiking in El Salvador was almost as good as it had been in Guatemala, and by early afternoon, we were walking across the bridge and into Honduras.

The thin western sliver of Honduras that

hosts the Pan-American Highway is nothing to write home about.[41] It felt kind of like a war zone. Guns mounted on jeeps sort of thing.

By lunchtime, we got out of a P-up truck in a small junction of a town and I noticed with interest that one of the small restaurants was serving turtle eggs, but Chavez started giving me such a hard time for even considering the notion, that I was prevented from indulging my culinary curiosity.

By late afternoon we disembarked near the shore and trekked down to the stony beach, stripping down to our underwear to rinse ourselves in the brown ocean water. *Ahhh!* Then back out on the beach, we tried to hide each other as we changed and then strapped our wet clothing onto the outside of our packs. The lingering locals watched the scene with distaste.

Hunger and thirst drew us across the road to a large, thatch-roofed bar/restaurant, where we ordered beer, seafood and rice, and by the time the check came, the owner was seated and drinking with us at our table. We asked him how farr one could expect to have to walk south out of town before reaching any kind of seclusion. In response, he introduced his wife and children, and suggested that once the doors were closed, we could pitch the tent right there on the floor of the restaurant.

So we had a couple more and waited for the place to close down, and then spent the night

---

[41] The Pan-American Highway is considered to be the longest highway in the world, stretching from Homer, Alaska, to the southern end of the island of Chiloe in southern Chile. The only section of the highway for which construction has never been completed is known as the Darien Gap, 180 kms of jungle between Panama and Columbia.

hanging out with their kids, with the tent pitched in the locked-off section of the open air patio, right next to a fruit-bearing garden that had an alligator in its water feature.

CHAPTER NICK

El Salvador, and they had just had a huge earthquake, and in a few of the villages that we drove through, the buildings were just toppled over and there was still smoke rising out of the rubble.

We got a ride in the back of a dumptruck, fully loaded, and that was interesting. The towns we were passing through had been decimated, and I remember calling home. It was a Sunday, and it was the first time that I had called home.

We slept on the beach that night, and the next morning, we circled around this HUGE mountain, it looked like a huge volcano, and it was right before the Honduras border. There was a woman on the bridge that we were crossing, and she had elephantitis on her foot, and it was disgusting. It was the most disgusting thing that I've ever seen.

In Honduras we go into the town with long streets, and it brings us out to the beach, and a bunch of guys were asking us about our packs and how much they cost and all this stuff. It was a real rundown town.

We went to go eat in a family restaurant, and the mom and dad took Christian pity on us and took us in for the night, with their pet alligator and their little kid named Jose, and the little girl who I think had a crush on Chavez.

And then the next day, we go into Nicaragua.

There was one time that we were in the back of a pickup: we were at a roadside stop-check, and right about level with us in the pickup were 3 or 4 guys with M-16s, and they were questioning us, but nothing happened, and it was all cool.

CHAPTER 32
In Church

Early the next day, we arrived into Nicaragua. The border itself was painless, but seemed to reoccur with military road-stops posted at irregular intervals along the highway. From the back of our P-up truck rides, we waved at the world and watched as the landscape began to take a definite turn for the better.

Our fifth ride was a charm.[42]

He was the eldest brother of a family that had been Nicaraguan nobility before the revolution, and back then, they had owned the largest coffee plantation in the country. Nowadays, he was an English-speaking, very politically minded, greying old man who soon

---

[42] There are no laid out specifications as to what makes for a charm ride. It may be the distance that they take you, the speed at which they're traveling, the character of the host, some combination of these, or something else entirely. You *do* know, however, when you get one. And for some tried and tested reason (coincidental or otherwise) it always seems like the fifth ride of the day is a charm.

pulled off the road to invite Chavez and Nick to squish up into the front with us so that he could bring us *all* up to date on his account of recent Nicaraguan history. Both his talking and his driving were equally fast and erratic, and when he turned off on a detour to show us *his* town[43], he drove with all of the reckless abandon seemingly afforded to a depraved upper class. We could tell that the townsfolk could recognize his vehicle due to the speed with which they fled the streets as he positively tried to run them down. He honked and scoffed, and spoke of them as though they were his chickens.

After this hair-raising tour of the village, he took us on to his house where he insisted that we come in for a coffee.

The old man rolled up a joint as his butler served us instant coffee. Then he showed us through the garden and offered to rent us the annex-room off of the back of the house. We politely declined, but mentioned that we might be coming back through again in the future, and with that, he drove us back along the highway and dropped us off in the next little town.

Later that evening, we were roadside and shuffling south out of town looking for a place to camp. The streetlights seemed to go on forever, and we began to contemplate a crafty pitch. We came abreast of a small brown church off to the right, and exhausted as we were, I was for camping in the moon-shadow cast by the small building. The boys wavered, gazing ahead in a hopeful attempt to identify an end to the interminable stretch of lights. Then they nodded

---

[43] That's what he called it: "Mi pueblo," with a stress on the "Mi."

to each other, and then back to me, and the three of us waited until the traffic cleared from both horizons before hurdling the fence into the shadowy churchyard and beginning to unfurl the tent.

We had the poles straightened out and one of them through the sleeve when I noticed that Nick was frozen up, staring over my shoulder. I turned around to see two men stepping forward. One carried a machete, and the other had an antique sword that he held halfway drawn from its scabbard.

I dropped the tent and made a small bow, "Buenas noches."

The one with the machete spoke, "<What are you doing there>?"

"<We are travelers, and we mean no harm...>" etc, etc.

"<But this is a church>!"

"<Yes. And what better place to stay for one night when travelers find themselves so farr from home>?"

The two men exchanged a look, and the companion sheathed his sword.

"<This is not a safe place to camp, and I am speaking now of your safety...>" and here he gestured around and over his shoulder, "<from some of the people that we get coming through here>."

"<But chief, late as it is and tired as we are, and with your permission and that of your comrade, we would like to put our tent here for

the night, and place our fate into the hands of Providence>."

Again the armed pair exchanged a look before the speaker said, "<Wait here>," and then the two of them turned and walked back off into the darkness.

We left the tent half-pitched, and sat down to have a smoke. The boys were asking me about the subtleties of the exchange; all of the important stuff they had pretty much already understood.

A couple of minutes later the armed pair returned, now accompanied by a fat woman bearing a large key and an old man who I was guessing to be the priest.

"<We have spoken with the father>," began machete man, "<and he invites you to sleep inside of the church>."

We started to make out like it would be too much trouble and all the bother, but the silent old man shook his head and gestured to the woman, who stepped forward with her large key and unlocked the door. She smiled and explained that we would be locked inside until morning, and that if any of us wanted to do our *deeds*... that we'd best do them now. The three men watched in amusement as we got our stuff inside and took quick turns at using the outhouse around back. Then they peeped in the doorway, pointing out the light switch, and then all four wished us goodnight. We sat on the floor and listened to the loudness of the latch as the key turned and locked us into our overnight sanctuary.

We immediately took advantage of the flat

floor and our windless setting to spread out all
of the maps, and eating candy as we crawled
around in our underwear, we communally recounted
our trip as we traced with a magic marker our
meandering hitchhike line. Appropriately pleased
with our progress, we pitched both tents up on
the alter, and Nick and I started playing music,
seated beneath the dome stuccoed ceiling between
the few pews in the centre of the floor. We
played some quasi-religious country covers, one
of my tunes, and a new song that Nick had been
working on. The resulting music struck us as
being acoustically (if not divinely) sublime, and
we ate candy and laughed out loud at ourselves,
and at our good fortune.

The turning key awoke us in the morning. It
was the fat lady. She had brought us some
crackers and some hot mate, and after a short
bilingual chat as we packed our stuff, she saw us
off with an easy smile, and assured us that we
were welcome to overnight in the church anytime
that we were passing through that way again.

By late morning, we were riding on top of a
large truck that was filled up with some sort of
powdery red gravel.

This is when the landscape became
magnificent.

Our truck made a slow climb up into the high
plateaus of southern Nicaragua, and to all sides,
we could look down the slopes and into the
mysterious tangle of jungle. It was a clear day,
with visibility running straight to the horizons,
and as we gazed ahead, we were certain that we
were beholding the green hills of Costa Rica
before us.

The truck let us down at the border, and we proceeded on foot towards the flock of flags denoting the boundary, attempting in turn to name each one.

The crossing was a slow one, and came with a twenty dollar charge. We exited eventually from the pedestrian side of the border only a minute before our trucker friend pulled out from the commercial side, and much to our karmic pleasure, he was smiling and waving as he pulled over onto the shoulder, jumping out to caution us that riding on top of trucks in Costa Rica was illegal, and that we would have to duck down and lay low for the remainder of the ride.

This legality would continue to plague us throughout our travels in Costa Rica.

CHAPTER CHAVEZ

We awoke in the morning when the church door was opened, and we thanked our hosts and hitched out of town.

Later that day I was sitting in the back of a pickup truck, facing backwards, watching things go by, when the wind caught by favorite ballcap, the one that my brother had given me, and it blew off my head and into the street to be gone forever. I watched it drift away in slow motion. Audacy and Nick both just kind of looked at me for a second, and then put their heads down. I was really bummed. We had been eating chocolate and we were almost out, and Audacy held up the little Hershey's bar and gave me the very last piece of chocolate.

Later on that day we hit the Costa Rican border, which was a pain in the ass, and with a lot of people crossing, we had a big wait. It was funny though, once we did get through and paid our exit and entry taxes, we had thought that Costa Rica, being the most Americanized of all of the Central American countries, would be the best country to hitch in. Gringos would be a more common sight, and would perhaps seem less dangerous. Much to our surprise, that was not the case; it was the *worst* of all of the Central American countries to hitch in.

We did get a ride pretty far right off the bat from the border, back in the big truck with the same guy as before, and he took us maybe a hundred miles into the country. We were trying to make it to these two girls' house, two of Audacy's old college friends who were living in Costa Rica. We were trying to get there by nightfall, but it just got later and later and later, and finally we got a couple of key rides and made it there in the early evening.

We took our showers and got ourselves cleaned up and did some washing, and holy cow, that was the first people that we knew in Central America, all the way down through. And it felt like we had made it to a piece of back home, and that we were in a safe zone again.

CHAPTER 34
Queen-side castle

Our trucker friend was headed to the capital, and we descended from our windy thrones at the turnoff to Guanacaste. We walked down and through the town of Liberia, which appeared to be in full preparation for carnival, and we eventually managed to hail a confused French-Canadian couple who were driving a rental mini-jeep. We assuaged them with our steady tones as we strapped our load onto their roof, and then coached them through a stop-and-start ride out onto the peninsula. They ended up leaving us off down in the boondocks, where we walked 7 kilometres from one town to the next as the heat of the afternoon sun began to fade. It seemed certain that we would not reach the girls' place by nightfall. I didn't really know where they lived anyway.

Our next ride was with Alfonso who was driving a fruit-laden P-up truck with his family in the cab, and he apparently considered himself to be farr enough away from the highway to leave the ride restrictions behind. I got to talking with old Alfonso, and it turned out that he knew of the school that the girls were running, and more importantly, he knew where they lived. He said that he had to do a few deliveries, and then that he would take us there.

*　　*　　*

"Oh my God," she said quietly as she opened the door and stepped out of the house.

"<Are these the girls that you mean>?" Alfonso asked as he smiled and closed the door of the cab.

"Si. Y gracias por nos haber llevado."

She was drifting closer now, and Ingrid too was visible from the street, peeping out through the doorway.

Alfonso turned towards the house in a knowing way, and waved to the girls, and then began offering Nick a melon from the back of the truck.

Background: I had recently written to P.M. through a post office box that they held in town, and had told her that we would soon be coming down.

The truth is that I was late.

I had been supposed to meet up with her at the 'Mar y Sombra Café' on her birthday the year before, but I had been up in northern Ontario at the time with Morgan.[44] There was lots of rain up in Canada just then and the phone line went down and stayed down for a week. By the time I could get ahold of a car-phone, it was only three days until our Costa Rican engagement, and I was forced to call her mother in Boston to 'please relay to P.M. the message of my impending delay.' We had since shared very little actual communication, but had been playing chess all the while through the mail.

I was winning.

"You're late," she smiled.

"We're here," I replied.

---

[44] I'm Canadian, dual citizenship.

CHAPTER 35
P.M. and the surfboard incident

The EXISTENTIAL RULES of the CODE:

I - you are entirely and only responsible for what you DO and for what you SAY.

II - do not tell others what to do, or allow for yourself to be told what to do.

*　　　*　　　*

Arriving empty-handed as we were, the boys and I quickly dropped our things and headed into town on foot to procure an appropriate amount of alcohol to celebrate the occasion. We each bought a bottle of spirits (rum, gin, vodka) and as much mixer material as we could carry.

Back at the house, we opened the door with our elbows and told the girls to prepare themselves for a proper blow-out. Ingrid was chopping vegetables, and slid our remark a nervous smile. There was already pasta boiling on the stove, and Chavez shook the ice out of the freezer, refilled all the trays, make-shifted some shakers, and proclaimed himself bartender.

I had rum. Nick had gin. Chavez drank vodka.

P.M. produced two boxes of CDs that had arrived in the mail the week before, and I opened a box and proudly gave a CD to each of the girls. (Back in business!).

Nick started talking to Ingrid, asking her about the house and that, and P.M. took me by the hand and started showing me around. Up in her room, she had a chessboard set up with all of our mail-order moves. She wanted me to look at some photos of the kids that she had been teaching. She told me all about how well the school had been doing, and how it was already all paid off, and that the Landcruiser in the driveway had been bought with their earnings. I stared at her and listened. The house took a deep breath, as if someone had opened a door downstairs. I raised my hand and touched her hair, and her sun-browned face turned down and away before it came back up to me. Her eyes were piercing. She asked if I had been thinking about her.

"Yes."

She winced at my answer.

"And now you're here... hitch all the way down, and just walk in."

"Uh huh."

She gave a sigh, and then pulled me towards her with her arms, not a full embrace, but with her elbows pointed downward towards the floor. I wondered if the move hadn't been intended to hide her face. She pulsed me as she spoke, "Oh Audacy, why couldn't you have come last year?"

"I don't know," I spoke into her hair, "It didn't work out."

"Aahuuggrharau," she growled, pushing away and collapsing down onto the bed. "And now, here we are!" she said.

"Yes, here we are." I leaned down onto the edge of the bed.

The photos dropped to the floor.

I was kissing her on her bed. Her breath wet,
her lips open. Smooth, stretching and strong.
Lifting and wondering. Remembering each other and
how we are.

Her desires came through as though of a split
personality: pulling me in and clasping, but
then: "Not yet... Your friends... wait, wait..."

And as though to affirm the timeliness of her
draw, comes Ingrid's voice cutting in from the
bottom of the stairs, "Hey you guys! Dinner!"

*   *   *

The dishes were done and the spirit bottles
were half empty when she and I left the kids
downstairs. She had broken out an old bag of weed
and I doubt if when we left the boys even noticed
our departure.

We slowly stripped each other of our
primaries, slipping back and forward into the
past. She hung on to me and shivered, as she was
prone to do, and asked me improbable questions. I
answered, recounted and evaded as the case may
be.

She had a low soft voice.

"Do you know what has been one of my most
favourite days ever?"

"What."

"With you, when we went swimming, and then
driving around naked in that guy's field."

"That was a fun day."

"With the forties and the rainbow, and that

farmer, and the crazy French music..."

"I remember. I like it all."

And then we kissed, and I took off her shirt.

*   *   *

The next night we all went to the carnival.

It was the same carnival, the one that we had passed along the way. With our much higher WPM ratio, it took us a while to adapt to the added attention. We felt like beekeepers now.

After finding a place to share a large pizza and have a few beers, we headed over to the bullfight arena which was the main-attraction of the fair.

There was an entry charge of about $5 USD, and as the girls went to get in line, we spotted a hole in the back of the bleacher-barricade and feinted off to make our way through the internals of the stadium. Coming to the fence on the inside, we emerged into the circular arena where most of the male population of the community had already assembled. Females weren't allowed in the ring, so it was just as well that the girls had stayed in the ticket line. We spotted them through the bamboo mesh in the stands, and we waved and made faces at them, and then waited with the rest of the crowd for the doors to be thrown open.

When the first bull got let out into the arena, he was already pretty pissed off. The Costa Ricans apparently bloody the horns and rubber-band-smack the balls of the bull before releasing it into the crowd.

The local guys had their handkerchiefs tied in loops, and they were running around trying to toss them onto one of the horns of the raving beast. This of course would be the most macho thing to achieve.

From the farr side of the arena, the bull didn't really look as big as all that, but as the seas parted and it entered my foreground, you could see all of the boys become a little less boastful, and everyone began eyeing for the nearest route of escape.

I had tied my green bandana, and held it now in a loop in my hand. The bull stampeded towards us and came up close, and then turned and veered, stopping and glaring around in humiliated infuriation; desperation never so clear. At the moment when it came closest to where I was standing, there was only one other person who stood closer, and the bandana idea kind of fizzled. I watched in slow motion as the bull gestured to take off back towards the other end of the arena, and that one other person looked away to wave to someone in the crowd. Just then, the bull unexpectedly turned back and caught the poor guy unawares.

When the bull first hit the oblivious standing guy, he lifted him up with his horns and continued to run straight through him. The guy went up into the air like a piece of ribbon, and then hit the ground like a sack. In that slow moment, the guy, not yet unconscious, raises his head to find himself staring straight into the eyes of *Taurus*. The bull holds the moment with everyone watching, and it takes a half a step back before lowering its head and again flinging him into the air with its horns. This time, as the man hit the ground, the bull was upon him. First with its full weight down on him with its front legs, and then the full weight reiterated with its haunches. The man was now desperately unconscious, and as the crowd crowed over the fallen man's destruction, some few stepped forward and bravely diverted the aggressions of the beast. The broken body was lifted up by the masses and quickly body-surfed over to the wall of the arena, where a sliding door had been slid open, and the remainder of this life was efficiently passed through a hole and deposited into the back of an awaiting ambulance.

We regrouped and exchanged our shared sense of disbelief, and then signaled to the girls and crawled back out underneath the bleachers to meet up and head on over to the dance club.

There was a feisty and excitable group of young boys at the dance club who weren't afraid to let it all hang. Chavez and I started up the fight-dance thing and the whole circle got wild. We had them doing the monkey, the robot, anything. There was break-dancing starting to happen. I pointed one of my youthful Costa Rican dancing doppelgangers onto P.M., and then took a step back to watch the two of them become unleashed. He danced with the inhibitions of a kid (he *was* a kid), and she was like a mad woman, with her long hair chucked forwards and her arms cast up and out like an incanting puppeteer, an enchantress. It was a total abandon, and it gave me a physical stirring. And an energy to keep on dancing.

Driving home, none sober but for tight-ass Ingrid at the wheel, and even *she's* having trouble. Drinks in the jeep and moon in the sky, and wrestling in the back and spilled drink with laughing and something to smoke and then sitting out the window with the jungle whirling by and "faster you ninny", and "sit back down inside goddamnit!" and everything reckless and open, and romp romp romp, and live while its now, and wait to be seen.

*   *   *

We didn't get up until late.

We grabbed some things from town before heading down to the beach where we set up in the sand above the tree line and made a sun-block out of dried palm fronds. We lazed around with the girls, eating fruit and reading books, and intermittently exerting ourselves with a bodysurf in the waves. I strolled with Chavez up to the north end of the beach and found a bar that sold take-aways.

As we stood at the bar, waiting for the bartender to grab some long-necks from the walk-in, we were engaged by a couple of Irish surfers who wanted to know where we had been, and whether or not we'd been surfing. Then they went on and on in praise of the wave breaking down to the south. They had just come up from Mal Pais[45], and I asked them if they had bumped into a character named Stirling Prescott from Vermont while they were down there: 5'10, short brown hair, five-day beard, loud voice.[46] They hummed and hawed for a minute and then the one guy snapped his fingers

---

[45] <Bad Country>

[46] I had only just met Stirling at the liquor store in Manchester a few months before. I had already kind of known *of* him, as the crazy older brother of a girl that I had gone on the French exchange with. He and I went to have a beer together, and he had mentioned that he was intending to spend the winter surfing down in Mal Pais.

and asked the other:

"Hey, wasn't he that big guy, sort of gruff-looking guy down at the beach who was trying to get with that girl?"

The taller Irish guy was slowly shaking his head, still drawing a blank.

The blonde guy continued, "Yeah, the guy who was running around wearing fluorescent orange..."

I smiled to Chavez, "That'd be him." Chavez shot me a doubtful look, and I added "...Hunter's orange. It's part of his redneck heritage," and then I asked the Irish guy if it was his jacket that had been orange.

"His jacket *and* his hat if I remember."

Now the taller guy was nodding too. The bartender had come back out and I paid her for the beers, and then we thanked the guys and headed back down along the beach.

*   *   *

The sun was getting low when we got back to the girls' house. P.M. got on the phone to order up some take-away pizzas and Nick started shaking up drinks with what remained in the spirit bottles. The girls had to work at the school in the morning, and suggested that we could have a mellow evening and watch a movie. This sounded good to all of us, and Chavez sat down on the floor and started looking through their videos.

I was asking about where we might be able to rent ourselves a surfboard, and Ingrid jumped up and padded out of the room. When she came back in, she was hauling a medium-sized surfboard that

she said her brother had given to her as he was
leaving the country some months before.

"And we can use this?"

"Sure. I haven't been out on it since he
left. It's not a great board, but..."

"No, it's perfect. Thanks Ingrid."

"Yeah, sure."

She turned to steer the surfboard back into
one of the back rooms, and then reappeared and
stepped into her thongs and asked if anyone
wanted to come with her to pick up the pizza.

"Yeah I'll come along for the ride," said
Nick.

I was at the counter, filling the ice trays,
and fixing up another round of drinks.

P.M. was sitting on the floor beside Chavez,
and was raising her voice to him in disbelief,
"Are you kidding? You've never seen
'Casablanca'?"

*   *   *

There was a small purple flower on my chest
when I woke up in the morning, and the sunshine
was already on the bed. I headed downstairs and
found Chavez making up a thick batch of coffee.
Nick was sprawled out on the couch. The girls
were already gone.

We rolled up some shwag that we swept up from
the coffee table, and woke Nick up to a toke and
a black cuppa' joe. As those guys started to come
around, I headed into the back rooms to have a

look around for that surfboard, and eventually found it wrapped up in a sheet underneath Ingrid's bed. I took it out onto the porch and put it in a pile with some towels and a large jug of water. And after a second coffee, we were off.

The boys became much less shy in their beach behaviour, and a burn-one's-ass priority was set for the day. They came into the water for a swim, and then I paddled out beyond the shallow shore break, mostly just fucking around and riding the wash up onto the beach.

When I came back in, Chavez quickly set off with the board, and I stripped down and started in on a Hemmingway novel that I had found at the house.

Five chapters later, Chavez came plunging into the hot sand beside us, panting and proclaiming that he had had his fill. Napping Nick expressed his lethargic ambivalence towards having a go at the surfing, and rested as I was, I took back off into the break.

The first wave that I tried to catch was passing me by, and I took a step forward to weight the front of the board. Shallow as it was, the move resulted in a bit of a nosedive into the sand, and as I tumbled in towards the beach, I surfaced to find that the tip of the board had been broken by the impact.

I grabbed the broken bit and headed up onto the sand, with Chavez whistling and shaking his head. Then he started laughing, "Oh, oh. Well, that's gonna fuck things up."

I responded with an edgy smile, "Hey, honest mistake. It'll be alright. I'm just glad it was me and not you."

"Yeah man," he answered, laughing, "So am I."

We stopped by the school on the way back to the house. P.M. introduced us to her class of 7 and 8 year olds and then set them to working on an art project while she showed us around the place. Teaching tools, mosaic walls, translation flashcards, and a school anthem later, we retreated out the front door of the place.

"And where's Ingrid?" I asked.

"She had to run into town. She'll be back soon. She's going to close up today. If you guys could just hang out the laundry when you get there, I'll be home in about an hour and a half."

I was picking up our stuff that we had left out by the gate, "Um, OK."

"What?.. What happened?" she asked.

She could tell.

"Um, well, I kind of broke her surfboard," and here I displayed the two pieces. "But it's OK. I'll replace it, and it'll be fine."

P.M. lowered her tone, her expression becoming more serious, "Oh shit... that's going to be bad."

"No. It'll be OK. Just tell her that I owe her a surfboard. That's all. I'll get her another one. It's OK."

And with a roll of the eyes and a bit of a smile, P.M. receded into the building of children.

When we got back to the house there was a soccer game going on at the place next door. We hung up the laundry and jumped through the outdoor shower before heading over to the neighbour's place to become involved in the game.

When the teams had grown in number to 6 against 5, and the score was tied, the Landcruiser pulled up into the driveway, and Ingrid wasted no time in jumping out of the driver's side and marching straight up to where we were playing.

"Audacy!"

"Hello, Ingrid."

"You fuck! How dare you to have taken that board out without my permission?"

"What?" I shrieked, looking around to P.M., and then back to Ingrid, "I *did* have your permission."

"Yeah, whatever!"

"Wauh? You told me last night that I could take it out."

"Yeah well... what? Last night after we had had a few drinks?"

"Yeah."

"Well that hardly counts. I didn't mean that you could take it out without telling me!"

"Are you fucking kidding me?"

"...And here you go stealing out on my brother's custom-made board in the low tide, and end up smashing it all up!"

"..." (She hadn't even seen it yet).

"Well... enough! You owe me 400 dollars, that's all. He had that board especially made, and I don't look forward to explaining it to him..."

"So now it is your brother's board?"

"Of *course* it's his board... custom made! And he left it with me. And that's fine if you feel bad," she put in, with a quick glance to P.M., "but you owe us 400 bucks to get him a new one, and that'll be fine."

"Like hell!" I shouted, and Chavez squeezed my arm.

Ingrid had already spun around and was marching back over to the house. She slammed the door shut behind her so that P.M. had to open it back up to follow her inside.

I turned back to the frozen game, and all of the kids were looking at me, wondering what I had done.

Nick came up closer and squatted down, chewing on a piece of straw. He turned his smiling eyes up as he said, "Well *that* didn't go so well."

I gave a laugh, "But I just can't believe it. The permission thing? Fuck. We were all there!"

"Best just wait till later," advised Chavez. And then turning and noticing our impatient playmates, he added, "Should we call the game?"

"What, over this? Hell no. We've *got* you guys. Let's play the tiebreak, win by two. Ganar por dos, hay que ganar por dos! Listos?"

The entire issue was thoroughly readdressed in the evening, and I repeated that I was willing to replace the board, but that I flat—out refused to settle the matter with an exorbitant cash pay out.[47] I said that I would find and purchase for her a similar or better board before leaving the country.

"But you don't understand. There aren't that many boards around here," she started, "You can't get them for what you think. We brought that board down from America..."

Yeah, yeah, yeah. I had a feeling I knew where I could find a damn surfboard, but I buttoned my lip and asked the guys to take a walk around the block with me.

When we got back to the house, we made our announcement: *We would be leaving in the morning for Mal Pais.* I would find her a board down there, and either hitch it back up, or they could come down and get it.

Ingrid said, "Well I'm not sure if I can even trust you on this."

P.M.'s words were all but lost as she mumbled, "You can trust him."

I responded hoarsely to Ingrid's insult, "Well you don't have a choice (you bitch!)."

That night, P.M. spoke with me up in her room.

---

[47] At the time of this incident, I only had 700 US dollars, and there was no way I was gonna give $400 of it away to this unreasonable little trust-fund prissy.

"I'm sorry about all of this," she said, pulling her hair back.

"So am I."

"Well, and I'm sorry that you guys are leaving. I hope that you don't feel like you have to."

"It's OK," I sighed, sitting down on the edge of her bed, "I think it's just time for us to keep going. But I guess I may be back up soon, bringing the fucking board... unless you guys decide to come down."

"I think we'll probably be down," she said, sitting down beside me, "We've both wanted to check it out down there anyway, and we've got school holidays coming up next week."

"Oh. Well that's good then."

She turned and looked at me for an awkward moment, and then pushed me with her spastic energy and growled, "You're impossible!" I fell back against the bed, confused, and was about to lean forward, but her head came down and rested upon my chest and she lay there completely still.

I decided to let it go.

We stayed like that for what seemed like a long time and I held her head against me with the weight of my hand.

When at last she spoke, she spoke very quietly, "Do you know that I waited for you, waited for you at that place, waited for you, thinking that you were coming?"

"No. I didn't know that. I thought you got

the message."

"The message... I got the message the next day."

"I'm sorry," I said, picturing her alone at a table.

"I couldn't wait forever you know."

"No, I know." And here I paused, thinking for a moment... "So now there's someone else."

"Well what was I supposed to do?"

"No, nothing... you haven't done anything wrong."

"...And I'm not even sure about him."

"Let's not talk about him. I don't even want to know about him. You'll make your decisions, and I have faith in you, but for now, let's just be here. Let's just lie here. (And I'll be gone from this town by tomorrow.)"

CHAPTER 36
Off to Mal Pais

By morning, Ingrid had eased up a bit, and conceded to the group that she and P.M. *had* been hoping to take a vacation down south during that following week. This enabled us to keep to a minimum the ceremony of our departure.

I came up with a note to be left out for Max, in case he should eventually turn up, and because for some reason Ingrid didn't want me to post it on the door, I made her promise that she would leave it posted when they left to come down.

And then we burped our coffees, filled our waters, and waved to the girls as we walked off into the hot dust.

And man oh man did we ever walk that day.

The coastal road that we were trying to hitch along didn't show up on the map that we had, and as we manipulated the first few forks out of town, it was through local roadside guidance that we steered our course. Even then, when we got to the edge of anything, there was nothing to do but just keep on walking. None of the traffic seemed to be leaving town. Chavez was soon complaining about his having gone and burnt his ass.

Walk, walk, walk. (Sun, sun, sun. Heat, heat, heat.)

Eventually we rounded a corner and started down a long straightaway. Halfway down the strip, there was a jeep pulled off on the side of the road. But the jeep was on fire, and was sending a black greasy plume up into the sky. This unlikely scene struck us as being extremely funny, and our disproportionate laughter seemed to indicate that we had become slightly hysterical.

We passed by the spectacle and there was no one around, or any indication as to what could have started the burn, and as we lumbered on, the conversation turned to the imagining and describing of possible causes and explanations surrounding the flaming jeep: murder, time travel, vengeance, spontaneous combustion...

Suddenly Nick perked up and said he heard a

motor, and turning around, we saw a white P-up truck, trail of dust flying as it weaved up the road towards us.

It was a family, and they all turned and gawked at the flaming jeep as they passed it by, and then shaking their heads, they pulled the truck over to offer us a lift. One of the daughters was ousted from the cab, and I sat up front talking with the father, turning occasionally to exchange a smile with the boys, who were visibly pleased to be riding in the company of girls.

I soon realized that the father had assumed the burning jeep to have been ours, and had given us the ride on that account. Without telling any lies, I let the older man believe what he wanted, and chatted with him, asking about the condition of the road ahead.

"<It gets worse. Four-wheel drive only. Very little traffic>," he told me.

The family dropped us off in a small town, and we traversed the baseball field to make our way over to the store, and then hurriedly ordered up a round of Fantas. We chugged them down in the afternoon heat, and then chased them with a round of cold beers before returning to the deserted highway.

We planted ourselves on the uphill stretch that led out of town and played hackisack while we counted the passing hours with hardly anybody passing by in either direction. Those vehicles that *did* come by would stop and ask where we were from, and then tell us where they were going, and point out why their ride would be no good to us. At one point, a western-looking couple in a large

jeep cruised up the hill, and despite our
desperation-whiskey-hitchhike, they smiled and
gestured and then swerved around us and kept on
going, intoning through the glass some reason of
supposed great importance.

Eventually a bulldozer came crawling by, and
stopped in the middle of the road to talk with
us. The sitting driver and his leaning companion
happily lowered the front-end scoop to provide us
with a seat, and in such a manner we were slowly
hoisted down the road for another few miles. The
farmers tipped us out of the shovel at the foot
of a humungous hill, and we thanked them and
began an hour-long climb up the winding dirt
road. Chavez ended up helping me to lug the
guitar up to the top.

After resting for a while at the summit, we
had started back down the other side when we
rejoiced to be picked up by a happy fat couple in
a P-up truck with a roll bar, and we stood up
there in the back, hanging onto the bar, three
abreast in our chariot, and watching the miles
roll by.

The road ended up turning straight onto the
shore, and there was a highway sign posted at the
edge of the sand with an arrow on it that pointed
left. We could hear the happy couple laughing
inside the cab as they made the turn onto the
packed sand that lay exposed during low tide. Ten
or fifteen miles of beach driving later, there
was a similar sign, pointing us back into the
jungle.

The fat woman yelled out that theirs was the
next town, but that they were going to drive us
the extra bit to Mal Pais. I yelled out our

thanks.

The truck started passing huts, bungalow-cafés and surf shacks as it weaved along through the jungle growth behind the shore. The traffic was mostly bicycles, and there were signs painted in English and in German.

The fat couple let us off at the one crossroads in Mal Pais and smiled and waved as they made the three-point turn to head back home. We walked straight down to the water and dunked ourselves in.

The boys stayed on the beach to watch over the stuff while I headed back across the road with our empty water bottles. In the café on the corner, an older woman had taken the bottles and disappeared into the back and I had got to talking with a young waiter who claimed that he knew of a Stirling from Vermont. I questioned him as to his whereabouts, and he shrugged and told me that he could be anywhere, but then added that he was often seen around with another gringo named Brent. And he knew where Brent lived and went on to give me directions on how to get to the house.

So back at the beach, Nick and Chavez drained one of the water bottles, and we returned to the crossroads and started up the hill. Half an hour later, we came to a partially constructed cinder block house that seemed to match the description given by the waiter.

There was no one home.

We ate mangoes off of a tree behind the house and had a look around in the shed: surfboards and kettles strewn about, and two hammocks hanging

between the beams, with 2x12's underneath,
creating for the benches of an improvised coco-
palm workshop. Scattered around on the benches
were a camp stove, various bits of sand paper and
surf-wax, a half-eaten plate of rice, a rag that
had once been a tie-dyed t-shirt, and then
hanging from a nail on the beam: a fluorescent
orange hunting jacket.

We spied around to ensure that we were not
being watched, and then stashed our bags in the
thick undergrowth behind the shed.

It was dusk by the time we got back into
town, and we headed to the little super market
behind the beach to get a beer. I asked the old
woman at the counter if she knew of a Stirling
from Vermont, and she told us that he had an
account there. We purchased some peanuts and
longnecks, and then turning to leave, I spotted a
familiar-looking guy with long blond hair coming
down the aisle.

"Hey there! Remember us?" I asked as I stuck
my thumb out in a hitchhiking pose, "Thanks for
the ride, fuck-head."

The guy looked up at me with a blank, and
then glanced over to Nick and Chavez. Recognition
flashed, and he started stuttering in a German
accent:

"Oh. Hi guys. Good you made it... Sorry about
that back there, but, we don't pick up
hitchhikers, *you* know."

"Well lucky for us, some people do. And here
we thought that you were signaling that you
weren't going our way or something. Not that you
would've known which was we were going..."

His darker-skinned girlfriend had now entered the store and was lingering behind him. He turned and cast her a look, and took in the watching storeowner as well. He changed his tact and addressed everyone in a Spanish that only Germans are capable of: "Ya... <he is angry because we don't give them a ride in our car, but really we didn't have space...>"

"Nada que ver!" I interrupted, also addressing the store, "<If I am angry, it would be because you felt the need to lie to us about where you were going. And now here again, you are saying that you didn't have space? He continues lying to us this> puto aleman!"

He looked at us with alarm, and his girlfriend lowered her head. He switched again, back to English: "Well we didn't know where you were going. And really, there was not enough space for all of the things you guys had..."

"Basta," I yelled, cutting my hand through the air, "<the day will come when you too will need a ride>" and then turning to the guys as if they had understood everything, "Vamanos amigos!"

We brushed past the German, and came out into the street to find his Jeep pulled up right in front of the store. I turned to Chavez, and sneered. "As if he didn't have the room. Check this thing out," and we all looked into the spacious interior of the empty and oversized SUV.

There came a nervous yelp from behind us, "Heyy! What are you guys doing to my jeep?"

I widened my eyes and hoarsely said, "Maybe we've come to kick out your headlights!"

The German threw his hands up in a panic and ran back into the store. We laughed and cracked our beers as we crossed the road and headed down the dark pathway towards the beach.[48]

Approaching the shore, we could see dozens of glowing campfires twinkling through the trees, pointing off in either direction. We turned south and began our search, campfire to campfire:

"Con permiso senores. Andamos en busca de un amigo Americano. Se llama Stirling, y es de Vermont. A caso de que si algien le ha visto?"

This question was repeated at every campfire, to surf-hippies of all ages, and of every nationality. Talking, smoking, lounging, drinking, music-making and story-telling, they all paused from what they were doing to hear our question, and then to take turns telling us that they knew not of where our friend might be.

We had almost reached the south end of the string of campfires, and the mere idea of having to double back was exhausting.

"...en busca de un amigo NorteAmericano. Se llama Stirling, y es de Vermont. A caso de que si algien..."

"I can't fucking believe it..." thundered a baritone voice as one of the dark figures began to rise to his feet, "Audacy fuckin' Myles!" He stepped forward into the firelight and smiled,

---

[48] Some of you, no doubt, are now imagining me to be a real asshole. I make no apologies, but will here point out that one seldom gets the opportunity to converse with one of the road's travelers who heartlessly pass you by. This nastiness bears the disclaimer of karma police. I will also point out that tellingly, and unbelievably, neither of the boys made any attempt to restrain this outburst.

orange sailor hat turned down, swollen lips and sunburnt face, white zinc smeared across his nose, "Holy shit," and then throwing out his arms as if it were his kingdom, he yelled: "Welcome to Mal Pais!"

We sat down with the community of the campfire and introductions were made all round. Nationalities: English, Irish, American, Swedish, Argentinean, Polish and Costa Rican. Prescott explained that "everyone just lives on the beach!" and there were tents everywhere, and hammocks strung up between most of the trees.

We told him that we had stashed our shit behind the shed of his buddy's house, and that we'd have to be climbing back up the hill before night's end.

"Your stuff is at Brent's house?"

The three of us nodded.

"Oh, well come on then we'll go up to Brent's house."

So we said goodnight to the hippies and started up towards the road.

"No no, this way," Prescott yelled over his shoulder, walking back up the beach, "We'll swing by the store."

When we reached the crossroads, Stirling was becoming distracted from the story that he was telling and began peering in through the windows of a nightclub that we were passing by. Then he shoved the bag of beer into my hands and said, "Hold on, I think Brent might be in here," before running off into the place.

Brent came out into street to meet us, and said that it'd be fine for us to spend the night up there. He was having a drink with his girlfriend, and told us that they'd soon be headed up as well.

When we reached the house, we pulled our stuff back out of the shrubbery, and sat and drank beer in the shed for a while with Stirling. He told us that there was a dry riverbed at the base of the slope behind the house, and that we could pitch the tents there.

When we had the tents up, we sat down in the natural hallway of the riverbed. Prescott passed on our offer of space in the tent and said that he'd sleep in one of the hammocks up in the shed. Nick was asking him about snakes when we heard a motorcycle engine and saw the beam of a headlight passing through the trees above. Then came the sound of drunken laughter, and a lower voice that would have been Brent's. Prescott told us that Brent had been sleeping with this German bird, "Just wait till they get started!" he said. I asked what he meant by that, and he smiled but didn't answer. Then he bade us goodnight and headed up to the shed.

The three of us got into the tents and stretched out on the hard-packed mud, listening to the voices above. Something got knocked over inside the house, and the girl's laughter pitched up in delight. This kind of romping around noise went on for the next few minutes.

Then they started humping.

"AAAUuUuuugghh, AAAUuUuuah, AhhhUUUahhhh, AAAUUAUAUAHh..." came resounding out into the quiet jungle.

It was her voice that we could hear, and we started giggling. Then it got louder:

"AAHHGGHAAU, AAUHGGAAU, AAHHAAUU, AAUUGGHH, AAUUGGHHI..."

Chavez's voice came from their tent, "No fuckin' *way*!" and I heard him undoing the zipper. Then we all got back out of the tents, and sat on the ground, looking up and listening in amazement.

"AAHUU, AAHUU, OOAHA, YES, YYA, AAHUU, FUCK ME, YES, YES!..."

We sat there listening, our laughter only barely contained by our fascination.

"I've never heard it like that," I said.

"She's putting it on," said Nick.

Just then, there was a *whoosh* in the branches high above the riverbed, and we stood up to watch a large band of monkeys making their way through the trees. They began squawking and barking as they approached the sexual ruckus, and then situated themselves high up in a tree, right outside of the lovers' second story window.

Meanwhile, the never-ending orgasm continued from inside, but now, the monkeys had joined in the orgy, and were actually competing in volume with the German girl:

"AAUU *<aaii>* OOHH *<eioo>* AHHH *<ooou>* YAAA *<eeih oooo>*..."

I'm pretty sure that the monkeys were actually fucking as well.

"This is too much!" exclaimed Chavez. And we all started laughing as the sexual symphony built onwards towards its climactic crescendo.

The next morning, we packed up and lugged our things back up to the shed. Stirling was already awake and was fixing some tea.

"Get much sleep?" I asked him.

"Oh, how about that eh? They come over and do it right next to their window."

"They always do that?" asked Chavez.

"Oh, only about every night," replied Prescott with a laugh.

CHAPTER 37
On the beach

The four of us walked back down to the beach and set up camp with the group that we had met the night before. Stirling ran off to do whatever it is that he does, and me and Chavez smoked a joint with the Irish and Swedish guys. Afterward, I started into a game of chess with a guy named Marcus, and Chavez sat around talking with the dumb American girl named Luna (who we were quick to dub 'Lunacy').

Prescott soon reappeared with a surfboard under each arm, announcing that the 'bonefish' was available for anyone who wanted to have a go.[49] As I was stepping over to the tent to grab a bathing suit, he was explaining that we had arrived to the second most consistent surf-break in the world. He was going on and on about it, and would gladly repeat his clinical estimation to anyone who would listen: "Yup, 2nd most consistent in all of the world!"

I followed him out, paddling the 'bonefish' through the crashing waves until I finally caught up with him at the calm beyond the break. He was waiting for me with a smile.

Over the course of my next many failed attempts, Prescott paddled alongside me, screaming out advise from his shorter yellow board.

"Step forward!"

"Two more paddles!"

"You got up too soon!"

Eventually, I managed to catch two of the waves to my (if not necessarily to his) satisfaction.

When we returned to the beach, I was exhausted. Chavez quickly suited up and headed off into the surf, and I made ready to start out on my surfboard acquisition mission. Nick had broken out the guitar and was sitting above the tree line in the shade, entertaining two little

---

[49] The 'bonefish' was an irregularly shaped surfboard that had been sawed down from a broken longboard, and so named for the fish skeleton that he had graffittied onto its topside. The makeshift board had a jagged edge on the front where it had been cut down, and he displayed the board with a wink, saying that there would be "zero liability". By this he was ribbing me for the surfboard that I had already broken, but also referencing the danger presented by the sharp front edge of the board.

dark-skinned girls that I hadn't noticed before (*Badabadooda, Badapada-da*). He shot me a wide smile and wiggled his eyebrows when he noticed me watching and I laughed and waved before turning to set off.

The surfboard repair shop had two used boards that they were willing to sell, but they were both of the 5 to 6 foot variety. I wandered around some more, engaging various groups of surf-types, and after following a false lead around for a while (the board had been sold), I returned to our spot on the beach to find the international collection of boys amping up for a game of soccer.

Later on in the evening, as we sat playing music around the fire, Prescott reappeared from one of his mysterious little jaunts, and stepping forward into the firelight with a smirk, he gestured back over his shoulder. Another figure emerged from the darkness, a Vermonter who I recognized straight away...

It was Finn.

Finn is a short elfin-looking hippie with an open smile and a striking shock of blond hair. His older brother had been one of my rivals back in high school,[50] and through this vague connection, I had met him a couple of times before.

Nick was much better acquainted with the young man, and his face lit up with the

---

[50] The older brother was a year my elder, and used to go out with the girl who lived across the street from me. I believe that his jealousy of my friendship with her had led him to suspect that we had slept together (we never had), and for this reason, he attempted to persecute me.

unanticipated arrival. Nick circled with Finn, introducing him to Chavez and the others, and as our group bunched in to make extra space around the campfire, Nick smiled across to Finn:

"I never figured I'd run into *you* down here," he gawked, settling back down into his spot, "And where's Jasmin?"

"Oh, it's a long story," answered Finn with an uncomfortable smile.

"Oh... Did she go home?"

"Really," smiled Finn self-consciously, running his finger in a line through the sand, "I don't know if I really feel like going back over it right now."

Prescott's smile widened as he watched Finn squirm. Then he turned to the circle to put forth the explanation:

"Finn lost his girlfriend to some hippie down on the Osa," he blabbed.

"*Honestly* Stirling, can you ever just fuckin' shut up?" cried Finn. I detected a certain measure of relief along with his overtone of incredulous disbelief.

Prescott laughed, and then went on to start explaining it to us, which in turn forced Finn to take over the telling of the story:

It turns out that Finn had come down to Costa Rica with his hot little number of a girlfriend named Jasmin.[51] His mother had had some sort of

---

[51] I was once supposed to have gone on a date with Jasmin's older sister, but fucked it up, having tried to double-book my Friday

connection down on the Osa Peninsula, and somehow, he and his girlfriend had ended up staying with this other hippie guy named Cane. During the period of their stay, Cane developed an eye for Jasmin, and even approached Finn openly with his declaration of intent. For some reason (maybe because of her whisperings in his ear), Finn did nothing. He didn't leave the joint, and he didn't kill the guy. So that eventually, the whole thing culminated with Finn's actually witnessing his own girlfriend being fucked by their interloper host, and as alliances realigned, he found himself forlorn in a foreign country with his girlfriend returning to the States without him, her attentions focused on enabling hippie Cane to follow her home in some months time.

Thus was Finn perhaps not at his usual levels of gaiety at the precise time that we met him on the beach of Mal Pais.

Furthermore, and as if things couldn't have gotten worse for the innocent lad, he had left the scene of the lustful crime (perhaps with not all of his blinkers working), and had soon fallen victim to a theft, finding himself to have been relieved of his passport, his airline ticket, and all of his money. At this point in the tragedy, he was hanging out with three young birds from Venezuela, who apparently took pity on the golden boy and took it upon themselves to recover his airline ticket and passport (somehow, it was common knowledge as to who had been the thief).

Fate plays us shabby tricks.
Charles Dickens

---

night. I had met Jasmin once before at a small party, and can personally attest to her desirability. She was very gorgeous.

Anyway, as Finn concluded the story of his misfortunes, he said that he was still travelling with the three Venezuelan girls, to whom he felt himself to be highly indebted, and that he had been camping out on the north end of the beach in their company (and supposedly not fucking any of them).

Finn pulled me aside to say that he had been intending to accompany the Venezuelan girls to the capital the next day to see them off on their plane, "...but now that you guys have shown up," he said, smiling, "I'm thinking that maybe I'd like to hang around for a while."

So the next morning Finn reappeared with the three girls. They helped him string up his hammock, and laughed with him in a knowing way, as if he could have been their younger brother.

I walked up to the store with Chavez to get some breakfast: sliced bread, avocados, hard-boiled eggs, and Trits.[52] Then we scampered back down to the beach with a melting ice cream sandwich for Nick, and got back to camp just as the Venezuelan girls were preparing to leave. They doted over Finn for a good while, and then circled through our group to half-jokingly implore us to take good care of their boy.

I took off into the waves for a little while with Finn,[53] and he turned out to be a much more patient teacher than Prescott had been. I was improving, and I caught one of the waves almost all the way up to the beach.

---

[52] "Trits" are delicious Costa Rican chocolate-chip cookie ice cream sandwiches that would become the staple of our diet all during this time.

[53] No one but Finn was allowed to use Prescott's yellow board.

Back on shore, Prescott was hatching a money making scheme that involved the exploitation of Finn's ability to climb a palm tree. He took off to the store, and soon returned with an oversized bottle of white rum and a pack of straws, expounding upon the earning potential of selling rum-n-coconuts to the tourists along the beach during the sunset hour. I came up with a name for the concoction, and everyone allowed themselves to be won over by the preposterous enterprise.

So we set off to the north end of the beach, where the trees were the shortest and the fruits most abundant, and then set about pressuring Finn into making the climb.

Once we had talked him up into the tree, he began twisting the coconuts off of their stems, and they would hit the hot sand with a *thump*. From where we were standing, we could see the fire ants as they began to attack Finn, who clung to the trunk of the palm.

"Ahhhr, they're fucking biting me!"

Prescott's gruff voice rose up to talk him through it: "Hold fast young soldier, there's just a few more. Grab that brownish one to your right."

"Ahhh!" he yelled, trying to swat his back with his free hand.

"Yup. And just those two above your head..."

So we whittled down the coconuts with a borrowed machete, and when we cut the first one open to add the alcohol, we sampled the warm fluid and unanimously conceded it to be a god-awful brew. Then Stirling and I took off along the beach to peddle our alcoholic wares.

"Coco loco! Prepared onsite for you. Coco loco! Traditional recipe. Coco loco! All natural and organic. Get 'em while they're warm."

The rest of the afternoon was a bit of a blur, as Stirling and I began to drink the rum straight out of the bottle. We did, however, manage to sell two of the coconuts to a couple of American girls, and one of them didn't even want any rum in hers.

The next day, I met a Tiko boy on the beach who said that he had met a Danish guy who was flying out in a few days time and was desperately trying to sell his longboard. He told me that the guy was advertising 300 dollars, but that he had offered it to him for $250. I set off in search of the Danish guy, and eventually found my way up to his shack on the farr edge of town. He wasn't in, but his roommate produced the blue and white 9ft. board and I tried to conceal my reaction. The board was perfect, like new, and seemed better than Ingrid's old board. I told the roommate that I'd be back around tomorrow, and to tell his friend that maybe we could do a deal. And with that, I crossed back through the fields, down to the road, and back down along the beach.

By mid-afternoon, when the bars were starting to open, I pried Nick away from freaking out on the iguanas, and he and I took a walk around town to see if we couldn't schedule ourselves a gig for that weekend. I had a couple of my CDs in hand.

"<Perhaps I can help you? I am the manager of the bar>."

"<Thank you but no. This is an issue that would best be taken up with the owner. Is he not available>?"

"<Yes, the owner does happen to be in right now>."

"<Ah! Well, this is my card. If he could just spare us a minute>."

It was the third place that we had tried, and the manager suppressed a frown and headed off into one of the back rooms to summon the owner, one of my CDs in his hand.

The owner appeared, and I stood up as he approached our table.

"<You are the owner>?" I asked.

"<Yes, Fabio>," he said, stepping forward to shake our hands, and then taking a seat opposite to us at the table.

"<Ah, good. Pleasure to meet you. This is my musician friend, Nick Santarino, and my name is Audacy Myles>," I stared expectantly at the guy, with my eyebrows raised and my head slightly tilted down, "<...perhaps you've heard of me>?" I pressed.

The guy's look of confusion said that he hadn't, and I threw a smiling shrug to Nick, and then turned back to the bar owner, "<Well, no matter. My name is Audacy Myles and I am the lead singer of a group up in California: a band called *Freewater*>(?)" And here again I paused and searched him expectantly, before magnanimously dismissing his ignorance, "<Well... and my friend here plays music with many groups up in Boston,

in the United States. He plays almost every instrument>".

And here the guy was beginning to nod, glancing at the CD that was now in his hand. I spoke quickly with very little pause between sentences.

"<...Well anyway, we are down here in your beautiful country on vacation, and yet the two of us find ourselves with the desire to play some music this weekend. After walking around town and checking some of the places, your bar seems to be the best venue in which to do this sort of thing. Now, there are many young people here on the beach who would like to hear us play, but we would really need a place to put something on. For your part, let me say, that we would not charge you a thing. We would not ask any money of you. Perhaps only that you would host us with generosity, and not charge our small crew for their drinks or any of those small things. And after seeing your menu>", I gestured to the large chalkboard hanging above the counter, "<I was actually just talking with Nick about what a pleasure it would be for us to sample your cuisine here. But other than that, really, we would be willing to play your bar for absolutely no charge>", I looked at Nick as if to ensure his approval. He nodded, and I continued, "<...We just have the urge to make some music, that's all. And most of our money is made through CD sales now anyway. So now, today is Thursday, and we really do prefer not to play on Saturdays, what with all of the disco music and that, because we're really much more of a *live* thing. Now, will you guys be getting much business in tomorrow night>?"...

...And so it was arranged.

We were to play *The Cocacabana* on the following evening.

* * *

The Polish guy at our camp had developed a sore on his chest from where it had been rubbing against his surfboard. A red tide had come in during the last few days, which is really just some sort of bacteria in the water, but as his wound worsened and his friends continued to warn him, he had at last decided to take a couple of days out of the water to allow for the disgusting thing to scab over.

Late in the afternoon, as we were sitting around deciding who's turn it would be to go off and find some firewood, Prescott started cursing and exclaiming from a little ways off, and then led the Polish guy over to where we were playing chess to show us the condition that he was in. The scab had come loose, and the poor guy could pull it out of his chest to reveal a silver dollar sized hole that went a full inch into his chest, surpassing the layer where one would have expected his ribs to have been. We cringed as Prescott made the guy show us, and then we all strongly advised the dude to stay the hell out of the water. He shrugged and plugged himself back up, inserting the thick scab into his chest as though he were putting a cork back into its bottle.

Then we smoked a joint.

Dinnertime came, and Prescott was making up a

stew of meat and potatoes.[54] The meat he had
gotten from somewhere, trading it with somebody
for something. It looked better than it tasted,
but we polished it off anyway as we sat around
the fire, passing joints and singing songs;
honing our story-telling abilities.

Later on, just after I had crawled into bed,
there came a sprinkling sound down onto the fly,
and I cautiously emerged from the tent to find a
monkey up in the tree, pointing down at me and
screeching as he finished up his urination. The
stick that I threw at the monkey's head missed by
about an inch, and he was laughing at me as he
swung off through the canopy with his horde of
friends.

*   *   *

Friday. At some point in the afternoon, it
was discovered that with the stalk of a dried
palm frond, you could fling a shriveled coconut
for a rather impressive distance. And more
importantly, that the coconut could conceivably
be caught by another palm frond wielding
participant. No sooner had this feat been
demonstrated than the entire male faction of our
base camp scrambled onto the beach for an
impromptu game of coco-lacrosse.

Afterwards, when two of the participants had
been injured by the flying coconut and the
diversion had reached its peak, we called the
game and headed up to the store for *Trits* and
some take away beers. On the way back down the
path, we spotted a blue Landcruiser trying to

---

[54] It is a strange but true, and little known fact, that Stirling
Prescott actually has no sense of smell (and therefore, no sense of
taste), and cooks his meals based on texture alone.

navigate its way down the bumpy road to the shore.

It was the girls.

P.M. sat up through the open window and stretched her arm up, "Yeee! There you are!" she cried.

Ingrid was at the wheel.

"Keep on going," I yelled, skipping ahead, "we're down at the beach."

We directed them through to the clearing behind our camp and helped them to unload their stuff. The girls were introduced to Finn and to Prescott, and then I helped P.M. to pitch up Ingrid's tent onto a vacant spot in the sand. Ingrid did a quick circuit around, and then came over to where we were finishing up to ask if I had yet to find her a replacement surfboard.

"Yeah, actually you're right on time," I told her, "I was just about to go pick it up. If you guys have a minute, we can go grab it right now."

"Is it a nice board?" she asked sternly.

"It's a beauty."

"Long board?"

"Nine foot."

And here she looked at P.M., "Well I wouldn't mind *seeing* it," and then back to me, "Is it far?"

"Not farr," I said, "Come on. Let's go now, and we'll get the fucker over with."

So the girls and I drove back up the bumpy road, and I told Ingrid that when we got there, she was to say that it was really *not* the right board for her, regardless of what she actually thought.[55] A simple hand signal was devised to communicate to me her true impression.

After leaving the jeep and crossing the fields, we found the Danish guy to be at home. I introduced myself and he brought the board out into the garden for our inspection where Ingrid began looking it over as he was telling me what a great board it was for 300 dollars. I told him that the word in town was that it was being offered at $250, and that I would perhaps be willing to pay that price if Ingrid were to give me her word of approval.

Ingrid came over to where we stood talking and said out loud that it was a good board, and that she would take it.

So much for signals.

So I made the big cash payout: five American fifty-dollar bills. And Ingrid took her prize and set off down to the road to strap it onto the roof of her jeep.

When we were almost back to the beach, I mentioned to the girls that I was considering catching a ride back up north with them when they left, so that I could grab the broken board and hitch it back down, and have something to surf on while we were here in Mal Pais.

"Yeah well no. You can't have it," said Ingrid.

---

[55] In this way, I was going to try to get him down to 200 dollars.

"Um... Ingrid, I've just bought you a replacement board."

"What Audacy? You think I'm just going to give you my brother's board? You don't understand. It was custom made! I'm not just going to give it away!"

"...!" The damn woman was beyond reason! I appealed to P.M. with a look, but she just shook her head and slowly blinked her eyes.

So I shut up. I corked it. But from that moment forward, part of me was just waiting for those girls to leave town.

*   *   *

That night at *The Cocacabana*, Nick and I set up some chairs overlooking the dance floor. I spoke with Fabio and introduced him to Chavez (our *"manager"*) and to Finn, whose eyes kept darting around the joint, until in his excitement, he ran off in search of a hand drum. Nick and I wolfed down some bowls of pasta as we sat together at the counter, and Chavez and the girls laid claim to a big round booth table, and were soon joined by Prescott, Brent, and the noisy German girlfriend.

When Finn came back in a few minutes later, he had a large congo drum up on his shoulder, and he was leading a group of our hippie beach contingent who had come to sip waters and listen to the show. So another chair was put up onto the platform, and I told Finn to stay attentive and that I'd wink at him before any major changes in tempo.

Our set list went like this: Farr from Home,

Where I Go, Carry Me On, Smile, Friend of the Devil, Freedom Song, Whole New World, Mr. Soul, Goat-Dog Sign, Marine, Viajero Perdido, I Am the Ocean.

When we took our set break, I started my circumnavigation of the room, peddling CDs from one table to the next. Ten minutes later, I was five hundred grams lighter, and *back in business*.

I stepped out with Nick and Finn for a quick puff down by the shore, and when we came back in, P.M. was lining up shots of tequila for our entire group.

By the time we took back to the stage, we were much more relaxed, and our second song set the group to dancing.

Look Out For My Love, Sparkle, Willie & Waylon & Me, Fish Guts, Bridge to Burn, Running Bear, Freight Train, Ave de Paso, Kerosene, The Gambler, The Theme, Sunshine Away.

By the end, we were all becoming a bit shit-faced, and I sold one more CD before joining the booth table with a fresh round of beers. Fabio seemed to be happy with the way the gig had gone, and continued to provide Nick, Finn, Chavez and me with Imperial beers, free of charge.

The DJ music came on, and there was another round of tequilas in there somewhere, and then things start to become a bit foggy.

T.D.T.F.

I woke up to the sound of the monkey pissing on my tent again, and I crawled out into the blinding light and started chucking stones. The monkey squatted back on its hand and then rose to its full height and flung a fresh piece of poo at me with great accuracy. In my hung-over state, I only just barely managed to dodge the bullet, and it deflected off of the tent-fly behind me.

"Holy shit!.. you mother little shit of a fucker!" I yelled in disbelief, shaking my fist, and then bending over to pick up a heavy stick.

P.M. emitted a painful moan from inside of the tent.

"OK, I know, but it just threw its own *shit* at me!"

Ingrid was already up, and came jogging over to scold me, "Audacy don't you dare! Why can't you just leave the poor little thing alone?"

"Leave *him* alone? The fucking thing keeps pissing on my tent!"

"Honestly Audacy! It's just a monkey!"

So I turned and flung the stick away. Ingrid huffed off and I grabbed a bottle of water before collapsing back into the soft shade of the tent.

When the heat of the early afternoon finally sweated us out of the tent, Chavez had already packed his bag, and he came swaggering over to me, googly-eyed and somewhat apologetic.

"Well," he said, "I'm off."

"Is it today?" I asked, stretching and blinking, feeling myself to have been too self-absorbed to properly perceive the outward passing time.

"No, her flight comes in tomorrow. But I want to get a place in San Jose, and see her in properly. I'll be back in a couple of days."

"Well then," I said into his ear as we embraced, "I won't say goodbye. Ride well."

"Yeah, I will," he said, heaving his pack on, "Just be here when I get back, eh?"

"We'll be here."

And with that, Chavez turned and made his way back through the forest, and up towards the road.

I turned back to the shore and noticed Prescott dragging a humungous log up through the sand. When he got to the section of beach that was between our camp and the shore, he dropped the huge pole with a muddled thud, and then got to his knees and began digging a hole. I went over to where he knelt digging and asked him what he was up to.

"Oh, I figured I'd show you guys how to make a proper fire. It's full moon tonight."

"But why the hole?"

"To stand the fucker up. You'll see. Help me dig."

So I did. And then I helped him to erect the huge log, with its base in the hole, and we filled in the edges and packed down the sand. For the rest of the afternoon, all of the wood that we could collect, we propped up against this centre pole, creating a narrow wooden tepee, maybe 18 feet tall, which we then stuffed full of dried palm-fronds.

When the sun went down and the moon came up, we lit the fucker and stepped back to watch the flames rise up and engulf the structure. Nearby campsites and cooking fires were soon abandoned as everyone trickled towards our beaconing torch.

Succumb to the rum and a little strum-strum.

The dancing began. Hand drums and bottles, guitars and harmonica, pots and spoons, someone had a didge.

And it was on.

And full moon it was.

At some point thereafter, a loaded down figure came lumbering along the beach, and into the flickering light of our inferno.

"Holy shit you guys!" he exclaimed, dropping his pack in the sand with a smile and a sigh of exhaustion, the flames reflecting in the lenses of his glasses, "I saw this fire and I knew it had to be you!"

We all turned, and Prescott was first to speak:

P: "Is this guy with you?"

A: "Yeah," I said laughing, "this is Max."

P: "Welcome to Mal Pais!" yelling, with his arms out as before.

M: Thanks. I can't believe I found you guys!

A: Well you got the note, right?

M: The note?

A: On Ingrid's door.

M: No, there was nothing there. It was all locked up, and the neighbours said that they had just left, but they didn't know where to. Hey there Nick."

N: "Hiya Max."

I: "I left it on the door!"

A: "Well, that's certainly what you told *us*."

PM: "Hallo Max."

M: "Hi there gorgeous. It's good to see you."

PM: "I'm glad you made it."

M: "Oh... Hey Ingrid."

I: "How you doing Max? Long time no see."

M: "Yeah. It's amazing."

N: "Mexico City?"

M: "No. Not all the way. It kind of became a slightly redundant parade. I rode with them to Oaxaca, and then decided to hitch down. Where's Chavez?"

A: "He'll be back tomorrow or the next day. He went to San Jose to pick up his girlfriend."

M: "She's coming down here?"

A: "I guess so."

F: "So you're Max Fortes."

M: "Forte. Yeah, hi."

N: "This is Finn. He's from Manchester."

M: "Oh. Nice to meet you."

A: "So how did you know to come down?"

M: "Well that's the funny thing. I was just about ready to give up. I figured there was no way, and I didn't know what I was going to do, so I went to this place and just sat down to have a drink, when I started talking with these two Irish guys..."

A: "No way!"

M: "Yeah, and they said that they'd seen you there at the bar, and that you guys were maybe gonna come down here."

N: "Wait, which guys?"

A: "These are the guys that me and Chavez were talking to when we went to the end of the beach to get those beers."

N: "Oh."

A: "I can't believe it."

M: "Yeah, otherwise, you know, I didn't know what I was going to do."

I: "I did leave the note up. It was on the door. It must have blown away."

M: "So you'd never believe who I bumped into, and who gave me a message to give to you."

A: "Who?"

M: "Teaching at a school up in the cloud forests of Monteverde!"

A: "Who?"

M: "Marilyn Campbell!"

A: "What?"

M: "Yeah, and she told *me* to tell *you* that she *really* wants to see you, and that we should all come up *there*."

A: "What?"

M: "Yeah... And its only one day's hitch from here."

CHAPTER MAX

I stayed with Australian Wayne in Chela, Quetzaltanango, and spent the night there in a two-dollar motel. The next day we got picked up by a Tiko truck driver who ended up picking us up four times over. He would let us out just before the border, and we would cross, and since trucks have to wait a long time, we would invariably be standing by the side of the road when our guy came through again.

So we went through El Salvador with him, which at that time was not too far from civil war, and they had just had an earthquake, and had also recently been hit by hurricane Mitch, so, infrastructure: fucked up.

There was a lot of *delinquencia*, and the truck drivers were afraid of highway robbery. They would drive in these convoys, and they would park at night and be guarded by guys with shotguns, and then they'd leave very early in the morning, you know, kind of like circling up your wagons.

We asked the truck driver if we could sleep on the ground in front of his truck, and he said, "Te van a culear!" And culear is a Central American verb that means 'to fuck up the ass', so we ended up sleeping in hammocks underneath the bed of his truck, which wasn't too bad except for the mosquitos, and we continued to do the same, crossing through a little bit of Honduras.

In Nicaragua, we stayed in Granada, which is a beautiful little colonial town. We got a ride from this Danish guy who had just bought a house there for 40,000 dollars.

When we crossed the border into Costa Rica, it was kind of a hard border to cross. There were a lot of Nicaraguan immigrants trying to get across that border, economic migrants trying to go over and work in Costa Rica.

We went up to Monteverde, which is this fantastically beautiful town up in the mountains. Wayne and I had realized that we had a friend in common, this girl Marilyn who went to Middlebury, and he knew her because she was friends with his girlfriend, and we decided to go visit her. She was working in a Quaker school, and we hitchhiked up.

Monteverde is about two hours up a dirt road, and the climate is fantastic. It was founded by Quakers, and they preserved this huge piece of rainforest, the watershed for their dairy farms that they had built. They were from Alabama or something, and came down in the forties and bought all this land, and it's one of the largest intact pieces of cloud forest in Costa Rica, right on the continental divide, with a climate like Vermont in the summertime, but with toucans and monkeys and strangler figs, and just a gorgeous and amazing place.

So we saw Marilyn, who happened to be roommates with a friend of mine from New York, just the strangest of coincidences, this girl Mackenzie. And then I hitchhiked by myself down to the coast to meet up with Aude.

I went and tried to find Aude at Ingrid's, but he had just left, but then as I was leaving town, some Irish guy told me that he had gone down to some beach at the bottom of the Nicoiya Peninsula, and I went down there and found them. They had fallen in with this whole crew, and had sort of set up surf camp on this beach in Nicoiya, and Prescott was there, and Finn, and we stayed up all night playing music and playing chess and drinking.

I went fishing with these kind of fishing lines that you just spin around and toss out into the surf, and I caught a fish on my first go, and Prescott came over and ripped its head off with his bear hands, which was quite horrifying, and then we cooked it.

CHAPTER NICK

We got to the girls' house in Costa Rica, and that was cool. We watched 'Casablanca' while we were there. Audacy broke her surfboard, we rode some bikes, we played some soccer, and Chavez burned his nuts. The first shower any of us had in an age was there in Costa Rica, and I was

laughing, watching all of the dirt just pour off
of me. That was amazing, dirt-grind; gotta love
it.

Costa Rica. The coastal highway was cool, and
we had a guy from San Francisco who we kept
prodding on that his little rental car would
make it, and it always did! Except for that time
that we had to cross a river and gorges, but had
to first wait for low tide. Ha!

But then we came into Mal Pais, and we
decided that we were going to like this town
because we saw this girl on the back of a bike
who looked just like a French model. She looked
like Elle McPherson to me. And she was so hot,
so *good*-lookin' on the back of that bike, that
we were just like: we're here.

It didn't take long to find Prescott. Maybe
he found us. We go back to a place, and then
hear them having monkey sex, and the girl that
he was having sex with, I slept in her hammock
for the rest of the time, about ten feet away
from the beach. I remember that there was a guy
who took a shit there, and the iguana was eating
his freshly dumped shit. Freaked the guy out.
Freaked us all out.

We played soccer there, and all of us kind of
went off on our own and did our own things for a
while. But we happened to all be together when
we first saw Finn, which was a random thing. And
he was hanging with these Venezuelan girls, and
he ditched them for us, and then we had another
One. And then Trudy showed up, so Chavez got
preoccupied, and as we were about to leave, Max
Fortes showed up, and we went up to Monteverde.

CHAPTER CHAVEZ

The day that Audacy broke the surfboard, I had been on the beach with Nick, and I had a couple of big beers in front of me, and I was reading in the nude, and I fell asleep. When I woke up, my ass was so red. I had blistered my ass. And when he broke the surfboard and we had to leave the next day, it had to be, for me, one of the worst days to walk, and we probably walked 15 miles that day, and my ass was just burnt.

Very uncomfortable.

And also that day, I offered to carry Audacy's guitar for him. We had walked over this mountain, and he'd been carrying his guitar for a long time 'cause there hadn't been any rides. So I offered to carry it for him. Big mistake. As soon as I took the guitar, we started going uphill, and unburdened by his guitar, he climbed on ahead and kept on going. I carried that fucking guitar up the mountain, struggling, because my short fucking arms and legs couldn't keep the guitar from bouncing off the ground, so I had to hold it like a baby, and up this mountain I walked, and there he was at the top, sitting on his pack, resting in the shade.

After that, we walked into some small little village, and sat down in the little saloon and ordered some orange Fantas in glass bottles, and then chased those with a couple of beers, and then managed to get a ride out of there.

It was later on that same day when we rolled into Mal Pais. We were in the back of a pickup truck, cruising along the coastal highway that only exists at low tide, and we had just turned back into the jungle and away from the beach. We passed this girl on a bicycle, this beautiful girl, and all of us were just like: "Whew! This is going to be a good place to sit for a while."

Mal Pais. We spent about a week and a half on the beach there, living in our tents, walking to the little store there to buy ice cream sandwiches and cold beer.

We met up with Stirling Prescott, and that night, there were spider monkeys in the trees, right above our tent. Not very far away there was some man fucking some woman quite loudly and robustly, and the more the woman got off, the more the monkeys got off, until the monkeys were just screeching, echoing the orgasmic screams of the woman, and we all just sort of lied there laughing, horny, and secretly wanting to kill the monkeys.

Then we went down to the beach. We met up with Finn and Finn's beautiful Venezuelan girls that he was with, that he *wasn't* laying, and we surfed on the fuckin' bonefish: the surfboard from hell, with the jagged fibreglass edges.

Prescott made his rum and coconut concoction that didn't sell at all, and that they just ended up drinking. Audacy sliced his face open on the surfboard. Met that crazy girl Lunacy, and the guys played music at the little nightclub there, and Finn played drums, and we just chilled out. I got a hammock there, and we just lived in the trees and on the beach and in the water for a week and a half or two.

Here's the point where a girl comes back into the picture: a girl who had dropped me off in a blizzard.

I left the guys on the beach in Mal Pais, and it was off to San Jose for me. I picked her up at the airport the next night and spent a night with her in a hotel, and then hitched back to Mal Pais the next day. I remember when we got back to the beach, and I walked up, and the guys were all sittin' around a campfire singing songs.

And from that point on, the trip was totally different, man. The girl had entered the folds. The dynamic completely changed from like a gung-ho boy forward onward mentality, to a compromise compromise compromise approach.

CHAPTER FINN

I was travelling with these three beautiful Venezuelan girls who had kind of saved my ass. I had lost everything: my passport, my ticket, my money. I had no... nothing. And they found the kid who had stolen it, or found it, or whatever... He had taken it, and they went and got it back for me — not the money, but everything else.

I was basically hanging out with them, watching their camp for them, so that they could go off and do their things, and they'd feed me.

I had ended up going down to Mal Pais just 'cause I had nothing else to do, and the girls were on their way out. I spent two nights down the road from where it turned out that the guys were, but I knew that Stirling Prescott was down there in that camp, and I didn't want to see him. I had already visited him, and I was like: *I'm gonna give it a break.* I didn't want to show up

at his place with three beautiful girls, 'cause
that would have just been too much. You gotta
understand how he is.

So I saw Stirling finally, and he was like,
"Oh, some guys from Vermont are here," and I was
like, "Vermont. Cool." So I went down there, and
those guys were sitting by a little fire. Audacy
had some zinc lip-stuff on, and a bit on the
nose, and he was chapped and burnt as hell. Nick
was there too, and he was the only one that I
really knew. He was playing guitar when I walked
down, and I was like just totally blown away, and
I was like: this is really weird!

The girls were leaving the next day, and I
was going to go with them to the capital to see
them off on a plane, 'cause I really had nothing
else to do, but I was like: cool, I'll hang out
with you guys. So I said goodbye to the girls and
it was kind of, "blah blah blah," and then I
spent a few days with the boys on the beach.

And man! That was the drunkest I ever got. I
watched the light bulb split in two, and I
couldn't get the two parts to go back together.
We had some real fun on the beach though. We
played soccer, and coco-football and coco-
lacrosse.

Stirling and Audacy came up with the bright
idea of selling rum-coconuts. The whole plan was
that Stirling Prescott had an account with the
store, 'cause he'd been livin' there for so long,
so he put a bottle of rum on his charge, 'cause
he had no money. And the whole plan was dependent
on me being able to climb the coconut trees,
cutting the coconuts down, and then opening every
single one to the point of almost-penetration, so

you could poke the holes in it and pour in the rum, right there for the people on the beach. Coco Loco.

So I'm climbing this tree, and there's like fire ants coming out of this hole, and they're like, "Just get the last ones down." And I finally do it.

They come back later on all wasted, 'cause they didn't sell any, and they drank all the rum themselves.

*   *   *

The funniest memory I have of Prescott is when we were surfing the Bonefish, and I was out in the water, and here comes Prescott and he's got a fishing pole. What are you gonna do with a fishing pole? And he's sitting on the board and he's casting, and I'm like, "You know, there's some pretty big fish in there," and he's like, "Oh, you know, whatever, it'll just drag me for a while." So I just go out for a few waves, and then come back and look over, and all I could see was Stirling Prescott, completely underwater, with his hands above his head, reeling in. He'd been yanked from his board, and was still trying to reel the fish in! And I caught a wave in, and I was laughing my ass off, and I asked, "What happened?" and he was like, "Oh, it snapped the line, blah blah blah."

And then the next scene in the water that I saw was that he had caught a wave somehow, and while he was standing on the board, he had cast out, and was reeling the thing in, trimming down the wave!

But he didn't catch a single fish.

He got back to shore and gave the rod to Max
Fortes, who is a total kind of dork, you know
like: really nice guy, but you don't see him
being a fisherman. And he's like, "Here, let me
try." And Zing. Five minutes later, he catches a
nice ten-pound fish, and Stirling's just like,
"Let me see that," and takes over, and they cook
it up.

They tried to get those two German girls into
bed, who *weren't* that hot, but were *definitely*
looking for it.

I was already hanging with the guys when Max
Fortes showed up. And I think that I immediately
started ragging on him cause the other guys were
ragging on him. I'm pretty sure that there was a
little bit of tension going on between he and
Nick. So when he showed up, I was treating him
like he was a goofy dork, and he was treating me
like I was a dumb-ass, and like he was some sort
of intellectual, and he was immediately like
that: like he was so smart.

CHAPTER 42
No matter how hard I whistle
(I still said those things last night)

It was early in the afternoon when Chavez
arrived back on the beach, holding hands with his
pale northern double-X, and blushing from the
extremity of the leap that he had undertaken from
rough road abstinence to sexual affluence.

For her part, she seemed like a young doe who
had just unknowingly snacked on mushrooms, and

was stepping out into a plot whose movie had long been playing.

In order to protect her, Chavez was forced to create a bit of a universe apart from the rest of us, and as plans moved ahead, and towards a move up into the mountains, Chavez confided his intention of staying behind to spend a couple of days with Trudy on the beach, in order to "help her acclimate to her new foreign surroundings" (sex his brains out without any disturbance from his comrades).

Later on that same day, I was coming in from a surf with Finn. Chavez had been awaiting his turn, and I was just coming into the shallows, holding the board out in front of me to catch a small already-broken wave up onto the beach. All of the sudden, the wave pulled and I lost hold of the board, and it flipped back around and stabbed me in the face, centering in between the right cheek-side of my nose, and the gum-half of my eye tooth. I was a bit blanked out, and stood up in the surf to ask the two closest guys how bad it was. They just stood there and gawked.

"Well come on guys, is it fucking bad or *not*?"

"Well dude," drawled the one guy finally, "I'd get out of the water if I were you."

I looked down and saw the dripping, and realized what the guy was saying.

Up on the beach, Chavez saw me coming, and after running over and together discovering that I probably was not going to loose my tooth, he ran off laughing to get his camera, elated with the notion that the reckless display might more cohesively match his heretofore descriptions of our entourage to his naïve little number of a girlfriend.

After much hemming and hawing, and comparison of various ignoramuses' medical understandings, I weighed the gravity of the situation against my explicit non-desire to experience the Costa Rican medical system, and allowed Prescott to flush the wound with whiskey, and then patch it with a splotch of crazy glue that one of the Argentinean guys had been carrying.

The wound held well, and bled only during extreme bouts of laughter, but the event would mark the end of my surfing in the red tide.

*　　*　　*

The girls announced that they were going to head back up north on the following day, and the boys all happened to bring home a bunch of liquor that evening (Ingrid is after all a pretty good-looking girl).

P.M. and I were mostly off getting drunk on our own, and we fell into this huge discussion that I didn't want to have, about the boy that she had met, who I didn't want to know about, and it seemed that she wanted either some kind of declaration, or else a resolve. I was for a resolve, but *may that it not come until morning!*

This was afterwards, and lying on the beach, and we were drunker than mama's ruin. The two of us lay there, caught somewhere in between our past sense of intimacy, and our oncoming isolation, and at last my tongue was won over by my id. "Yeah, and so is so, and that's the case, but it doesn't mean we can't have another night of it. One final night. After all of our things, and here we are, alone now, here on the beach."

"I know, I just don't know," she wavered, her long hands fidgeting in the moonlight, "It's not you so much as that it's me. And I just have to find some sort of period at the end of the sentence, some sort of finish line."

I resolved myself at last to the growing certainty of a pre-emptive termination of our sexual relationship, and steered myself over to the tent to grab the flask before coming back over to reposition myself next to her in the sand. I rolled a cigarette as she stared out to sea.

A sad irony was our love.

The moon was over the water now, and each of us took a pull from the flask, and then lied with our backs flat down against the beach. She wordlessly took my hand, and the two of us just swam there together, with just the faintest sound of guitar strumming drifting in and out through the waves and the ocean.

*   *   *

The girls were all packed up in the morning and loading their stuff into the Landcruiser that still had the surfboard tied to the roof. The boys began to assemble, and as everyone said their goodbyes, I pulled P.M. closer and we shared one final kiss.

Then they got in, Ingrid at the wheel, and started it up and turned down the music (Paul Simon, Diamonds on the Soles of her Shoes), and off they went, honking as they bumpingly crawled away through the forest and up towards the road. There would be no more chess through the mail.

I waived to Purple Maiden as she flew away.

CHAPTER WHO CARES WHAT?
This book may contain traces of nut

We assembled our mutated posse and prepared for the hitchhike up into the mountains. There would be no straw-drawing this time. The boys decided that it was Nick and Finn, and that I was to go with Max.

Max was giving us directions on how to get to the town, and everyone magic-markered the contact phone number onto their wrists and arms as we sat with Prescott and the lovers, passing a joint around the breakfast fire.

After thanking Prescott for his excellent hospitality and bidding Chavez and his girlfriend a restful respite, we hauled our stuff back up to the junction and took our positions, with the two pairs of us spaced about 500 metres apart.

Max and I were the first ones to get a lift out of there, even though we were positioned further on down the road.[56] The ride was in the back of a P-up truck that had a cap on it, and we sat in that sauna of an enclosure, alternating our tactic between propping the rear window open because of the heat, and holding it shut because of the dust. We headed east with that ride until

---

[56] We would later infuriate them by maintaining that this was purely due to our hitchhike expertise.

all road traffic loaded onto a ferry, and we got out and bought some ham sandwiches before joining the rest of the passengers on the top deck.

Nick and Finn ended up rolling in with one of the last vehicles that made it aboard.

There was a cheese grater band set up along one of the side benches of the upper deck, playing music for tips. Rasta and Cajun music mostly. Nick became fascinated with them, and we all rested and listened to the music as the boat carried us across.

Arriving to the farr shore, Max and I dismounted quickly to hitch the cars as they unloaded from the boat, and even before the rope had been pulled across to let the traffic off, two old guys in an ancient blue Datson offered us voyage with a gesture. We left the other guys setting up, and took the ride over to Arenas Negras, from where we got a lift with Patricio, rolling up a joint as he picked us up. We also rode with Felix who ran the hotel taxi, and then with a smelly worker from the cheese factory. By late afternoon, we were riding with a Canadian tourist couple when we came switchbacking up the long road that leads into Monteverde.

There were clouds in the sky when we got let out at the bottom corner of town and made our way along to the store, painted all yellow and blue, and looking like it had been operating there unchanged since the thirties or forties.

"Do you want to call and tell them we're coming?"

"Not if you can get us there."

"Well I know where it is, you know, but it's kind of hard to find."

"How farr?"

"Maybe a half hour walk."

"So let's walk. We can call if we don't find it."

I soon saw how it could have been confusing, what with the long lanes, a stream and a bridge, and then across a double cow paddy and down through some paths into the jungle, but Max led the way and found it, and it was dark when we descended the path and out into a field with a small house off to one side.

A figure came running and screaming at me from out of the darkness, galloping over and jumping straight up onto me, entwining her long legs around my waist and pack. I dropped the guitar and greeted my unpredictable assailant.

"Hello Marilyn."

Background: Marilyn Campbell is another girl from college, but not just another girl. She's absolutely crazy, and communicates mostly through laughter. She was fated to be paired with one of my best friends in school, and although everyone could perceive their inherent amorous cohesion, they had never maintained much of a sexual relationship. He was more of a religious ascetic nature, and she would find release for her physical desires through an unruly relationship that she maintained with an old boyfriend from high school. The high school boy kept her conflicted for years, and would threaten to kill himself if she ever strayed too farr.

Marilyn had, at some times along the way, spent nights in my bed, and we enjoyed each other's closeness. But all during those years at school, we had never once trespassed the unspoken and invisible barrier, due mostly to our shared understanding and respect for Laker.

Besides being close to Laker in the normal way, he and I are forever bound together through our having shared a single most important and life-changing experience, which I will here digress to include...

*   *   *

It was actually Mike who saw it first. It doesn't really matter where we were, but we were walking. In a field. He didn't say anything, but the weird kind of inhaling-gasp that he emitted made Laker look up, and made me look over towards them. And then I looked up.

It was like a bright, double ended bullet that had somewhere to get to, and it went straight along, fast but not too fast, totally quiet, almost right above us, east to west, definitely within the atmosphere.

We were all terrified silent till it went over the horizon, and then what ensued was an indescribable shirt-ripping-off scream dance, and an immediate kind of a grand re-evaluation of everything.

I'm not guessing when I say that we all went a little crazy from that day forward. Laker tried to live on nothing but sprouts for a while, and then dropped out of school and started doing natural psychedelics with indigenous peoples, travelling from this jungle to that and "apprenticing" with medicine men and sorts. Mike changed his major to physics and astronomy, and refused soon thereafter to ever discuss the incident. I started hitchhiking. This book may or may not explain why this was the case.

*   *   *

So a little while later the phone rang, and it was Nick and Finn, calling from the store. Marilyn gave them directions and then she and I walked back to the road to intercept them at the bridge. Max stayed back at the house, chatting it up with Marilyn's roommate, who he had apparently met once before in New York City.

After we had led the boys back to the place, wine bottles were opened up, and the group of us sat around a mosquito coil out on the lawn. Nick and I pitched the tent up in the corner, and Max was pointing out that the tent would only sleep three, and he was therefore volunteering himself to sleep on the couch inside (or perhaps in bed with the roommate). Marilyn laughed out loud with what passed as an irrefutable statement: "Well Audacy is going to be sleeping in my bed with me."

And that night, I did. Here we were in the jungles of Timbuktu, and never before had everything from the past felt so farr away. I was off, I was moving forward, and I would not be denied the fruits of my journey. Marilyn took me to bed with a half a bottle of wine in her hand, and led me as we rehashed our way through the way things might have been between us.

And staring at her in the candlelight, her prickly thatch and her beckoning self, the thought flashed through my mind that word of this would definitely somehow make its way back to Morgan, but instead of deterring me, this bridge-burning notion rocked me forward, and led me onward.

CHAPTER 44
Monteverde

The next day, we were down at the store. The girls were off working, and Nick and I had an appointment to go and meet the owner of the Jungle Boogie Café in an hour's time.

Finn and I were eating *Trits* on a bench outside the store, watching a tour bus unload its cargo of tourist bird watchers. They all approached this one big tree at the corner of the parking lot and quietly began to examine along its branches with binoculars and zoom-lens cameras.

One of the hippie locals that we were talking to explained that the buses would stop here for a few minutes in hopes of spotting some particular kind of bird in this one tree. They all carried these little pads that had little boxes to check off, and they would check off each one until they had seen every bird.

By the time we noticed the next tour bus making its way up the hill, Finn and I were just finishing our second round of ice cream sandwiches. I ran over to where Max was reading in the shade to borrow his camera, and then headed up into the tree.

Crouching quietly on one of the higher
branches of the tree, I waited until the bus had
completely unloaded and the birdwatchers were
approaching with their instruments drawn. When I
was sure that I had been spotted, I started
squawking like a monkey and taking pictures of
the tourists, shuffling back and forth across the
branch and creating a real drama. Finn was
laughing below as the group began to make various
gestures of annoyance, and made to get back on
the bus.

"Some people, honestly!"

"Well it only takes one to ruin it..."

Later on, we went back up to the Jungle
Boogie to meet (and fall in love with) the owner.

Mariana was originally Cuban, and after
living in, and then fleeing Venezuela during the
revolution, she had just recently set herself up
here in Costa Rica. She was in her early thirties
and absolutely beautiful, a true Latin American
princess. Long, dark unruly hair, worn up but
spilling out of its bun, plump lips encircling a
wide mouth, and big dark eyes that it looked like
you could have dropped a pebble into. She spoke
Spanish with the Cuban tendency to leave the "s"
off of the end of her words, and then seamlessly
switched the conversation into English upon being
introduced to Nick.

From where she stood, mesmerizing us at the
bar, she also ran the entire system around her,
and all of the business that was taking place in
the room seemed to revolve around the fulcrum of
her presence. She said that there was to be a
television crew coming through in the next hour,
doing a segment on the town, and that she was

anxious that the café be conveyed in its most positive light. Nick made some comment about how nice it looked already, and she smiled.

The place looked like an elaborate tree fort, everything dark, solid, and organic. There were chessboards and crystals placed about the bar, with burlap weavings hanging from the wooden walls and a driftwood mobile from the ceiling. Just next to the bar was a thick wooden table, the cross-section of an ancient tree, which could easily have supported the elbows of Vikings.

I brought the conversation around to the possibility of our making music at her café, and she shrugged and gave us the gig with a wink and a smile, immediately setting one of her café girls down to making up some signs.

"Things are busy right now," she said, "but I would like to talk." She paused and glanced back towards the kitchen, "Come in early on Friday, with your friends, and we will cook for you a dinner before you play."

"That would be very nice."

"...And who knows?" she said, raising her eyebrows, "Maybe I will sing a song too." And the twinkling smile with which she punctuated this statement could have broken glass. It could have laid a fifth ace down on the table without raising an eyebrow from even the Devil himself. And I was just thinking, "Wait until Max meets this girl."

*   *   *

Back at the house, Marilyn was sitting in a chair on the patio affixing gold stars to her students' artwork. I was beside her on the lawn scrubbing and hosing down the tent with some dishsoap that I'd found inside. Max was thinking globally and acting locally, with Mackenzie's laughter drifting out from her bedroom, and the door left slightly ajar. Nick had my guitar out inside teaching Finn the changes on some Grateful Dead song.

"How about this one?" she giggled.

"Is that supposed to be a person?"

"No, it's the school, but drawn from a bird's eye view, see? This is the soccer field and the playground where they have recess, and the front building here. And this would be my classroom, like, kind of here. Pretty good for a nine year old, don'tcha think?"

"Sure. Is that one gonna get a gold star?"

"With the bird's eye view? That's two gold stars I think."

Another fit of laughter from Mackenzie's room.

"How often do you do that, wash it out like that?"

"Well, I'm going from never to once right now."

"I could probably find you a better scrubby if you want."

"No, It's cool, I'm done, just given'r a rinse.

Nick stepped outside. "Hey Audacy, I broke

one of your strings."

"Well that's not like you thrasher. Which one, third?"

"Yeah. I think it's cutting on the fret."

"That's alright. There should be another in the flap part of the case."

Max poked his head out from Mackenzie's room, laughing, "Hey Aude, I was just telling Mackenzie about that ride that we got over the Spanish/French border in that car carrier. She doesn't believe me that we got to sit up inside the cars, she thinks I'm full of it."

Nick rolled his eyes and went back inside.

"Mackenzie," I yelled out, "Don't believe a thing he says. Car carrier?"

Max chomped at me with a smile, "Bastard. I wasn't going to tell her what *you* were doing up there in *your* car."

"Good, well don't.

"Hah," Max asserted before stepping back into her room and leaving the door just a little bit more closed than it had been before.

"...Doing up there in *your* car?" echoed Marilyn, with a crook in her eyebrow.

"Oh, a ride that I jerked off in. He likes to think that he holds it against me."

Just before we started getting any ideas, Mackenzie came out from her room and she and Marilyn started making up some dinner. Finn helped them to chop some vegetables and Max sat

on the counter telling stories. I stepped outside
to rotate the tent, and Nick followed me out and
went to take a piss in the long grass behind me.
Then he strolled over.

"So," he said, "So how's it going for you?"

"It's going good man. It's going fine."

"Yeah, I'll bet," he said, raising his chin
to gesture inside, "You haven't done too bad for
yourself, huh? Is this the one then?"

"What? Ah no man. Marilyn and I are just
really good friends. She's slept heaps of nights
in my bed; we've got a mutual friend, and it just
goes back..." I assured him with a dismissive
wave.

"Really good friends huh?" he sparkled,
blinking his eyes and leaning up close.

"Yut," I sputtered, breaking into a smile.
"...I think you're gonna luck out and not have to
sleep in a puddle tonight, but I'm just gonna
leave it up on its side anyway, and you can put
it down. It's tied down here."

"Alright," he smiled, and we went back
inside.

*　　　*　　　*

The next day when we got to the stream, the
water level was up, which was kind of strange
because it hadn't rained, but Max was saying that
it would have been raining up in the cloud
forest.

We arrived into town and Finn got to talking
with some hippie who told him the location of a

big avocado tree. He was going on and on about it, and how we should load up before heading back. Once again we were next to the picnic table out in front of the store, eating *Trits* and hacking on the lawn.

When Finn went off to look for some sort of herbal ointment and Max left to get on his e-mail, I took off to go find tobacco, which took me longer than anyone else's mission, but I finally struck gold with two ancient and faded packs of Samson that I found at a gas station on the farr side of town.

When I came back down the hill, I saw that Chavez and his girlfriend had arrived. Chavez and Finn were hacking with two young kids and some other hippie guy, and Newbie Trudy was standing over with Max and listening to one of his stories. Nick was off to the side, reading the English text on a mural that was painted on the store wall.

I stepped into the hack circle as Chavez was still recounting their hitchhike up from the shore. He made a point to ensure that I knew that they had hitched the whole way.

"And how's things down at the beach?"

"Oh, same as ever really. We didn't really hang out with Prescott very much. We mostly just stayed on our own."

"Must'a been tough," I said.

"Yeah, I'm still recovering," he grinned. "Nick, are you gonna come play?"

"In a minute. Hold on."

"Did Nick tell you that we got a gig?"

"Yeah, that's what he said."

"It's just over there, and up the road. Actually... do you see that sign?" I pointed to the post at the bottom of the lane, where a colourful sign had been put up that read, 'LIVE MUSIC FRIDAY @ The Jungle Boogie Café'.

"Oh, that's you guys?" asked the hippie.

"Yeah."

"Nick said it's a nice place," said Chavez.

"Yeah it is. We're going to go up at about this time tomorrow, and the hot owner lady has offered us all a feed."

"Sounds sweet."

"I hope so. Have you guys got anything to do today in town?"

"No, we've kind of been waiting for you guys. I'd kinda like to get the stuff up to your friend's house and drop it off."

"Yeah, we should probably get going."

Just then, Trudy burst out laughing, and we all glanced over to where she and Max were standing as he continued with his story, "...but the funny thing about *that*, is that the next time that I was up there..."

"So what have we got here?" said Nick, coming over and hovering just outside of our circle.

"Alright. Nick's in. Look alive... Let's go for a triple hack, and then we'll make our move."

"OK, OK. Triple hack, no fucking around," said Chavez, striking a kung-fu pose.

Finn chuckled, and then started chanting as the hippie lobbed the hackisack up towards Nick's side of the circle.

*   *   *

Chavez and I went off with Finn to help carry avocados back from the tree, and Max got inspired and picked up a bunch of vegetables from the store before we started back up to the house.

When we came to within sight of the swelling stream, there was a red jeep stuck halfway across in the sandy mud. It was a Colombian family, on vacation, and the handsome father gratefully accepted our offer of assistance. Chavez and Trudy's things were dropped on the farr bank, and we started organizing the push, with the guy's wife at the wheel. We soon bounced some traction into the spinning wheels, and the guy's children, who were running up and down the bank, laughed and applauded as the jeep came loose and jumped up onto solid ground. The couple thanked us, and the mother started rounding up their children as I stood talking with the father.

"<...And have you been to Columbia>?" he asked.

"<Not yet, but I would very much like to go>."

"<Yes, you must. Columbia is the jewel of South America>."

"<Yes, so they tell me. We might even go down there on this trip, from Panama>."

"<Ah... but that is not possible. The road doesn't go through>."

"<Yes, I know. But one could hike through the Gap, no? From the highway's end, and down to Turbo>."

"<Aha! Turbo. Well... no. There was a boy like you who tried a few years ago to hike down from Panama. A French boy. He made it halfway through before being discovered by a tribe of Indians who live in there. They found him lying unconscious, next to a stone into which he had carved his name and his date of birth. So you see, it's really not possible to get through>."

"<What did they do with him? The Indians who found him>."

"<Well, they took him to a hospital — saved his life>."

"<A hospital in Panama, or a hospital in Columbia>?"

"<Why... in Columbia. That's where they ran the story. That's how I know about it>."

"<Aha! So he *did* get through>."

"<Eh>?"

"<I said that he *did* get through, with a little help, from Panama to Columbia. So it is possible>."

"<Ha ha, well then, I suppose it is. But be careful in there, if you do decide to go through the jungle>," and here he gave me his card with his address in Bogota, and said that we would be welcome to stay with him if we made it down.

"<Thank you>," I said, taking the card, "<May that you go well>."[57]

"<Thank you, and thank you all, for your help. Go with God>."

*   *   *

The girls heard us coming and came out to receive our new arrivals with hospitality. Chavez and Trudy were brought into the fold, and then they sallied off to pitch their tent on the farr side of the field. When they had staked their claim and settled into their spot, they came back over with the first of two joints that they'd squirreled away from back at the beach. Nick and I were playing a song, and Marilyn was singing along. Finn was kind of testing out different pots from the kitchen.

Max found some olive oil and started frying the tortillas up into crispy chips, and he had Finn mashing the avocados up in a big white bowl. Nick and Trudy were mincing up the garlic, onions, cilantro, tomatoes, and whatever else Max had bought for his guacamole thing, and I started cooking up some beans on the stove and bringing a large pot of rice to boil.

Mackenzie came back in from collecting limes, and mentioned that there was a large cow lulling around behind the house, and Chavez and I took a break to grab a pail and run outside to try and milk the old heifer. (Not so much).

When aromas had saturated the house and things were close to ready, the two tables were joined together in the living room, and chairs

---

[57] <Que te vaya bien>.

enough were put all around, and we feasted in a merry fashion, with laughter and wine, in a scene that to me invoked a modern day drifter's image of the last supper. It was such a moment; it seemed like we all felt it.

Nick took out the guitar when Max and I started doing the dishes, and he played from an old songbook that had been discovered up there at the house. Waltzing Matilda, Home on the Range, Sloop John B., On Top of Old Smokey, Yellow Submarine, we sang together from around the room, with hands in the sink and Finn on the spoons.

That night, once again, I bedded down with Marilyn, and the amount of pashing noise that would have bled through the door was going to make it infinitely harder for me to convince anyone that she and I were just sleeping together as friends.

She woke me up in the morning with a hot coffee, and asked if I would come by to visit her class at the school. I sleepily consented as I sipped from the mug, and she slipped me a kiss before turning to go with a quick blast of morning light spilling into the room as she stepped out through the doorway. I laid back down and listened as she got onto her bike and went peddling off up the jungle path.

When next I woke, the smell of food drew me into the kitchen where I found the rest of the army already up and cooking eggs. Max had gone into town, and the lovers were finishing their breakfasts and fixing to go out for a walk. Finn passed me a coffee and Nick asked what kind of playlist I had in mind for that evening. We found a marker and penned up a tentative set-list as we sat eating toast, and I had the guitar out and was going back over the changes for 'Red Queen'.

A: "Hey, um, would you guys want to come up to the school with me in a little while and visit Marilyn's class?"

N: "Ha! Yeah right. That's your can of beans, buddy."

A: "Ah c'mon. Just to see the school and say hi to the kids... Apparently she's told them all about us. We'd be like the featured items for show-n-tell."

N: "Yeah right."

A: "...It'd be like a fly through. We could play them a song. Maybe fifteen minutes."

N: "No. I have to go into town to get a phone card. I've got to call the airport."

A: "Bitch."

N: "Don't call me bitch, bitch."

F: "Why do you want to see the school anyway?"

A: "Oh... I said that I would. I just really don't want to go over there by myself."

F: "Why not?"

A: "I don't know. Somehow, it would just be too... serious."

N: "Ha, you see? Here it goes. "Just friends" he says..."

A: "How about you Finn?"

F: "What, to the school?"

A: "Yeah. Come with me. I really need a wingman."

F: "Sure I'll come along."

We entered through the wooden gates and into the front yard of the school grounds. Marilyn spotted us through the louvered windows of her classroom and pitched her voice up as she turned to the kids, saying, "Oh my god, get ready, cause I have a feeling that a certain *someone* is about to get here."

She ran out to greet us, and then led us through the hallway and around into her classroom. I don't know what she would have told the kids, but they were all beside themselves to meet us, and she had them come forward one by one to introduce themselves and give us pictures that they had drawn up of who they had imagined us to be. Many of the drawings had my name scrawled across the bottom (mostly misspelled), and some of them included depictions of Marilyn as well. It was really embarrassing.

I whooped out my guitar and rattled off the first two 'general audience' songs that came to mind ("Puff the Magic Dragon," and "You Are My Sunshine"), and they watched with wide eyes, and then some sang along on the choruses. Finn set them to clapping on the second song, and then cast me a hope-that's-OK look, which cracked into a wide smile. The whole thing was very strange.

Once the guitar was back in its case, the speed of our departure became my highest priority, but we stood in front of the class and endured their rendition of a song called "Adios and Goodbye", through which Marilyn led and conducted. Then we made our move towards the door, and Marilyn thanked us for coming and dropped me a cheeky kiss. The kids went: "Wooooooo!" and I was probably blushing as I fled the classroom, thinking angrily to myself, "Who runs this bloody school anyway?" as I tried to recall if I had ever seen any of my teachers from school behave in such a manner.

Finn caught up to me at the front gate, and then turned to wave to the kids who were still watching us through the louvres, as I all but jogged off down the lane.

Finn was ribbing me for a little while about the school episode as we walked together down the lane, and I was kind of laughing uncomfortably. Then he asked me:

"So are you looking forward to tonight?"

"Fuckin ay. I think it should be a good time. Do you want to sit in with us?"

"I haven't got a drum, or else I would."

"Well if you figure something out, you're certainly welcome to join."

"...Let me ask you something"

"Shoot."

"When you guys leave here, where are you headed?"

"Well, Nick's got his flight back home in a couple of days."

"Yeah."

"And Max is gonna be flying out as well. And
I expect that Chavez'll probably follow Trudy
home. She got a round trip ticket."

"Yeah, but you're going down to Panama
right?"

"Yup."

"And you're going to catch a boat?"

"Yeah, if I can."

"Is that something that can be done, I mean,
have you ever tried to hitch a boat before?"

"Once. I got a ride across the English
Channel once. Justin and I were playing in
Dunkirk, in France. And we were due to catch the
ferry to England the next day. Justin was the
drummer in my band in San Francisco, you know?
Anyway, we finished playing the third place that
we played that night, and we were hanging out
with these two girls who were both named
Virginia. They were kind of older than us. Like
32. The Virginia girl that I was with was
literally dancing up on the bar in the place
where we were at, kicking over glasses and
breaking things and that, and they wanted for us
to come along with them to some discotheque, but
by that time, we knew what it would be like,
walking into some place like that with our packs
on, and not having anywhere to put them, so we
decided instead to say goodbye to the girls and
walk out of town to camp on the beach. Well it
was about a two-mile walk to the beach, and
halfway along, we had to wait for this bridge
that had opened up, and the sirens were going
off. One of those swivel bridges, you know?

"Yeah. I know those."

"Well this was like two o'clock in the morning, and we were pretty drunk, and we had just finished smoking our last joint. So I decide to climb up over the barrier to see what the hell we were waiting for, and just there off to the left, coming out of the marina, is this little yacht, and I can see it bright and clear 'cause it's a full moon, so I climb up over the thing and stand out on the edge of the pier and put my thumb out. Well, sure enough, as the boat comes by, this guy laughs out from where he's at, at the helm, and in this thick English accent, he yells out, "*Right* then, where are ya goin?" And I go, "England!" And he says, "*Right* then, well you'll have to stay up all night," which was no problem for us, and then he asks, "You haven't got any drugs on you, have you?" and I was like, "Ahh... no!" So he pulls over and we load aboard, and we sail with him across the English Channel under the full moon, and he said that it was the best wind that he'd had in his three-week trip. Jim John was his name, or John Jim. Anyway... so I know, at least, that it's not impossible to get a boat."

"And that's the basis on which you're gonna cross the Pacific?"

"Well, yes, in that... I expect that it can be done. I'll just have to wait and get down there to see. Someone told me that this is the big season now. March and April."

"And what if you don't get a ride?"

"Well, then I'm thinking I might try to hike the Gap and down to Colombia. I've been trying to hitchhike the whole of the Pan American Highway, you know? And the only stretch of it that I've got left is from here to Quito. Either way, I'm gonna keep going."

"Well, that's the thing that I wanted to ask you... is that I want to keep going too. And the flight that I've got back isn't for another month. And I really just don't want to go home. I was wondering if I could come along with you. I've got this time, and I don't really have any plans."

"Well, I'll tell you what I told Chavez and the others: If the boat thing works out for me, then I want to cross the ocean alone. But up until then," and here I stopped him in the middle of the road, "I'd be glad to travel together and have you along, and if the Darien Gap is what happens, then I'd sure like to have some company for that mission too, but if it's across the ocean, I'm going to go alone."

Finn smiled, "Sweet. Agreed. So, to Panama."

"Yes," we shook hands, "To Panama."

CHAPTER 45
The Jungle Boogie Café

We found an ancient bottle of apple schnapps under the sink and had a shot with the girls before all together heading into town. Finn carried a cardboard box for me. We walked spread out, morphing between two and three different groups, and chatting all along the way.

Mariana welcomed us when we arrived and I

hovered with her in the doorway, introducing each one of our clan members as they came walking through. She told us that she was expecting a good turnout, and Nick and I excused ourselves to make our space and stow our things.

When we had tuned up, we came back over to the counter where Max was leaning in towards Mariana, and asking her about her opinion of Hugo Chavez. He was also folding a Quaker pamphlet into an origami bird (which he would be sure to present to her upon completion)[58].

Nick and I surveyed the menu, and decided it best that we ask Mariana to select our fare. The result was a tremendous Caribbean-style feed for the two of us, and various plates of tapas and finger food for the rest of our crowd. We sat together at the Viking table, consuming our feasts as the others mingled about the room. Max found a shelf in the back that was piled high with board games, and when he came back out to the big table, he had a flat purple box in his hands.

"Hey you guys! How about a game of Scrabble?"

My mouth was too full to shut the idea down in time, before a handful of others had consented to play. I sopped up the juices on my plate with a fresh tear from the loaf, before allowing myself to be drawn over to the counter, in towards the fulcrum.

"<Thank you very much for an excellent

---

[58] This is one of Max's MoJo things: Origami. He can make all sorts of things, right up to a three-headed dragon. There was one time, and a girl, a while back in Bulgaria, that he and I both competed for, and as I serenaded her with song, Max madly folded paper animals, delivering them to her with wistful phrases of poetry. (Max has a near-photographic memory for verse).

dinner. It was well enjoyed by all>."

"<Ah. Desert is yet to come>."

"<Oh, not for me>."

"<Ah, no>?"

"<Thanks, but I'm full up>," I said, rubbing my belly and lighting up a smoke.

She put her dishcloth down and leaned onto the bar with her elbow, "<...So where did you learn Spanish, because you don't sound like you learned it around here>," she yarned.

"<Oh my family lived in the Dominican Republic when I was young, and then later I studied in Chile>..."

"<Ah! That's why. I knew I recognized it. My sister now lives in the Dominican Republic, in Samana. Do you know it>?"

"<Samana? Yes. Very nice. We lived outside of Puerto Plata>."

"<Ah yes, Puerto Plata. And what were you studying in Chile>?"

"<Well, studying is a strong word for it. It was in '97 when all the universities got taken over by the students...>"

"<Ah yes. The national paro. I remember it in the news>."

"<Yeah so, we didn't have very many classes, but I was *down* there to study music and art, but mostly we just got teargassed>."

"<Music and art>!"

"<Yes>."

"<These are two of my greatest obsessions>."

"Would you like to come away with me this instant, and we'll be married and breed like savages?"

I didn't say that.

"I would like to fuck you right here and now up on this counter, but there's a girl sitting over there with whom I've already cast my local tryst."

I didn't say that either.

"<So, when before, you mentioned that you might sing with us... will you do us the honour>?"

She gave a wide smile, and bowed her face before answering, "<When you guys take a break, if you will lend me your guitar, I will sing you a song>."

"AhHa! Seven letters!" exclaimed Max from behind me, rising to his feet.

"That's not even a word," murmured Finn.

"It *is* a word! It's a synonym for buccaneer. First word, seven letters! Have you ever seen that?"

"I think it *is* a word," put in Mackenzie, sounding impressed.

"No hold on, we'll look it up."

"Hey Aude!" yelled Max, "First word of the game, seven letters! Have you ever seen that?"

As he turned to verify Mariana's comprehension of this scrabbular feat, I got out of my seat and went over and have a look at the board on the table.

CORSAIR.

Nick was lighting up a smoke, and the last of the dishes were being cleared away from the table. People had been drifting in, and by now all of the tables were occupied.

"Well. What do you reckon, like five or ten?"

"Yeah, let me just have this smoke, and then I'm good to go."

"OK. The owner woman is going to play a song when we take a break."

"Cool. That'll be cool."

Playing a bar can be a bit of a chore, and more often than not, people really don't give a lick about your music and you have to spend your whole time trying to trick them into listening, and then trying to hold them until they hear. But every now and then, you get a series of circumstances that create for a situation in which people have come to listen, and are trying to hear — as if they'd bought tickets. This was the incredible feeling that we got when our first song brought the whole room to silence. And it stayed that way, with everyone listening to the words of each song. I could have played like that forever. I would have paid to have played.

When the time came to take a break, I gave a big introduction to Mariana, and roused a loud and encouraging bout of clapter from the crowd.

And though protocol would have had me do the rounds right then with the CDs, I squatted down to listen to her indescribably sweet rendition of some Cuban folk song about the life and death of a tree, as it paralleled the life and death of a young girl who becomes an old woman. Her voice was beautiful and plaintive, hopeful but fatal. She sang with her eyes closed. Max's jaw hung open. The applause was ginormous.

By the end of our second set, my voice was starting to give out, but when we got through the last song and made our way towards the bar, we got cheered back over to our kill-zone to perform an encore. I sold eight CDs.

Afterwards, we packed away our things and resumed our guise as anonymous drinkers. Mariana came up and singled us out to one of the bar maids, instructing that our drinks were never to go empty. I translated this comment for Nick, and he was delighted by the imagery and immediately switched to bourbon.

I sat down across the table from Marilyn, who I knew had been wanting to talk to me all night. We went over the gig and some trivial stuff before the conversation turned back to the past, and before long, we were talking about Laker.

"I really don't know what you guys saw that day, and he tells me that he can't explain it, even though I feel that I could certainly imagine... but anyway, whatever happened, it really seems to have fucked him up! He's off on all these strange trips, and barely keeps in touch with anyone. I don't know. I called his place in Minnesota a few months ago, and his mother started asking *me* questions about how he's doing. *She's* asking *me*. And I just wish that he'd stay in close touch with me, because I care about him, and I want to know what's going on. And like *now*... I'd *love* to tell him that you're here, and how *great* everything is, and to be able to *share* these things with him."

"I'm not so sure about how anxious he would be to find out all that's been shared," I said, pinning the tail on the donkey.

"No Audacy, he loves you."

"That's not the point Marilyn. Guys are funny like this, and I know it's been a long time since then, but I'm not sure that..."

"Are you kidding me?" she interrupted, "Laker has had his chance. And he left. And he's still gone. And it's not like I'm going to keep either of you from doing it."

There was a long silence, and I was making ring designs on the table with my beer bottle. Suddenly Marilyn started laughing as if she had just remembered something funny, but then quickly resumed a serious demeanor.

"So what about you? Tell me what *you're* looking for," she asked, "Tell me what you're off to find, and what you're *really* looking for." Her tone had changed, and she smiled at me like a buddy who was asking me to confide some secret.

These radical changes in her manner no longer took me for such a spin, and I was willing to adjust the conversation in accordance to her whim.

"Well. I won't shit you Marilyn. It's not

what I'm looking for, it's a *who*. Same as before, and same as always."

"Audacy's looking for a girl," she sighed, exasperated.

"What, that's so wrong?"

"No, its not that it's wrong, it's just that you sound exactly like Laker. Laker's looking for a home. That's what he always says: 'I'm just looking for a home.'"

"That's what he says? Well... maybe it's the same thing..."

"Yeah. But what if Laker never finds a home, and Audacy never finds a girl?"

I slowly echoed this possibility out loud, and then admitted that I didn't know.

"Oh well," she said quickly, "It's not like you won't find her, with all of the places that you're going. I suppose everyone can end up finding anything if they really look hard enough."

I raised my glass to her, "May that it be so."

And she raised her glass to mine, with her terrific giggle, and the two of us made plans to marry at the age of thirty-five.

Max was seated over at the bar, storytelling with Mariana. He would have been very pleased with himself because he had her bubbling and laughing out loud. He shot me a wink when he caught me looking over.

The atmosphere started to cool off, and I stepped over to touch base with Chavez and his girlfriend who were seated with Finn at the Viking table. Those two were ready and I exchanged a nod with Nick, and then he and I went into the back to get our stuff. Mariana strode over to tell me that she had moved my guitar into the back hallway, and as she showed me into the narrow corridor, she turned me with a grab to the arm. I could see that she was a little bit drunk.

"<You guys have good friends Audosi. And Nicolas, I was enchanted to hear him play. And your other friend, Maximo>…" and here she was laughing with her hand still on my arm.

"<Maximo is a good friend>," I chuckled, "<He can be very entertaining>."

"<That's it, That's it>..." she said laughing, her eyes cast up and over as if she were apparently trying to remember something more about Maximo.

"<Well, I want to thank you for tonight>," and here I took her hand and we shared a kiss to the cheek.

"<The pleasure has been mine>," she smiled warmly, "<You are most welcome>."

I stood for a moment, transfixed by her openness, before I began to feel the others waiting for me, thinking things.

I stooped down to grab up my case, and as I did so, my eye wandered over the board games that were stacked on the shelf. ...RISK(!) Mariana said that we could take it with us as long as we brought it back, and as we disjointedly departed,

I received a second electric kiss to the cheek.

We positively danced back to the place. With our huge pack, it didn't take a second. We probably glided. Back at the house, the bigger of the two tables was cleared off, and the map of the world was unfolded before us.

I was black (THE BLACK PLAGUE!), and the girls played with us for the first game, but not the second. The second game didn't start until just before sunrise, and by the time we were attacking each other with 70+ armies, the girls were getting up to do morning things and wondering if we had gone stark raving mad.

"Kamchakta will hold, goddamnit! Kamchakta will hold! Come on mama sixes!"

CHAPTER CHAVEZ

The boys stayed at the beach for another few days after I got back, and then they headed up to Monteverde. But right before they left, Max Fortes had showed up, like magically, along with Ingrid, who was the bitch whose surfboard Audacy had broke, and the other girl. Max showed up on the beach and met back up with us, and told us a big lie about hitching all the way down. I mean... I'm not sure, but I'm pretty sure that he took a bus.

So the boys decided to head up to Monteverde because they apparently knew somebody who was living up there, and I stayed on the beach for a few more days with Trudy, and then she and I hitched up. It took us a day to hitch from Mal

Pais to Monteverde, and when we arrived we set up camp near the girls' house.

We stayed up late and got real drunk all of the nights that we were there. We played Risk, and there's some debate as to who actually won. We were there for like three or four nights, and the boys played at the Jungle Boogie, with some beautiful bartender/owner, and it was just a really fun night. It was a fucking crazy-fun night.

CHAPTER 47
The Cloud Forest

Later on in the morning, I opened my eyes to find myself being straddled by Marilyn. She was looking down and making funny faces at me.

"What time is it?"

"It's time for you to get up."

"Ohh. One more sleep," I groaned, trying to roll over.

"No. I've got the day off and I want to show you guys this one place. The boys are up. Chavez has got a coffee for you. So get up, ...you all-night Risk-playing fool.

Coffees were drained and hiking boots were laced, and aside from Mackenzie, who apparently had to work on Saturdays, the whole group of us started back in towards town.

The others went into the store to buy ice

cream sandwiches while Max and I walked up the hill to return the board game.

"I think I'm in love," he said to me on the way.

"Who? Mackenzie or Mariana?

"*Mariana, man!*"

"Oh yeah?"

"I can't even begin. She said that I should *come by to see her house.*"

"Liar!"

"I'm serious."

"She said that?"

"Uh huh."

"In English or in Spanish?"

"In English."

"Come on!"

"Yeah," he said, with his eyebrows in hyperextension, and then more seriously, "Your bread's already being buttered. You gotta let me work my thing."

"Hey, I'm not gonna touch you on this one bud."

"Yeah well, as well you *can't*."

"Exactly. Otherwise, are you fucking kidding me?"

"Bulgaria reborn, right?"

"Yeah, forget it. This one is you."

"We'll see. You were never going to get that Bulgarian girl anyway."

"Yeah right. At least I didn't feel the need to go and propose to her!"

"Yeah, well."

Desafortunadamente[59], Mariana had not yet arrived. Max scrawled some love lines onto the lid of the board game before leaving it off with the girl at the counter, and then we headed back down to the store.

Ice cream sandwiches.

Marilyn gave us the grand tour as we went through town, explaining which buildings were which, and what they had used to be.

We crossed through the village and up away from the valley, past the tobacco gas station and up a dirt road. Finally, we turned off through some gates and down a path that led into the national forest. After five or ten minutes, we came to a little swimming hole that was fed by a tall waterfall. The water was cold, and Marilyn led us across the stream and up the steep bank on the other side. The trees were humungous, and many of them were covered with strangler figs.

Apparently the strangler figs grow up around these huge trees and eventually suffocate them. The inner tree rots and disintegrates, and the hard wood of the strangler lasts for many more years as an exoskeleton, so that the way you climb these trees is from the inside, and the one

---

[59] <Unfortunately>

that Marilyn led us to, near the top end of the
bank, had a ribbed interior that went up and up,
and we climbed through in single file, watching
each other's bums squirm on ahead.

Coming out onto the topside, it was
spectacular.

Do you know those plants that grow out of a
stick, and that hardly need any water at all? The
ones that you just squirt with a spray bottle
every now and then, and that somebody probably
tried to sell your parents once at a home-show?
Well, those kinds of plants were growing
everywhere, together with furry mosses and
Tarzan-vines, and the whole scene was high up in
the canopy of the jungle, overlooking the
waterfall that we'd passed below.

Marilyn had her arms up and was reciting
poetry about spacial infinity.

Looking upwards through a tree
Vision filled with sky and limbs
Our craning heads
Follow vertical trunks into the
Pale Blue Emptiness.

The branches splayed against the sky
Spin us into unmarked time,
Where progress ceases to exist.

From the ground, the tree, the sky
Tip us into vertiginous states
Where the sense of limit finds no trace.
Francesca Valentine

Chavez brought out the second of the two
joints, and we sat talking for a long while, the
boys daring each other to fire-pole it down one
of the vines. Marilyn talked about her kids,

Trudy talked about back home, Finn talked about buying property, Max talked about New York City, and I was thinking about God. Chavez was quietly perving on Trudy, and Nick was squatting against a wooden backrest, sporadically whistling between his teeth and just spacing out on everything.

*   *   *

There is a hypothetical philosophy over which I like to contemplate.

The idea is this: **God as a movie-watcher**; as a Siskel and Ebert movie-watching Buddha, and he doesn't get to watch your movie until the moment you die. So he's not there meddling with your things and casting judgment down upon you the whole time. He just awaits your inevitable demise, and then receives your video through the intergalactic mail and loads it into his player.

It's not an ordinary video, and His senses aren't reduced to the ordinary medium. He can feel and smell and everything just as you've experienced it all the way through life. And the viewer of course is not an ordinary person, he's God, so it doesn't take him a lifetime to watch yours. He can watch the whole thing in just seconds. But the important thing is what happens once he's finished viewing your movie, for there are only two outcomes that can result from one's life as a whole: Either to be ejected from the player and placed into his private collection (perhaps to be viewed again at some later time, *at God's leisure*), or to be chucked out in the atomic disposal, which is a gaping black hole that immediately causes for the equivalent of your never having existed at all.

So the idea in life, according to this line

of thinking, is that one's primary objective as the director of their movie is to make it into The Collection come hell or high water. This thought must be taken into account upon regulating the continual interestingness of one's own life, for treading cautious roads may run the risk of boring the viewer divine.

Did you have a good world when you died?
Enough to base a movie on?
Jim Morrison

Now as farr as the control that you wield over the way that your life is going to go, it is both limited and infinite, because you, as the director, only have one choice. And it's a continual one. YES or NO if you like. SPEAK or DON'T SPEAK maybe, or ACTION or INACTION. Some would consider this decision to be binary - 0 or 1. And the decision is being made by each person perhaps a hundred times per second during every waking hour. (Is it any wonder that the universe is expanding?). And any given combination of this ongoing decision-making could lead you to where you may most want to be, or straight to the worst. You choose through your choices, and this is what you have control over.

Now as for the other thing, the thing over which you have no control, people usually call it fate. (Bear with me Reader). If you can relate this diatribe to playing poker: you play your cards with your decisions and your control, but the cards that you are dealt: well that's fate. But having lost some money at cards, I can tell you that it usually isn't fate that decides the winners and losers of the game; it's the decisions that you make, and the way that you play your cards. Even Kenny Rogers knew this.

So what stands between you and everything
that you could ever want, is merely a combination
of decisions, maybe 1010110111010000101010101...,
or maybe 0010000011101010010101010..., and your
measure for action in response to what's thrown
at you by the world is calibrated through good
judgment, as derived from experience.

So don't pretend that you don't have control,
'cause you have just as much control as anyone
ever does, or as anyone ever did.

And don't bore God, 'cause God'll just chuck
you out.

*   *   *

When the aspect of the daylight had changed,
we squirmed back down through the hollow tree and
descended to the stream. Chavez and Trudy stayed
back up there, and I think that they were working
themselves up to having a fuck. Marilyn and I
braved the icy water and dunked ourselves into
the deepest pool, and Finn was laughing and
whistling up towards the canopy as we headed back
up the path.

We crossed back through town and Max ran off
to make a telephone call. The lovebirds caught up
with us at the bridge, looking flushed and a
little bit embarrassed, but Chavez wore a grin
with a crease that only grew deeper with each
insinuation.

When we got up to the house, Mackenzie had
made up a big pot of macaroni which we spooned
into bowls and devoured with very little
ceremony.

"OK. We've got a problem," said Marilyn,

coming back from the cupboard, "This is the second to last bottle of wine."

A: "Oy shit."

M: "That was stupid. We just came through town."

C: "Do you think the store's still open?"

Mknz: "Maybe. But maybe not."

F: "I kinda doubt it would be."

M: "I think that something's probably still open."

N: "I'll bet that our Cuban friend would hook us up with a bottle from the café, if everything else was closed."

A: "*Now* you're talking Nick."

C: "Ok... Not it!"

N: "Yeah, not it. Ha."

A: "Hold on. Let's take a collection, and then we can draw straws or something."

N: "No fuck it. I'll go."

A: "Yeah?"

N: "Sure, I'll go. Finn, are you gonna come with me?"

F: "Sure. Let's do it."

N: "Alright. Me and Finn'r goin. You boys just cough up some dough."

So those two set off into town and the rest

of us sat out on the lawn, sipping wine from our little clay cups. We sat in pairs and played twenty questions, and then a sit-down version of charades.

At least two hours went by.

Finally, for some reason, we were playing 'what-kitchen-appliance-am-I?' when all of the sudden, someone heard a noise from up in the forest. It was the tune from "Bridge on the River Quai" being whistled amidst much intermittent laughter, and growing more distinct as it came closer, until at last the boys came stumbling out of the jungle. They were passing the bottle back and forth and it looked like there was only about three fingers left.

"Well so much for that," said Max, turning back into the circle.

"Hell of a booze run boys," Chavez put in, laughing.

"Yeah, I can't believe we fuckin made it!" shouted Nick, and he and Finn both bent over and started laughing uncontrollably.

CHAPTER NICK

Finn and I had a ride with a guy who was about 25 or 30, truck driver, nice guy. He told us that there were 19 kids in his family, and that every time the power went out in Costa Rica, his parents would have sex, and that's how he explained it.

And we took the ferry, and there were guys

who played 'La Bamba' and 'Jamaica Farewell'
with a washtub bass and a banjo. And when we got
to the other side, I was hitching with Finn and
we saw a guy who had just crashed his
motorcycle, walking around all dazed, and he was
all fucked up. His arm was halfway hanging off
and he was just out of it. Blood. And that was
about twenty feet before the town of Monteverde.

Monteverde was cool. It reminded me of
Vermont: the smells, the look. And we played the
Jungle Boogie Café and went to that very cool
banyan tree that we climbed up, and the big
field that we hung out in for a while, and we
played an epic game of Risk, and I'm not sure
who was the winner, but it went way past dawn.

We put a centipede, a tarantula, and a
scorpion in a bowl, and the centipede won. Finn
and I went into town to get supplies, and we
drank the whole bottle of rum on the way back,
and I puked. And then the next morning, we left
Monteverde.

CHAPTER FINN

F: When we left Mal Pais, all four of us went
to the corner, and I didn't even know what was
going on at the time. I didn't even know we were
hitchin. But we ended up splitting up, me and
Nick, and Audacy and Max, cause there was
definitely like, *whatever* going on.

Those guys hitched off first and they got out
of there, and me and Nick got picked up in a
bread truck, and we did all of the bread
deliveries with him, and then he brought us over

to the ferry.

We got to the bottom of the road that goes up to Monteverde, and it took us forever to walk up. Audacy and Max were ahead of us, and me and Nick called them from town, and they walked down to meet us, and took us back to her place. She had a roommate, and somehow Max Forte knew her, and he was really trying it with her, but she was not taking. Her name was something that sounded like a female detective.

We were there for a week maybe. And the Jungle Boogie Café, and the enchanted forest, and the puppies, and the tree that we climbed up inside of, that Chavez had sex in. Ha! And I remember when Max found out that I was going to continue down to Panama with Audacy, and he got all pissy and took me aside to start saying how it was Audacy's trip and everything, and that I shouldn't tag along or whatever, as if I needed his approval. And then we played Risk there all night. We played two games that night. Audacy thinks he won that final game, but the game ended in a draw, and he said that he would've won 'cause he had a set of cards to get the extra armies, but Nick told me that he saw Audacy's cards and that he didn't have the match, and I had the match on the next one, so if he had missed his match, I was guaranteed to have the win...

A: (I did have the match.)[60]

---

[60] Nick is a shit-disturber.

CHAPTER 50
Pass through each other

Later on, Marilyn and I laid together in the candlelight, sweating on the bed. She began talking to me in the most lucid voice with which I had ever known her to speak. Gone was her hippie sprightliness and her ditsy manner, and I realized that the whole thing had always been somewhat of a guise. She spoke to me now in a low voice, sober and serious, and I came to realize that I had underestimated the grounded intelligence of this girl.

"I feel so good right now. Just lying here. Not thinking, but just feeling what's going on. You know what I mean?"

"Yes."

"Isn't it such a simple and easy feeling to just feel good?"

"Yes."

"And the way that it's been with you here, as though it could have been like this all along, and that we'd still be here right now, and that it wouldn't have made any difference."

"I know what you mean."

"...But we all have our things, don't we? And we pass through each other on our ways towards our things, and along our lines, like so many strands of some great web."

"Some great web, in which each person is a strand."

"Right. And they touch and go, and move around in different ways. Sometimes together, but then shooting off to make new connections, and the beauty of the web if it could be looked upon as a whole."

"So you reckon the web is getting woven, it's not something that gets unravelled?"

"No. Woven I should think, if we're the ones doing the weaving. Or else it would have already been there before. Unravelled maybe in rewind, as a destiny, as looking back."

"So destiny as a future: not so much?"

"I don't know. You are what you eat, right?"

"Um, yeah."

"Well, you hear of people fulfilling their destinies, but you never hear of someone who didn't. Maybe it didn't exist until they did it, until they fulfil their thing."

"Yeah, maybe not... OK wait. Now I'm thinking about what you said before, about the web. Imagine this. Imagine that you took that Risk board from the other night and stuck it into the bottom of a glass aquarium. And then each one of us took the end of a coloured piece of thread (all different colours, you know?), and put the end of our threads onto the map in the place where we're at now, here in Costa Rica. So then you start like a super-glue drip into the aquarium... some sort of glue that you can see through perfectly. And as each one of us continue to move around the world, our threads would trace our tracks, and would rise up off the board over time with the dripping glue. So that when any of us came back together, you could see it in the clear cube..."

"Oh my god. And all of our threads would dance around together and then separately, with all of the near misses and different colours, creating this huge design that went up and up..."

"...Until the day we died."

"Oh, it would be beautiful."

We both sat there and imagined this sculpture for a moment, and then I turned over and propped myself up on an elbow: "I'm glad I know you Marilyn. I feel like we haven't spoken enough like this."

"It's always me speaking," she said, backlit by the flickering candle, "Just different sometimes."

"Yeah."

We laid there in silence for a while. My eyes became unfocussed.

"What are you thinking?" she asked.

"Oh, I was just thinking about tomorrow."

"You guys are definitely leaving tomorrow?"

"Yeah."

"Well I think those guys are a great bunch. And I think that it's great what you're doing."

"Well they all like you a lot. I haven't even thanked you for having us all up here. It's such a place."

"Oh, just shut up?"

"What?"

"I said to shut up."

"Why?"

"Come here and I'll tell you why."

CHAPTER 51
A brief puppy

In the morning, there were puppies at the house. Marilyn and Mackenzie had gotten up early to take a walk, and they had seen a litter of puppies get dumped into a ditch by an out-of-town pickup truck. The bad luck of it was that on their way back home they bumped into their landlord who immediately ruled that the puppies could not be kept at the house. The girls protested, but the landlord was insistent, saying that he would give the girls two days get rid of them, but then that he would come down and drown the dogs himself. The girls were beside themselves with compassion, and were ooing and ahing as they chased the pups around outside in the yard.

Meanwhile, we were inside drinking coffees around the map that we had spread out on the kitchen floor. Nick's flight was due to leave from San Jose in 36 hours time, and the idea was that we would see him in to as close as we could get to the airport, without actually going into the city. So a small suburb on the western outskirts of the capital was selected as our 'primary', and pairs were selected. The lovers would obviously go together, I was with Nick, and Finn was with Max. It was decided that we would meet at the gas-station beginning with the lowest letter in the alphabet, or at the bar or café closest to there.

By this time, the girls had worked themselves into hysteria, and Marilyn appealed to us to take at least one of the four pups with us. I talked it over with Nick, and we consented on the basis that we would give the puppy away to one of our rides. We told the girls to choose the puppy that would be the hardest to get rid of, and they gave us the jet-black runt of the litter.

We had packed our things and Nick was playing guitar. I was drinking a coffee with Marilyn on the porch, and Chavez and Trudy were just back from another walk. We were mostly just waiting on Max who seemed a bit shaggy this morning and was pondering around for his sleeping bag case.

Eventually all of our shit was outside and we did a sweep before loading up. The girls led us along a different path behind the house, and we went up to visit the uncle who had seen us play at the Jungle Boogie, and who we'd promised to visit before leaving town. They were a Costa Rican family, and Uncle smoked a joint with us as his sister-in-law served tea. She and the kids doted over the puppy until Marilyn finally made them agree to adopt one of the other dogs. Speaking for the boys, our minds were pretty much already on the road, and we kept the visit short.

When we left their house, the girls accompanied us through the woods, and along to where our two paths split. We mingled there at the fork, with everyone doing their rounds like at the end of a soccer game.

She and I didn't kiss, but instead clasped both hands and touched our foreheads together.

"Goodbye darling."

Down the path our procession went, over the bridge and through the stream, past the store and past the café, heading back down towards the lowest corner of town. As we passed the butcher's, a call rang out and we turned to see Mariana running over.

"Asi que se van?"

"Yes, we're off."

She looked as gorgeous as ever as she stood in the sunshine, claiming to be hung over, asking about the puppy, and then telling Nick and me that we would always be welcome to play at her café. She smiled and gave each of us a kiss before pulling Max aside to the edge of earshot, and absolutely sinking one into him (!).

At this point, Chavez and Trudy were already at the corner, and started yelling as a truck was pulling off onto the side of the road for them. They ran up and exchanged a brief word with the driver, and then turning back to us, Chavez extended both hands into the air in a 409 double-breasted, I've got ride, highway 81 victory salute.

Nick and I were the next ones to get going, and our puppy ended up getting adopted by that very first ride.

CHAPTER MAX

So it was the night before we were going to leave Monteverde. I had met this girl a few nights before when Aude was playing music at the bar that she owned, and she and I were pretty much fated to have a love affair. Her name was Mariana, and she was from Cuba, absolutely gorgeous, flirtatious, powerful girl. She had told me during the day that she was going to be closing up her bar, and that I should come by and visit her at her place, but that I shouldn't come until the moon was high. That was the turn of phrase that she used, "until the moon is high" in her fatal Spanish accent. She was absolutely spellbinding. And she called me in my Spanish name; she would call me Maximo.

Now, some of the guys had gone into town and were supposed to be bringing back a lotta drinks for our entire gang, and I was going to go but I knew that she'd still be working, and that it was too early. They came back and they had gotten drunk, having imbibed the supplies as it were, and when things started to tone down a bit, I went up to see her.

She had a place across town on the plateaued section just beneath the cloud forest, and I knew how to get there because I had gone up a bit earlier to check it out.

She wasn't there when I first got there and I had a strange feeling of sneaking around, in a romance-mystery-novel sort of way, and my heart was beating, but she arrived and came up to me in the dark. And I'm not one to kiss and tell on this, but she was as passionate and determined as she was beautiful, and when she kind of pulled me in through her door, I realized that it was just gonna be like that.

She made me wait while she took a shower, and then she came out completely naked, and oh my God! She had this beautiful antique singer sewing machine in her room... she was like a nature goddess, very uninhibited, you know? And then after when we were going and just as I was about lose it, she pushed me in a place that I can't even tell you, like right here, and just dug in really hard, and I let out this cry and looked down and was having an orgasm all at the same time, but I didn't actually do anything. Nothing actually came. It was totally mystifying but she immediately took me onto the bed and we did it all over again. And again and again, and man! She was the most sexually knowledgeable woman that I've ever met in my entire life, and I'm not exactly a spring chicken when it comes to this sort of thing. And she was beautiful. When I wasn't in fear, I was in love, and I was in love with her for most of the night and early into the morning.

She had this scarlet duvet on her bed and candles all around the room, and she was cultivating herbs on her counter and she had this humungous aloe plant in the corner, and I don't usually smoke pot but I smoked some pot with her, and she was talking about Cuba and Che Guevara. She had lived in Venezuela and had been there during the riots that led up to the revolution, and she was telling me about the CIA's involvement and the corruption of the Venezuelan military, and we sat there ashing her little joint onto the incense holder that was on the windowsill. There was only one neighbor to the place, who was apparently an old deaf woman, so it was just perfect really.

I didn't get back over to the house until dawn. I went and got a couple of hours sleep before we left in the morning, and just before we hitchhiked away, I saw her again. She had come down into town to see me off before I left.

CHAPTER 53
Mundo de Culebras

The daylight was fading when our ride passed a Texaco on the outskirts of Grecia, and then a Shell station on the way in, but we stayed on, gambling these few miles on foot that there would have to be a lower-lettered gas station somewhere here in town. From the lights where our ride dropped us off, Nick and I could see another one two blocks further down. An ESSO station. We thanked our guy and made our way towards the illuminated sign.

Crossing the road, we spotted Trudy sitting on the curb with their two packs stacked up next to her, and Chavez was stepping out from the fluorescent interior of the store, unwrapping a candy bar. Trudy saw us first:

"Hey you guuuys!" she drawled in relieved excitement.

"Well, well, well," smiled Chavez, walking over.

"Hey, you guys are fast," I said, as Nick and I unshouldered our packs.

"It must be my girlish good looks," said Trudy.

"Yeah, or Chavez's," said Nick, and he and I started to snicker.

"No. As someone once said...", beamed Chavez, "It's just a simple matter of expertise," and here he smirked in delight.

"Yeah, yeah. How long've you guys been here for?"

"Only about twenty minutes," he said, "We came in with a truck full of chickens.

"Yeah hey," cried Trudy, "We passed you guys about an hour ago, but you were walking along and didn't see us."

"Oh yeah?"

"Hey wait a minute, I think I remember that truck," said Nick, stroking his cheek.

"Any sign of the boys?"

"Not yet."

"Is this definitely the lowest-lettered station in town?"

"I think so. I was trying to ask the guy inside, but he looked kind of confused. You might want to go in and ask again."

According to the attendant inside, besides the Esso and the two others that we had passed, there was only one other gas station in town, and he said that it had no name.

When I came back out, Nick and Chavez were

comparing distances to the two nearest places that were open. One was a bar and the other was more like a café. Trudy was recommending that we leave a note. I was looking off in both directions, trying to gauge the distances, so that I didn't even notice the VW Bug that had come rolling up, until it started honking. The door opened up onto the curb, and Max was smiling at us from the passenger seat, with his hand still across on the driver's horn. Finn was squished up into the back.

"I'm almost surprised that they haven't changed it to E-S-O in these Spanish-speaking countries."

"Yeah, and then they're slogan could be 'Eso Es'."

We didn't choose either of the nearest places, but instead headed along until we found a local-looking sandwich-making place, and we all ordered *bocadillas* to go. Chavez reminded me that it was Nick's birthday, and we all chipped in and then kept Nick's attention diverted while Chavez and Finn ran across the street to the liquor store.

Once we had the sandwiches packed away, we started off in the direction of the least amount of development. When we had cleared the streetlights, there was a series of dirt roads that ran uphill from the street, and dumping our packs down, Chavez and I each ran off up one of these lanes.

When I got back down to where they were, Chavez said: "Well it doesn't look too great, but I think I've got a place."

"Trust me," I intoned, "the perfect campsite is at the top of this road."

Mundo de Culebras was painted in blue on a sign to our right as we began our climb.

"Mondo de Kolebras," Nick read out loud, "Hey Audacy, what does Kolebra mean?"

"Um, I'm not sure," I answered, suppressing a smile.

Max spookified his voice: "Snake World, Nick. Audacy's leading us up to a campsite right above Snake World!"

"Yeah right Max," laughed Nick uncertainly.

The road petered out as it approached the crest of the hill, and we walked along rivets in the mud that had been left by bulldozers. We crashed through the brambles and then out into a clearing that overlooked the city of San Jose. The lights were all twinkling below us and the boys agreed that it was a good spot to pitch. I ducked off to find some wood as the rest of them erected the tents, and once the fire was crackling, I grabbed the guitar out of the case and started everyone in a grand chorus of Happy Birthday. As we sang, Finn and Chavez made a great display of presenting Nick with the bottle of Jim Beam that they had purchased in town.

"...Birthday, dear Nicholas, Happy Birthday to you."

"Whooooooo!"

"Happy Birthday Nick!"

"Here's looking at you boy!"

"...Thanks guys," he said with a genuine smile, before adding, "I suppose you want me to share it with you, ha ha ha!..."

CHAPTER NICK

We did go to one place on my last night, and it was my birthday. We went to a pool hall/sandwich shack, and got some sandwiches and ate them in the park, and Audacy and Chavez wrestled, and then we were walking out of town, looking for a spot, in a world of snakes, and we slept on top of the big hill which overlooks the valley. It was a cleared-off hill, waiting for a house. And I got a bottle of Jim for my birthday, and we drank Jim, and Audacy was the only person that I had ever seen pass out like that. He took a swig, gave me back the bottle, and BAM, inches from the fire. I woke him up and he went into the tent and tried to get in the sleeping bag with Max, and we heard Max yelling, "What the hell are you doing? This isn't your sleeping bag. Yours is over there, get in your own fucking sleeping bag!" And that was my last night in Costa Rica of hanging out with the guys. The final night was just by myself.

After we left there, I went down to the airport with Max, who was trying to book a flight to somewhere, and I had to catch my own flight. I couldn't wait to get on a plane and see what flying was about. I had never flown before. So I spent the night in the airport there, and they had about eight seats that were all uncomfortable, and I ended up sleeping underneath a stairway there, and thinking to myself: "Yes, I have the capacity to be a tramp." It seemed to come very naturally.

And then I got onto the plane, and it took less than 4 hours to fly back over all the way that we had come.

CHAPTER 55
Nick's departure

The brightness of the morning light up on that hill seemed extraordinary, and I suppressed my feeling of nausea as we struck camp and headed back down into town. We ate breakfast at a little place, and I drank about four pints of water.

Chavez and Trudy were telling us that they were going to spend the night there in the capital, and that they wanted to make a side trip to some place called Matapalo. Max had to stop into the airport to book his flight back to Arizona, so he was going to continue with Nick, and see him off.

The map came out, and Finn and I eyed the two possible routes down to Panama. Finn wanted to loop through the Osa peninsula, and he said that he was pretty sure that there was a ferry that ran from Puerto Jimenez and over to Golfito. If that were the case, it seemed that it would certainly provide us with a shortcut to the border.

Bring me the horizon.

So Puerto Jimenez was established as the grand rendezvous point, but it looked a bit farr off for me, Finn and Max to be able to reach in one day, so we chose a small town in the mountains named David, and decided to have another go at the gas station game.

From the breakfast place we all started out of town, following the little airplane signs that were posted here and there along the highway. We slugged along for about forty minutes before reaching the turnoff to the airport, where we dropped our bags and the conversation kind of slowed. This was it: the first break from our original four.

A: "Hey Max. If you can find any Drum in there at the Duty Free, would you pick me up a pack, and I'll pay you back?

M: "Yeah. Just one?

A: "Well no, like three. Or five if they're in one of those traveler packs."

M: "OK."

C: "Well Nick, my friend, this is it."

N: "Yeah, I guess it is."

F: "Are you getting nervous about taking a plane?"

N: "Not really. I'm actually kind of looking forward to it. I can't wait to see what *that*'ll be like," he said, pointing to a plane that had just taken off."

Nick started to say goodbye to each of us, and Chavez and Finn seemed very sad to see him go. For my part, I was quite proud of him. He was a different person from when he had started the trip. His smiling face was tanned and wind-blown, and he held his shoulders a bit looser.

"Are you glad you came?" I asked him.

"Yes. I'm glad I came. But you guys take care of yourselves, and I'll see you when you get back," he said, heaving his pack on.

"We will. Thanks for coming down with us Nick. It's been an absolute pleasure. You seem a bit older now."

"Ha!" he laughed as he turned away, "I am miles older now."

And that was the last thing that he said.

He and Max started drifting away towards the airport, and Finn yelled out against the wind: "See you in Vermont, Nick!"

And I don't know if Nick heard, but he didn't turn. Instead Max half-twisted around and gave us a wave.

CHAPTER 56
Flip-flops

Chavez and Trudy decided to hitch back into the city, and they crossed the road and set up on the opposite side from us. Finn and I pushed our stuff together beside the onramp and began attending to the airport traffic. It didn't take the lovers long to get a ride in a little Audi two-seater, and they were waving back to us as they pulled away.[61] Finn and I waited for another hour and then decided to start walking. We could see the next exit sign in the distance, and we started walking down to try our luck there. As we went, a bus pulled off onto the shoulder ahead of us, and when we came up, the driver opened the door.

"<Hey! Alright boys. Let's go>."

"<Hey bud. Thanks for stopping, but we're not travelling by bus. We travel purely by thumb[62]>."

"<Ah ha. But where are you guys trying to get to>?"

"<We're going south. We're just trying to get out of the city>."

"<No problem. Hop up. I'll take you as far as the factory>."

"<You're not going to charge us>?" I asked, stepping hesitantly up onto the first step of the empty bus.

"<Come on>," he said laughing, "<No charge>."

The bus dropped us off on the outskirts of San Jose, and we shortly caught our next ride with a high school English teacher named Gustavo. Our third ride was in the back of a P-up truck, and we agreed to lie down and out of sight as we drove. When that couple dropped us off, they became the second ride in a row to caution us about travelling through the stretch leading into the mountains.

---

[61] It's always easier to hitch into a city than it is to hitch out of one.
[62] "…viajamos a puro dedo."

"That's weird," said Finn after they'd gone, "I wouldn't have thought of this as being a dangerous place."

We were walking down the side of the highway, making for the shade of the next road sign. "Well, it's probably nothing," I said, "But we might as well be on our toes just in case. And stay in good touch with each other."

"What do you mean, 'in good touch?'"

"Well, in case we have to bail from one of our rides or something."

"Oh *right*. Do you want to have some sort of code word or something?"

"No, I just want you to be ready for anything that could happen."

"That's me. I'm ready. You just say the word."

I shot Finn a look of annoyance.

"What?" he asked, defensively.

"You're ready for anything?"

"Well, yeah."

I was on a bit of a mean streak, hung over and all:

"Then why don't you take off your fuckin' flip-flops and lace your fuckin' boots on, so you can kick and run and real-life stuff like that. And maybe while you're at it, you could get rid of that tie-dye T-shirt, and put on something, I don't know, solid colour or neutral."

"OK," he said, taken aback, "You just have to *tell* me these things, OK? Will you wait for me?" he asked, making a move to change his things right there by the side of the road.

"Yes," I said, feeling a bit guilty, "I'll wait."

*   *   *

We probably couldn't have chosen a smaller 'primary' destination than the town of David. It was high up in elevation, and the temperature dropped sharply. There was only one gas station, and just up the dirt lane was the one bar and restaurant.

It took us about half an hour to find the owner and organize a gig for the night. He was going to 'food and drink' us in exchange for a two-hour slot, and once we had shaken hands on that, he asked us where we intended to spend the night. "<We sleep wherever we want>," I declared, and Finn apparently understood this reply well enough to roll his eyes and become a little bit embarrassed. The man then mentioned that he may have a place. He showed us outside and down the sloping lawn, and then along the back of the building to a built-in shed that was kind of underneath the restaurant.

"<Well, if you like, you boys can sleep in here>."

"<Um, thank you. Perfect. Do you mind if we pitch our tent right inside>?"

"<As you like. The door doesn't lock from the inside, but you can leave your things in the kitchen if you want>."

"<Thank you>."

"<Will you eat before you play>?"

"<After — if it's the same to you. Otherwise, I may have to have a siesta>."

"<OK>," he chuckled, "<Then maybe in one hour>?"

"<Yes good. We'll just pitch our tent, and then we'll be back up>."

The gig went well, but I only sold three CDs (including the one to the owner).

His wife fed us afterwards at the corner table. I ordered tongue and Finn was grossed out and kept leaning across to touch the tastebuds on my steak. Finn ate a heaping portion of spaghetti bolognaise, and then the wife offered him a second bowl, which he went on to polish off.

We were pretty tired by the time we had finished dinner, and we thanked our hosts, pocketed our last beers and headed down to the shed.

Just outside of our little room, we sipped beer and smoked cigarettes for a while, talking about the bar and the one girl who Finn had decided was really hot.

"...Well you should've tried to give her a kiss," I said, teasing Finn for his 'woulda-couldas'.

"Yeah right! What I probably didn't know is that her husband or something was maybe right there with her."

"Maybe."

"Maybe he was that big guy who wanted your pin."

"Maybe, maybe not. You'll never know now."

"Oh c'mon man! What am I gonna go up to her and say? It's the *language* thing, man! *You* don't think so 'cause you just go up and say whatever you want. What am I gonna just go up to her and smile? And be like, 'Hey baby!'"

"She probably would'a liked that," I laughed.

"Yeah right."

"There's more to language than just words Finn. That girl may have had your number. Maybe she was just sitting there waiting and hoping that you would."

"Yeah right, maybe. It's not as easy as you think."

"It's whatever you make it bud."

When the beers were finished and we had spat our toothpaste water, we got into the tent and pulled the door shut, with the strap of my pack tied to the latch on the inside of the door.

After about a minute, I was already drifting off when Finn reached over and squeezed my arm, "There's somebody trying to get in," he said in an anxious whisper. I listened, and heard the pack shift on the gravel. I grabbed my knife out from under my clothes-stack pillow and got to my knees. Just then came a knocking on the door.

"Quien es?" I asked, in my deepest voice,

"Estamos durmiendo. Dejadnos tranquilo."

"Hey you guys! Are you in there? Let me in!"

And again the pack scraped along the gravel as Max continued to try to pull open the door.

* * *

In the morning we had coffees and ham sandwiches, and Max stepped on the tail of the family's black housecat as he was coming back from the bathroom. This made the youngest daughter start to cry.

Then we thanked our hosts and headed back down the lane to just the other side of the gas station, where we aligned our things and started hitching as a trio.

"Oh... by the way Aude, I got you some tobacco," said Max, stooping to rummage through his pack

"Swedish.[63]" (We'd been smoking Faros).

"Yeah, they didn't have any Drum, so I got you a pack of this." And from his FFT[64], he produced two thirds of a pack of some rollie tobacco called Lion.

"Oh, I think I've tried this before," I said, looking dryly into the pouch at the halfzware shag mix, "I'm actually not too keen on this stuff Max."

"No, it's not bad. I've had a few myself. Anyway, it's eight bucks when you get around to

---

[63] Sweet-ish.

[64] FFT = Farr Farr Top (compartment of one's backpack).

it."

"You paid *eight bucks* for this?"

"Well I got it for *you*!"

"Um yeah well, no thanks. I don't want it," I
said, passing the pouch back.

"What do you *mean* you don't want it? You
asked me to pick you up some tobacco, and I *did*.
I wouldn't have gotten it myself."

"Max, I asked you pick me up some Drum if
they had it. And instead you go and pay way too
much for some kind of tobacco that I don't even
want, and then you go and smoke almost half of it
yourself, and then you want me to pay eight bucks
for it because you wouldn't have bought it
yourself? Are you kidding me? I have to agree
with you on this one, because I wouldn't have
bought it either. And I still don't want to buy
it now. I *am* thankful to you that you tried, but
seriously, this was not the order."

"Yeah, you can't do that Max," added Finn,
shaking his head with a laugh.

"Oah, that's bullshit. That's just not right.
I don't even really want the stuff now."

"Well here, I'll take one... if you don't
mind," said Finn, and Max chucked him the pouch
in annoyance.

Meanwhile, I had been running over to the gas
station whenever a vehicle pulled in for fuel.
Finally, this tactic paid off and we got a ride
out of there with a young kid in a fast car, and
the boys squished into the back while I sat up
front and listened to many tales of how cool the

kid's older brother was. The kid was a bad
driver, and at one point he fumbled the car into
a skid that had us all bracing for a crash, but
he turned out to only be going a couple of
villages along, and he left us off on the near
side of the next town.

Halfway down the main drag, there was a
suspicious-looking van, loading up with people.
The driver told us to hop in if we were heading
south.

"<We're hitchhiking>," I told him.

"<Yeah hop in, we'll give you a ride>," he
said.

<No charge>?" I asked, and he scoffed and
waved us in as he turned around to get behind the
wheel.

So we loaded in with a random assortment of
school kids and old ladies, and it was lucky that
we had our map out, or else we would have missed
our turnoff. "<Whoa, whoa. This is us. This is us
here. Yes. Thank you very much for the ride>,"
and we were getting our stuff out of the van.

"<That'll be 12 colones>" the driver said.

"<What? No. I told you that we were
hitchhiking, and you offered us the ride...>"

"No. 12 colones. Tendran que pagar!"

"What? Does he want us to pay him?" asked
Finn.

"Yeah, he's a fucker. He thinks that he's
tricked us."

"Oh just pay him," said Max, digging into his pocket for some coins."

"NO! Don't pay this bastard. At least don't pay him in money... Shit!" I was frustrated by the driver's flip-flop, but he wasn't pulling away, and the other passengers were beginning to take interest in the hold up. My mind was reeling to come up with some sort of compromise. I reached down and shoved an arm into my pack to grab out a half-full, flask-sized bottle of whiskey that I had, squirreled away since El Salvador. The driver mumbled an obscenity as he took the bottle and wedged it in behind his seat. "Yeah same to you motherfucker." And then the guy looked over his shoulder and pulled away with a sneer.

"I don't get it. What's his problem? He took the fuckin' bottle didn't he?" asked Finn.

"Honestly Aude, I don't know what's wrong with you."

"Forget it. He changed his story. One mustn't reward the fuckers of this world. We're hitchhiking."

We heaved up our stuff and walked into the small town to grab some lunch before continuing down and planting ourselves at the end of the strip.

We were back on Highway 1 now.

After a pretty long wait, a passing big rig gives us the ol' thumbs up and flicks on his air-brakes. His name is Manuel, father-of-two, Catholic from El Salvador. The boys slide back into the sleeping compartment with the bags pushed up on both sides, and the guitar across their laps. Manuel says that he can take us all the way to our turnoff to Puerto Jimenez, and then he starts asking if I would play him some music. Jammed in as we were, it was difficult to keep a steady rhythm in the bouncing shock-absorber seat, but I sang "Viajero Perdido" and then the boys backed me up for "Sunshine Away" as we rolled down the highway, with the sunset washing through the cab and the boys framed in the vertical rearview mirror.

When the guitar was away, I asked Manuel how farr he was going.

"<This load, I am taking to Panama>," he said.

"<Oh. Panama>?"

"<Yes>."

"What? Is he going to Panama?"

"Yeah."

"<You have been to Panama>?"

"<No, but that's where were heading now. Well... not right now, but soon>."

"<You want to go to Panama? C'mon, I'll take you to Panama>.

It was a tempting offer, but the plot had become thicker than a mere destination, and by nightfall when we reached our turnoff, all three of us descended from the ride.

> **This trip is greater than I, and as such, its demands are also greater.**

There's a long dirt road that separates Puerto Jimenez from the highway, and we stationed ourselves where it steps down from pavement to sand. There wasn't much traffic, but as the darkness crept in, humungous trucks carrying forested logs began to pass by in the other direction. The tree trunks that they were transporting were so big that they would have had to have been cut from some serious old growth. And as we waited there, talking about the forest, a forth truck came along and bumped its way up onto the asphalt. It was carrying just one huge log.

"So how farr in is this place?" I asked.

"Oh, it's about a half hour drive," said Finn, "Forty minutes maybe."

"Well, there's no place to camp around here. Do you guys wanna start walking?"

"Sure."

"OK."

After a couple miles, our shadows were thrown onto the ground before us, and turning around, we squinted into the headlights of a black Mercedes that slowed to offer us a lift. The driver was an English-speaking business man who said that he was headed to his vacation home on the shore and that his wife and family were already there.

At one point he had to pull way off onto the side of the road to allow for one of these log-trucks to squeeze by in the opposite direction.

"That's the fifth one of those trucks that we've seen."

"Yes," he said, "It is a shame. The government tells us that the peninsula is not being logged, and they have said so many times, but the trucks haul them out at night, in the dark," and here he made the money-rubbing gesture with his right hand, "Everyone gets paid."

"So where are they cutting them from?" asked Finn, "Do the loggers own the property?"

"No. All of this is National Reserve Forest," he said, gesturing in a circle over his head, apparently indicating the entire peninsula.[65] "Do you see those signs?" He slowed the car to point out the little white signs that were tacked onto some of the trees. The picture was of a tree being felled, with a red circle and a diagonal slash through the middle like the Ghostbusters sign.

"So then how can they cut them down?" asked Finn in disbelief.

"How?" asked the man, taking the question literally.

Max reformulated: "So they just cut from the public forest, and then run these trees out as if they owned them?"

"Yes."

"The old cut and run," I put in.

"Well that's fucking not right," continued Finn. "*You* should do something about *that*, Max, instead of going back to Quebec to protest this

---

[65] If you take a look at a map of Central America, Costa Rica's Pacific coastline is summed up by a large peninsula to the north, and then a smaller, similarly-shaped peninsula to the south. The Osa peninsula is this smaller one.

shit."

"Now there's an idea Max," I said, turning to face the back, "How many of these trailers do you think would have to get blown before there'd be like international exposure all down on this thing?"

"What... and blow them up?"

"Yeah! You could use one of those old plunger exploders and just hit the trailer once the cab went past. No one would even have to get hurt. You'd have a price put on your head by the logging companies before your third hit. You'd be like the Conservation Bandit..."

"The Forest Avenger!" added Finn with a flourish.

"Activism come to life," I read from an imaginary headline, "...And the one man who gave a damn."

Finn was laughing, and even our ride started to chuckle.

"You guys don't realize," countered Max, "The Quebec thing is going to be really big."

The Mercedes dropped us off just above town, and the three of us walked down. I had asked our driver his advice on places that I might try to play, and the first bar that he had recommended was farr too sketchy: standing room only, everyone drunk, glass on the floor. We had a beer and I didn't even bother to ask.

We went next door and shared a pizza, and then headed down to the bungalow bar on the shore. I inquired after the owner and was told that he wasn't in, but that he was expected back within the hour. So the three of us settled onto the grass by the pier, and I stepped off to get some take-aways.

Later on I walked back up the slope and the son introduced me to his father. I propositioned him about having me play, using as leverage the fact that his son had imagined having heard of *Freewater* from California.

So a round of beers was offered and the boys ascended the slope and I pulled up a chair and delivered my best rendition of "Viajero Perdido", and then "Smile". I had the old guys at the bar tapping their feet and the owner came back over to talk to me.

"<Maybe Friday. Are you going to be around on Friday>?"

"<What day is today>?"

"<Wednesday>."

"<Yeah, I can play here on Friday. But we want to do it big, right? Always big. So maybe it's best if you buy one of my CDs now and start playing it behind the bar. Advertise the whole thing and that. And I won't ask any money, because I'm on vacation, but we would like our few drinks for free. There will be five of us>."[66]

"<Is the Spanish song on this CD>?"

"<Yes. Number six>."

"<OK. Agreed. Leave one of these with me.

---

[66] <...Seremos cinco>.

Jaime will pay you from the till. Jaime>!.."

So after a second beer, we walked down to the shore and across a bridge that led over to a small beach. We pitched the tent in the shadows there, and slept till sun.

CHAPTER 57
Looking Back

In the morning we were eating ice cream sandwiches and loitering around on the main drag. There was a bit of a craft market going on, and we strolled along and had a look around, and then Finn and I started hacking in the park with some kids and a couple of other gringos. Max read his book and did some origami as he watched over our stuff on the sidelines.

After lunch I went to ask about the ferry, and it turned out that Finn was right, and there was a ferry that departed twice a day for Golfito.

"So we were just talking," said Max, after I had told them about the ferry, "And I guess Finn knows someone who has a place where we can stay tonight. Those guys aren't going to get here until tomorrow, and I for one could certainly go for a shower."

"Yeah, that sounds cool. How farr away is that from here, Finn?"

"Not too far. It's kind of a pretty long walk, but maybe we could catch a ride."

There were cashew trees growing along the road as we started our walk from town, and Finn stopped to show us how you could eat the fruit that hung underneath where the nut grew. Then we got a lift in an old-school, narrow-bed P-up truck that wiped a few miles off of our journey in the same number of minutes, but we were walking for the last stretch, and this is when I starting questioning Finn on exactly who it was that we were going to stay with.

"This is the *guy*," he said.

"What guy?"

"The guy that I told you about. The guy who stole Jasmin."

"What? And we're going to go to his *house*?"

"Well, it's not really *his* house, but he lives there."

"And you think that we're gonna be welcome there?"

"Yeah, we'll be welcome. This guy fucking owes me."

"Geez Finn, this seems pretty strange."

"...he fucking *owes* me."

Max had apparently already understood all of this, and I tried to see whether he didn't think that this was a rather questionable idea, but he didn't meet my gaze and instead turned to ask Finn how much further the place was.

"That's it just over there."

At first only the thatched roof was visible,

but soon we could see that it was a big house, mostly all open on the inside, with blooming gardens all around. There was a gringo standing at the side of the house addressing an older black man, until turning to take the few steps out to meet us as we came down the driveway.

"Heeey! It's you! How's it going, man? I wasn't sure if I'd see you again."

"Yeah, well... These are my friends, Audacy and Max."

"How's it going guys?"

"Yeah, pretty good," I said, shaking his hand.

"Nice place you've got here," said Max.

"Yeah come on around to the back and check the view. This is Antonio. He does the garden."

We all said hi to Antonio.

We followed Cane around back as he was asking Finn some breezy questions, and trying to figure out what we were doing here.

"Well, we're just going to stay for the night," said Finn, "We've got to go back into town tomorrow to meet some other friends of ours, and Audacy's gonna play some music at the bar."

"Oh that sounds cool. One of my friends across the road has got a guitar. Maybe I should call him over. Have you guys had dinner yet? I was going to do some pasta..."

I started talking with Antonio, who was standing off to the side, sharpening knives with his machete, and I got him to sharpen mine up as well. Then Max and I took off with Finn down to this little stream that was cold as hell and full of dark sand and smooth black river rocks, and I waded around sifting for gold.

Back up at the house, Max took his shower in an outdoor bathroom that was up on stilts[67], and Finn swung in the hammock while Cane cooked us dinner.

Fast forward now to three hours later and Cane's father had come home drunk, and he had a bit of a passive aggressive row with his son. The neighbour with the guitar had also come over, and at this point, the six of us are seated around in a circle in the middle of the courtyard, and Cane has got a didgeridoo, and there's a bong set in the middle that's been going around for a while.

"So have you talked with Jasmin again, since she left?" asked Finn, seated to my left, and directly across the circle from Cane.

"Um, yeah..." replied Cane, avoiding Finn's glare, "I've talked to her a few times."

Finn dropped his chin and widened his smile, "And what'd she say?" he asked.

"Oh, you know..." began Cane, visibly becoming more uncomfortable, "She said it's still snowing up there, and she's working with her mom, and everything's pretty sweet. She's doing well."

"You fucker," Finn slowly chuckled. "And what'd she say about me?"

---

[67] The one that had the window through which Finn had spotted the obscenity.

"Um..."

"Finn can you pass me that bottle of wine?" I asked. He reached and passed the wine without glancing at me or at the bottle.

"What'd she say?" he repeated, pulling his chin in further.

"Um, she just said that she hoped that you were doing OK, and that she'd spoken with your mother and found out about the robbery, and just that she hoped you were OK, and that she sends along her best."

"Through you? Ha!" There was a moment of silence as something clicked over in Finn's mind, "Do you know how much I want to cross this circle right now and just fucking *kill* you? Just strangle you with my hands until you are *dead*?"

The neighbour who had been strumming his guitar now started playing more softly, and I felt obliged to murmur an "Easy, Finn," in light of the hospitality that we were receiving from the perpetrator. Very uneven playing field. Max was rolling a Lion, and he kept his eyes down at his paper as he kind of stammered a giggle over the awkwardness of the moment. The father was sort of semi-passed out, and either didn't know what was going on, or didn't care.

"Look man, I know how you must feel, but..."

"You have *no fucking idea*, so you just *shut your face* and take it..."

"Come on guys," I interrupted, with a hand on Finn's shoulder, "Girls are the plague of the universe. This is old news. What are we doing?

Have another drink."

"I don't want to drink from the same bottle
as this fucker!" said Finn.

"So then kill him. Kill him now, or else have
another drink. What the hell are you doing?"

Finn made a low growl and took the bottle. He
turned it up and took a long swig. Cane was quiet
and careful. He slowly leaned into the centre of
the circle to grab the bag and repack the bong.

"OK, let's play a song that we all know.
Finn, you gonna play the didge? Finn plays it
good. Cane, why don't you lend Finn your didge,
and we'll do a song..."

*   *   *

I still don't really know why we went to
visit Cane, but he was already gone when we woke
up in the morning, and it seemed that he had
managed to escape the encounter relatively
unscathed.

The three of us went down for a dip in the
stream, and when we came back up, Finn
methodically stripped all of the ripe fruit from
the trees in the garden. Then we started our long
and vehicularly-unassisted walk back into town.

There were three games of soccer happening in
the town centre when we got there, and Finn and I
wanted to play but Max didn't want to have to
look after the stuff, so we detoured over to the
bar and knocked on the back door to ask if we
could stow our stuff there until evening. Request
granted, we headed back over to the playing
fields all-hands-free, and Finn and I got into

one of the soccer games and played together on the same team.

When we went to take a break, I saw Chavez and Trudy over with Max by the park bench. Trudy was busy unpacking her bag and Chavez was doing handstand push-ups.

"Hi there strangers!" I yelled out as Finn and I walked over, "How long have you guys been here for?"

"Not long," smiled Chavez, sitting down to lace his boots on, "I was just coming out to join you."

"Hi there guys," said Trudy.

"Hi there skinny," I replied, as Finn was giving her a hug. "Well it's halftime I think. They're taking five anyway. If it doesn't go, we can probably join in on that game over there."

By late afternoon, we were playing hackisack again, and this time, the circle grew in size to the point of becoming cumbersome. The local kids hadn't played before, and they chided each other and found the whole thing to be absolutely hilarious. As our hack circle waxed and waned, Max lounged beside us, holding talks with a random and variant group of internationals.

"Altitude hack! Altitude hack!"

When the clock struck seven, we headed over past the bar and back down to the grassy bit beside the jetty. I went up and spoke with the owner, and he suggested that I ought to wait for more people and play a little later on.

Chavez and Trudy went off to find some food,

and I made a trip over to the ferry office to check the schedule that was posted to the door.

SABADO. Pto. Jimenez >>> Golfito: 06:00 & 18:00.

When I got back to our spot on the grass, there were styrofoam containers of hot Chinese food for everyone, and Chavez and Trudy started telling us about their rides and the things that they had seen in Matapalo. Then Max and I had them laughing with our account of Finn's outburst from the night before, and as our stories collided into the present, I mentioned to Finn that the next day's ferry was suppose to leave at 6:00 in the morning.

A: "...It's either that or we could take the one at six in the evening, but we'd be throwing the day's hitch away, and we'd probably end up having to camp over there somewhere around Golfito."

F: "Yeah, Golfito doesn't sound very nice from what I hear."

A: "Well, ideally we'd make Panama in one day from here, and get through and away from the border."

C: "How far is it to the border from the other side?"

A: "I think it's only like forty miles."

M: "Well you guys should take the morning one then."

F: "Yeah, we should probably take the morning one."

C: "Yeah right! Like you guys are gonna get up for the 6:00 ferry. Did you go and organize free beers for tonight?"

A: "Yeah, we all get our beers for free."

C: "Well then there's no way you guys are going to make the morning ferry."

A: "Yeah, you're probably right... Does anyone have an alarm? Max, do you have an alarm?"

M: "No, my clock hasn't been working."

A: "Well... I guess we could stay up all night."

F: "Yeah, fuck it. *I'll* stay up all night."

T: "Wooooo! Break 'em out boys."

A: "Well there it is. Bender. I guess we should go get some booze then, for afterwards when this is over."

F: "Yeah, probably."

C: "I'll come with you if you want. I know where there's a place."

So an hour later, we had provisioned for the long night ahead, and there was a good crowd starting to show up at the bar. We smoked the first half of the satchel that the owner's son had given us, and then left our spot by the pier and headed up the slope and into the bar.

Another hour and my chair is up on the bar and I'm stomping along as I sing "Viajero Perdido" for the second time, with drinkers leaning in against the rectangular bar from all around.

"La espanola!" they cry.

"<Ha! But I've already played that song twice tonight>."

"<We don't care>! They yell.

"<The Spanish song>!"

"<Play it again>!"

I sold four more CDs before the bar closed, and took the cellophane off of each one to magic mark them with personally tailored quips and audaciously messy signatures.

Afterwards, we bumbled out of there and made our move down across the bridge and back over to the shadowy beach.

The empty ferry dock was only 2oo yards away.

We started a fire and broke out our wares, and Chavez sat across from me in the sand, rolling up the rest of the pot, while Max was pitching the smaller tent behind an almond tree on the high side of the beach "just in case".

CHAPTER 58
The Break Down

A: "So Max, when did you book your ticket for?"

M: "Five days from now. It goes via Mexico City, and then straight to Phoenix."

A: "And the Quebec thing?"

M: "Yeah, I'm not sure if I'll take the bike up for that. I might fly."

F: "So wait... why is he going to Phoenix?"

C: "Max left his motorcycle in Arizona when we met up, down in Bisbee. Yeah, hey. Are you gonna stay with those girls again?"

M: "I don't know... Hey Aude, do you mind if I have sex with Morgan on my way back through?"

A: "Do you guys hear this? These are the things that he really says."

C: "Geez Max..."

M: "I'm just kidding. Ha ha. I'm just kidding."

A: "It's hilarious."

C: "What a bastard."

M: "No, I'm just kidding. Aude and I have this arrangement where we don't sleep with each other's girls. I wouldn't do that to him, and he doesn't sleep with any of mine. Isn't that right?"

F: "You guys have an arrangement?"

A: "I don't know. That's our arrangement, is it?"

M: "Well, yeah..."

A: "Cause that brunette that you were keeping in New York struck me as being a pretty fit bird. And keen too. She wouldn't take her eyes off of me when I went to visit him. It was weird..."

M: "OK... No. Let's not get serious."

A: "Serious? I'm just trying to tell you what she was like with me when you weren't around..."

M: "OK, OK, forget it. You're in the clear, OK?"

*   *   *

F: "So wait, did Max get laid the other night?"

C: "Ah, what?"

A: "I should say that he did."

M: "Ah, lesser minds have never conspired to conceive of greater things."

A: "He definitely did."

C: "What? Not with the Cuban owner lady!"

M: <shit-eater grin>

C: "No way!"

A: "You should have seen them pashing in the morning when you guys were taking off."

C: "Oh my god!"

T: "Way to go Max!"

A: "He *is* a sly dog, one *does* come to find."

C: "But when was this?"

M: "When the children were asleep."

A: "The night before we left."

C: "Oh c'mon Fortes, give us a little bit of

it then Romeo."

M: "My dear Chavez, she was a woman such as
that I shouldn't wish to taint your innocent
mind."

C: "Oh ho ho, what a bastard."

A: "We'll probably never hear the end of
this."

(Trudy went to sleep in the tent).

*　　　*　　　*

M: "...No no, that was before Aude had shown
up. It was my girlfriend's father's place that he
had bought back in the late sixties for a song,
and it's basically in the middle of the mountains
amongst all of these olive trees and avocado
trees, and grapes and almonds growing everywhere,
with a cistern and a kitchen. Very rustic, you
know? Anyway, she and I had the place to
ourselves for about a week, and I had just
finished my novel. Audacy was late, and I didn't
know if he was still coming, but it turns out
that he was still up in Paris, chasing after some
girl that he had decided he was in love with."

A: "Can somebody help me break this one?"

C: "Yeah."

A: "I'll hold the end, you just jump in the
middle."

F: "What happened to her?"

M: "She and I ended up breaking up."

F: "No the girl that Audacy was chasing in
Paris.

M: "Oh. I don't know, ask him"

F: "Audacy, what ever happened to her?"

A: "To which?"

C: "You've got it?"

A: "I've got it."

F: "The girl in Paris."

A: "Oh. She didn't like hitchhiking. Bit of a city girl, dressed all in black." *<crack>*

C: "That'll do it."

A: "Swedish."

F: "You took her hitchhiking?"

A: "Aye, for a little while. Much to her boyfriend's frustration. She ended up telling me that hitchhiking was boring 'cause it was always just the same thing, over and over."

F: "Ha ha! And you were like, 'See ya'.

A: "Yup. Goodbye..."

*   *   *

M: "Aude thinks there's some kind of perfect girl out there waiting for him that he has to find..."

A: "Not a perfect girl. A perfect match."

M: "Perfect match, whatever. Here you've got five billion people in the world, and half of them are girls..."

A: "Right, right..."

M: "...And three quarters of them are too old, or too young, or too ugly..."

A: "Exactly. So now you're down to like, half a billion."

C: "Yeah well there's gonna be a lot of pretty compatible girls in a group of half a billion..."

A: "Yes. Say maybe a million, spread out all over the world.

M: "Right, well Aude thinks that he's gotta find the one of all of these girls that he's gonna be most happy with.

A: "The Red Queen."

M: "Right, he thinks that there's this one perfect girl who's like, waiting for him."

A: "Well."

F: "I don't know if I can go along with that. There'd have to a lot of different girls who could be perfect for someone in different ways.

A: "Sure, I don't disagree with that. The old 'Betty and Veronica' thing, like the Lovin' Spoonful song. But what I'm talking about is that hypothetically, you could apply a grand kind of playoff method to it. Think if you were say, king of the world. What you could do. Well. If you were to Stanley cup, Betty-and-Veronicize your way all the way to the top, *that's* the girl I'm talking about."

C: "Yeah, whatever *that* means..."

*   *   *

C: "...Yeah, so I'm at the bar and trying to figure out where I'm gonna spend the night, and there are probably only about ten people there, and it's this little country town. So I start talking with this hippie couple and they end up inviting me back to their farm for the night. So we go back there and they call up some friends, and pretty soon there's a party going on, so I drive back into town with the guy and one of the girls from the farm, and we're smoking a bong along the way, and we head back to the bar to pick up some more beers. So when we get there, the guy goes in to get a case, and I'm sitting in the truck with the girl, and the two of us can see through the big window and into the bar..."

A: "This is the same bar where you met them?"

C: "Yes."

A: "But not the same girl from the couple?"

C: "No, this was like his sister-in-law or something."

A: "OK."

C: "So in through the window we can see this woman from before, and she's sitting and talking to someone who's beside her at the bar, but just out of sight from where we can see. And it looks like she's in love with whoever it is that she's talking to, or at least that's what I was thinking, and I suspected that it was the strange-looking guy who I'd noticed at the bar earlier on..."

A: "Right."

C: "So me and the sister-in-law are sitting

there, and we're both watching this woman flirt with someone we can't see, and then the sister-in-law notices me staring in at the scene, and tells me the whole small-town story.

F: "Which is?"

C: "Turns out that the woman was married to this guy who got in a drunk-driving accident, and killed a couple of people. Locals. Just totally fucked it all up. He lived through it, but he was kind of a vegetable and needed lots of looking after. So through all the hatred and small town torment, she stayed with him, and had been nursing him along for years. But the guy obviously couldn't have sex anymore, and she had started having a love affair with the strange-looking guy that she was talking to inside. The thing about it is that she and the crippled husband had two grown redneck sons who didn't like to see her be unfaithful to their father, so every time she hooked up with the strange-looking guy, they would pay him a visit, and would kick the shit out of him. So that the strange-looking guy wanted to love the woman, but was forever wary of getting beaten down by the sons, and the woman wanted him as a lover and she would keep on pulling him back in, again and again and again, and the crippled manslaughterer was oblivious to the whole thing. But she kept taking care of him anyway."

F: "So what happened?"

C: "Nothing, I mean, I don't know. The guy came back to the truck with the case of beer and we went back to the farm."

F: "What?"

C: "Yeah. It just kind of struck me as a strange and tragic situation.

A: "What kind of a story is that?"

*   *   *

A: "...She was a terrific girl, but such an incredible liar, which at first was kind of handy, 'cause she could tell her parents that she was staying at her aunt's house, and tell her aunt that she was going back to her parent's place, and then we'd cruise off for a week at a time. But anyway, the first time I took her hitchhiking, the schools were on strike and we had all this time, so we headed south and had to pass right down through the town that her family lives in..."

M: "I know this story."

A: "...and she was hitchhiking with her jacket over her head so no one would recognize her. So it was pretty sketchy. And at this point we hadn't had sex yet, because she wouldn't do it with a condom on, and I wouldn't do it without one. But our relationship had kind of been sped up a bit after I had accidentally told her that I loved her, when I was actually just trying to say that I wanted her..."

M: "That's happened to me before."

F: "Wait. She wouldn't use a condom?"

A: "No. It's a catholic country, you know? They're told not to use them. I had to like, gradually persuade her."

M: "Not that it ended up doing any good."

A: "That's not part of the story Max."

M: "Ahem."

A: "So we reached this little town in the dark, and I went in to buy some things, and lots of wine, and it was just starting to rain so we jumped on the local bus that went south along the highway, and rode it to the end of the line."

M: "He took a bus!"

A: "...And when we get off, it's starting to pour and she's kind of nervous, so I'm like, 'No problem baby, we'll just get the tent up nice and quick in this field down here,' but when I've got it halfway up, this flashlight is coming along in the rain, and it's the farmer who owns the field, and I ask him if we can just camp out there for the night, and he's like: 'You can if you want, but this whole field is gonna flood,' so he told us to go up onto the other side of the road. Now by this time it's really pissing down, so I kind of spool the tent around my arm and we make for the high side of the road, crossing over a wooden fence, and then through these trees 'til we we're like, thirty metres off the road and we pitch it there next to a big tree, totally invisible from the road..."

F: "This is the same tent that you've got now?"

A: "Yeah, same one. So we get inside the tent and everything's pretty wet, and we're eating our chocolate and peanuts and stuff, and drinking our wine, and kind of screwing around a bit, but we still hadn't slept together because of the condom thing, so we're talking about religion and we're talking about God, and eventually we fall asleep together. This would have been at about midnight, and it was a Saturday night. So I'm laying next to her on my back, and she's on this side, and I'm in the middle of a dream when I get woken up by this crash, and I sit up like this and see this pair of headlights coming right towards us, and I just grab her and kind of jump to the back of the tent, and the car veers a bit in the final moment and smashes into the tree right next to us. I mean: the bumper is poking into the wall of the tent! And the first thing she says to me, is she sits up and points, and goes: 'That is God!'"

F: "Ha!"

A: "And I unzip the door and look out through the screen, and this guy appears out of nowhere on the other side of the car, and instead of helping or anything, he rips the driver out from the car and starts kicking his ass! Totally working him over. And she's swatting at me from behind going, 'Put your boots on!' but the guy knocks him until he's unconscious and then disappears back into the woods without even noticing us in the tent."

F: "What the fuck?"

A: "Yeah. So like an hour later when the cops and ambulances start to arrive, there's this inspector who finally notices the tent, and he comes running over to ask if everybody's all right, and I tell him that we're fine, and he and his buddies have a good laugh over the whole scene."

F: "But what was with the guy getting beaten up?"

A: "Well, that's what I asked the inspector.

It turns out that the car crash driver had been in town getting drunk to the point that when he wanted to go home, he ended up stealing someone's taxi. You see, the crashed car was a taxi. Anyway, as he's pulling away, some friend of the real owner of the taxi spots him and starts chasing him, and they get into this high-speed pursuit until eventually the drunk guy veers off the road and explodes through the fence, and almost has our number."

F: "And what about her? Did she get turned off of hitchhiking by the whole thing?"

A: "No. Exactly the opposite. We got back up in the morning and she brings out this little joint that she had squirreled away, and as we're going back over to the road, she's like, 'Is hitchhiking always this exciting?' and I'm like, 'Yeah. Pretty much.'"

(Max passed out in the sand on the other side of the fire).

*   *   *

F: "The thing that I don't understand is how she could have fucked around like that when I was there. It could have been a lot more... above the table, at least. And not something that came to a head when I actually fuckin' see them doing it. I mean, we've been friends forever..."

C: "She's a bitch Finn. That's something a guy should never have to see."

F: "And now she's back at home being like... well, who the fuck knows what she's saying? And here my family and stuff are wondering about what's going on, and she's just waiting for *him*, who's gonna go up there and completely invade my own fuckin' hometown, like some jungle disease that ruins your life and then follows you home."

A: "Take courage Finn. Things'll turn out better than what you can imagine right now.

C: "Yeah. If she's the kind of person who would do this to you then it's better that you find it out now rather than wasting years of your life with her."

F: "Yeah, maybe... but part of me is still in love with her... Maybe I really should have just fucking killed him."

*   *   *

A wash of blue gradually began to creep up into the night sky, and the three of us sat huddled together beside the smoking remains of the fire. We were swigging down the last of our bottle just as a foghorn came echoing from across the bay.

"The ferry's coming. I can see it."

The whole scene began to sketch itself back out, and the streetlights blinked and then turned off in town. Max was curled up next to the fire where he had passed out in the sand. We spoke quietly as we walked around him and stepped over him, organizing our things. Chavez blew on the fire, as Finn was collecting our garbage up into a pile off to the side. Trudy was still asleep in the tent. We did a final sweep before pulling our packs on.

"Do you want to wake him up?" asked Chavez.

"No. He looks too peaceful. Tell him I said

goodbye."

The sun itself was not yet visible, but the light was pouring up over the horizon now, and Chavez came with us and walked us over to the docks.

CHAPTER MAX

The Osa peninsula is like a proper rainforest; beautiful, and very tropical. We were in Puerto Jimenez, and the trees there have all these scarlet macaws, these huge red birds that make a really ugly cackling noise. We camped out on the beach near the ferry landing, and in the morning Aude and Finn were going to catch the ferry over to Golfito and make their way down to Panama City and the canal. I wanted to go with them, but part of me was kind of itching to get home, 'cause there was this protest scheduled to take place in Quebec City that I had fantasies about getting back in time for.

So we were camped out on the beach by the ferry landing, and I remember sitting around the fire with Aude, and Aude and I, we love each other but we've always fought and argued with each other, especially on trips, 'cause we're both very strong headed and like to stick to our guns. But I remember Aude telling me that he was getting to the point where he was unhappy if he stayed in the same place for more than a day, and that he just had this impulse to keep moving, keep looking for something, and it had become the sort of base condition of his life: that he was always looking for something. But it wasn't necessarily something that he wanted to find, you know, it's just that he wanted to look, which is an exhausting way to go through life, but I understand very well the compulsion. I have it too.

And we all just kind of faded out along with the coals of the fire, or I did at least, and I woke up in the morning, and he was gone.

LAST CHAPTER

The three of us started down along the beach. Chavez carried my guitar.

"So I've been talking with Trudy, and we've been thinking about maybe coming down to Panama as well, but it probably wouldn't be for another couple of weeks."

"Well, there's a pretty good chance that I'll still be there. At one end of the canal or the other. I doubt that you'll have a hard time finding me if I am."

"Yeah. I never really do," he said.

Finn was walking a few paces ahead, and Chavez nodded forward: "You gonna take good care of him?"

"Nah, he's gonna take good care of me. Ain't that right Finnius?"

"You guys want a banana?" he asked, turning around.

"Yeah."

"Sure."

The sun breached the outline of our horizon, and reflected sharply off of the water. The light was all pink and orange, and of a strange early morning variety.

We slowed our pace, swallowing our bananas as we approached the dock, which now had the boat tied up alongside. A few people had collected along the shore carrying chickens and bags of fruit. The foghorn sounded again, and we stepped onto the dock and clonked our way along the boards. I had a word with the shipmate who saw us aboard, and we dropped our stuff onto the deck in a pile.

Chavez stood alone on the end of the dock with the locals stepping around him. He was only six feet away, and he stood there with a sleepy smile on his face as he squinted into the sun. Our campsite was just visible in the distance.

"Well. Give our best to Trudy. Tell her that she's done well."

"I will."

"And keep your powder dry, and your thumb held low."

Chavez grinned and flashed his best hitchhiking pose as two young boys from the boat began to untie the ropes.

"Shall we not say goodbye then?" I laughed, with my arms out.

"Not goodbye," he said, raising his voice up over the sound of the engine, "Que te vaya bien. See you in Panama!"

"See you in Panama!" echoed Finn, throwing his hands up into the air. The engines wailed as our planes breached, and our floor beginning to pull away.

"Ride well," he mouthed, the sunlight illuminating the hand that he held aloft. All alone on the dock.

I stood, his mirror image, and watched him disappear as the boat slowly slipped us away.

THE END

ANDREW WHYTE

ABOUT THE AUTHOR

I am against war.

Artichokes are my favorite food.

My glass in the air to all of the adventurous
seekers who came before me, as well as to
all of the trippers to come.

Made in the USA
Columbia, SC
25 April 2024

34613621R00173